Other Books by J.E. Knowles

Arusha

May their memory be a blessing:

D. H. Knowles
M. M. Haisman
F. S. Knowles
N. B. Hunt
M. J. Blaufuss
D. E. Knowles

Acknowledgments

An excerpt from this novel, in an earlier form, appeared in *Toe to Toe: Standing Tall and Proud* (Bedazzled Ink, 2008).

Thanks to: Trish Hindley, for love and support. All of you, my readers. Canada, where my writing career began, as did my adult life as an equal citizen. Members of my longtime writing group, past and present, for keeping me Canadian. The Toronto Public Library, and my favorite independent bookseller in the world, Glad Day Bookshop. Shirley Yoshida, for renting me a room with a beautiful bay window that looked out through the trees, when she knew I could only afford a basement.

Denise DeSio, Penelope Radley, Jeffrey Round, Cathy Rowlands, Lara Zielinsky, and the writers at Langton's Books here in Twickenham. My editor, Katherine V. Forrest; my publisher, Linda Hill; and everyone who worked on my novels, especially the proofreaders. My teachers who imparted more love for American and Tennessee history than the Elizabethton City Schools required.

My parents; my aunt Janet and uncle Bob; Ben, Elizabeth, Rachel ("It's so great to be part of a family of friends"), and Rebecca. The animals who provided cameos. Music I have loved all my life, especially the wonderful, immortal voice of Mary Travers.

And Major Fritz Bernshausen, who said of his service in the US Army in Vietnam: "I fought for a protester's right to burn the flag."

Soli Deo Gloria.

About the Author

J. E. Knowles is from Tennessee, via Toronto. Her first novel, *Arusha*, was a Lambda Literary Award finalist. She has also edited the collection *Faith in Writing: Essays in Honor of Jack L. Knowles*. She is based in London and online at jeknowles.com.

When you besiege a city for many days, to do battle against it, you shall not destroy its trees by wielding a pickax against them; you may eat from them, but never cut them down. Are the trees in the field humankind, to come under siege from you?
—Deuteronomy 20:19

CHAPTER ONE

Every United States senator looks in the mirror and sees a future president. Raybelle McKeehan had been seeing that future president since she was ten years old.

Not that hers was the best mirror for looking into. The bedroom light didn't flatter her, but there was no one around to see. People probably thought senators had security around them all the time, but usually they didn't. When she ran for president, of course, that would change.

She sat on the edge of the four-poster bed and pulled on her pantyhose. Raybelle hated pantyhose. Hated the whole business of it: the endless losing battle to keep her legs shaved smooth, as pointless as most committee meetings; the constant runs from always being in a hurry; the unnatural flesh tones or the equally unappealing choice of opaque black, which she avoided because she didn't want folks thinking she was hiding her legs, that she didn't shave them at all.

Politics was all an act, and she was no actress. She was what once would have been called a lady of a certain age—old enough to be a senator, which was all that mattered. Five feet nine inches tall without high heels, which she also disliked, but wore when she had to. Blond hair, kept stylish (not to mention blond) by a nice young woman who did not charge four hundred dollars, so no scandal. Raybelle wore a lot of black and blue, to match what her opponents looked like once she'd given them a pounding. She avoided wearing earth tones, like the colors of the room, and she reserved red for occasions, like today, when she had to make a power impression on someone she didn't yet know.

There had been a major shakeup in Washington. The Republican president, his popularity at an ebb, was facing a Congress that for the first time was made up primarily of the opposition party. One of the groups of voters he, and by extension Republicans like Raybelle, had pissed off in the election was veterans, and a bipartisan committee had been formed in the Senate to investigate how the government had failed them. And one of the dominoes falling in this year's scheme of things was that Raybelle McKeehan of Tennessee was on that committee.

She didn't have to impress her longtime Democratic colleague from Tennessee, Grant Rivers. The Secretary of Defense, on the other hand, didn't yet know Raybelle. But he must never forget her after today. She would wear red. And heels.

Just as she was applying the last touch of red lipstick, squinting into the grimy mirror (Lord, what would Mama say?), the phone assaulted her senses. "Yes, Patricia?"

"Senator, this is Melody."

"Who?" came out of her mouth, too fast for manners. "Where's Patricia?"

"Ma'am, this is Melody Park. The new assistant to the assistant—"

"All right. What is it?" Of course. Everything in Washington was new. Why not a new assistant? Never mind that she didn't remember meeting this Melody.

"It's your brother, Senator."

"I'm not speaking to my brother," Raybelle said, and she meant that, in every possible sense.

"No—he's not on the line," Melody said. "Someone called about him. Tomas Jefferson."

"Is this some kind of joke?"

"No, ma'am. That's the doctor's name, Tomas Jefferson."

"All right. You have the number? I'll be in the office in a little while, Melody."

"Yes—"

"I'll call him from there." Raybelle clicked the phone off, sorry only for an instant that she had adopted the habit of hanging up without ever saying goodbye. It wasted time, seconds of every phone call. And she was on a lot of phone calls.

On the ride to Capitol Hill she focused on her paperwork, allowing the mounds of memos to crowd other thoughts from her mind. She had gotten on this committee by being nice and shaking lots of hands. Where she came from, a handshake meant a deal. She'd shaken hands all the way to the Tennessee General Assembly and then the Congress, at a time when Tennessee was represented by two Democratic senators, one of them Albert Gore, Jr.

Everyone in Washington knew she lived for the winning resolution, whether passing one or just resolving a particular problem. She refused to be caught up in any affairs, legal or otherwise. She could talk farm, nuclear plant, bridge-building or ditch-digging, and she didn't privilege people because of who they were.

Certainly not her brother Dennis, whom she hadn't seen in years. Dennis's name was not going on her to-do list, today or any other day.

She powered into the office and past its warren of desks all hopping with activity, productive or otherwise. Raybelle trailed "Mornings" after her and the staffers caught them like candies from a GI truck. "Where's Melody Park?"

A petite young Korean-American woman said "Good morning, Senator" and handed her a cup of coffee. Freshly brewed.

"Bless you, Melody." She raised a cup to the newest member

of staff, continued to her computer and leaned over the desk. Sitting wasted time. She heard Melody behind her: "Senator, the agenda for today is—"

"The Secretary. I got it." If it weren't for that meeting, Raybelle would have eaten breakfast—the most important meal of the day—but she couldn't risk slopping anything all over the red dress.

"I was going to say that I've e-mailed your agenda to you, and I'll have it automatically sent to your PDA, if you'll give me the number please."

Raybelle frowned between clicks on the mouse. "I have never been caught in a public display of affection, and you needn't concern yourself that I shall."

She took Melody's pause for confusion. "No, ma'am. I meant your personal digital assistant. Your Palm or BlackBerry or—"

"I've hired you. You seem competent. You walk and talk, so why would I want some vibrating appliance that doesn't do either one?"

"Yes, Senator." Melody cleared her throat. "I know you have a busy day with the committee meeting, but—"

"We."

"I'm sorry?"

"We have a busy day." Raybelle turned from her computer with the special sigh of frustration she reserved for it alone. "Listen, Melody, I know you didn't get this job because you like making coffee or explaining abbreviations to dinosaurs. You're here because you want my job someday. Right?"

"I'm just a law—"

"But you're here. You're here, and so from now on I'm going to assume that wherever I am, that's where you want to be. I'm in a committee meeting, you're in the committee meeting. I'm stuck in traffic, so are you. If I have to go to the ladies' room, I expect you to be right outside waiting for me. I want you sticking like a burr to my backside. Understand?"

"Yes, ma'am."

Raybelle might have imagined it but she thought Melody had snapped to attention.

"No need for 'ma'am,' either. You're a grown woman too."

"Yes, Senator."

"So." Raybelle held her coffee over the desk, so that when it spilled, it would not be on herself. "We're leaving in five minutes. Tell me about my brother."

"A Doctor Tomas Jefferson called and said it was a medical emergency," Melody said, her posture more relaxed. "That's all she would say."

"She?"

"It did sound like a woman, despite the name."

"Where is this Doctor Jefferson?" Raybelle grabbed a dull pencil and a trusty wad of paper. Personal digital assistant, indeed.

"Chicago."

What kind of mess had Dennis gotten himself into this time? "Tell you what. While we're walking to the chamber, I want you to help me figure out how to make a long-distance call on this thing." Raybelle pitched her cell phone to Melody and moved toward the door. "I can't waste any time figuring out stuff you already know."

"Thank you, Senator," Melody said, running to catch up.

***

Beads of sweat dripped into Dr. Tomas Jefferson's eyes and she swiped at them with the back of her hand. Thinking of Alicia made them feel like tears, though Tomas couldn't remember the last time she had cried. Not when Alicia left, or since. *Don't count months; count reps.* She pressed her spine more firmly against the weight bench and lifted the barbell on a long exhalation.

It would almost have been better if Alicia had left her for another woman. Or hell, a man. Anything would have been better than the day she'd announced that Tomas just didn't make her happy anymore, didn't "satisfy" her. Tomas had acted wronged and uncomprehending, not that she didn't have every right to be, since she was the one being left. But now that it was too late to do anything about it, she could finally admit to herself that she had known.

A doctor treats symptoms, but she was supposed to diagnose as well, to rule out one possibility and then another until she got to the underlying cause. That's what she should have done with

Alicia—looked beneath the symptoms of her lover's discontent to find out what was really wrong, and address them. Instead, Tomas had thought not like a doctor but like an accountant, totting up pluses and minuses and concluding that, on balance, they were happy.

This train of thought was going to wreck her if she wasn't careful. She sighed, pretending it was an *ujjay* breath like in yoga, wiped her moist hands on her black workout pants and adjusted the T-shirt from her scuba diving trip to the Red Sea. It said SHARM EL-SHEIKH—SHUT UP AND DIVE. In a Chicago March, it comforted Tomas to be reminded of the warm sea.

The one thing Tomas wished she could change about the way she looked was her hair. She longed to do something with it, braids or dreads, but even her black patients seemed not to want that in a doctor. In other respects, she was conservative in appearance. She always changed into street clothes before she left the clinic or the hospital, and could never understand how her colleagues could run around the streets of Chicago in their scrubs, smoking of all things. Not that she didn't have her own compulsions, but at least hers were healthy, and working out at the gym every day relieved stress.

Her cell phone rang and the woman on the next bench made a disgusted sound. "Wish people wouldn't bring their phones in here. What are you, a doctor?"

"Yes." Tomas returned the barbell to its rack with a grunt. She grabbed the phone from where it rested on her towel. "Doctor Jefferson." The "Doctor" felt like a waste of breath—one word more than necessary.

"How do I know if it's ringing?" someone on the phone said, not to her.

Tomas looked at the number, but it told her nothing about the source of the mysterious Southern voice. "I'm sorry, who's calling please?" Three words more than necessary.

"This is Senator McKeehan. I have a message to call Thomas Jefferson in Chicago."

Tomas laughed. Wasn't the first time somebody had made that joke. "Senator, it's Tom*as* Jefferson," she said, stressing the —*as*.

"I don't know you, Doctor Jefferson, and you don't know me. Get to the point. Please."

That one word, *please*, must have been costly for McKeehan, who otherwise sounded like a total bitch. "It's about your brother."

"What about him?"

"I don't know how much you know about Dennis's situation—"

"More than I want to."

"Look, Senator. I don't like to waste words either. Mr. McKeehan is living on the streets, and his condition is deteriorating."

"You know I haven't seen Dennis in years." McKeehan said it as a statement of fact, not something she gave a damn about.

"Yes. But what we need here is a—"

"Listen, Doctor, I'm on my way into a very important meeting. Do me a favor, will you, and call my assistant, Patricia. She'll sort out anything you need from me. Melody's number is—"

"I thought you said Patricia?"

McKeehan rattled off a number and said, "Thanks," and hung up without saying goodbye. Tomas hated it when people did that. It wasn't good procedure, to click away without confirming the exchange was over.

The gym wasn't warm, and Tomas had been sweating. Sitting still for several minutes had left her chilled, and her body ached from weariness as much as the strain of her workout. She decided to quit for the day and, after less stretching than she'd recommend to a patient, headed for the shower.

***

Raybelle started to toss the phone to Melody, just to get rid of it, but put it in her understated black leather handbag instead. "Thanks. Sorry about calling you Patricia again."

"That's all right. Congresswoman."

She grinned at the sparkle she saw in Melody's eyes. "Point taken. We're going to get to know one another quite well, and I meant to get off to a better start."

"Is your brother all right?"

Raybelle was surprised, and slowed for a moment. Melody didn't look at her again; she was busy trying to match her boss's much longer stride. "My brother suffers from delusions, but he won't let anybody help him. He and I have nothing to say to each other. So we don't."

"What kind of delusions?"

Instead of answering, Raybelle pointed to the door of the senate chamber. "Tell you later. It's showtime."

***

The droning of her fellow committee members had been going on so long that Raybelle felt the need to poke herself with a pin. The arcanities of Senate procedure required old business to be taken care of first. Old business*men* was more like it. Raybelle was sure she could smell their aftershave and less pleasant odors as the room baked hotter and hotter under the camera lights. She felt herself beginning to perspire under her blazer. The red power dress would be going straight back to the dry cleaners.

At moments like this one, Raybelle would raise her eyes slowly to the ceiling, to remind herself of the chamber's grandeur and the reason she was there. Robert Byrd, grand old man of the Senate, said it was the highest trust in the land, the office of senator. Unlike many of her colleagues, Raybelle took seriously her responsibility to be there for daily votes, not just "important" issues, the ones that made the news. The light broke through the window panels of the dome and gave her hope that the country could, indeed, get "through the night with a light from above."

At last, the Secretary of Defense was announced.

Henry Perry was shorter than he looked on television (weren't they all?). Shorter than she was. He was bald in almost a defiant way, as if he'd scrubbed his head clean of any hint that hair had ever grown there. She couldn't tell the color of his eyes behind square glasses, yet he seemed to look right at her. Red dress. Bull's-eye.

"Mr. Chair?" Perry said, and that always made Raybelle think the person was addressing a cartoon character.

"You have the floor, Mr. Secretary."

Perry began his peroration, thus: "The United States armed forces, as you know, are the finest in the world. Our military has never been stronger." He then immediately stated that it needed to be stronger still, and that, were not his plans put in place for the "tightening and streamlining" of the US military, it would be in dire shape indeed.

From across the aisle, Senator Grant Rivers shot her a look that said *Ain't that the total contradiction?*

She was tempted to guffaw. It often felt like she and Grant were kids in school together, rolling their eyes at whatever the teacher said. They shared the same beliefs in personal liberty and the same irreverence for the executive branch they each, of course, hoped to head one day. No doubt Grant would get to the White House before Raybelle did, but that didn't bother her too much. He could help her in the meantime.

"What we must understand," Perry was saying, "is that the realities of the new conflict have swept away old timelines, old ways of keeping the peace. In the time it takes for this august body to make a declaration of war, this city could be vaporized. Our armed forces must be sleek, swift, ready to pounce on the enemy and destroy him wherever he may be. Our brave men and women in uniform—" He said this looking at Raybelle and Olympia Snowe of Maine, as though reminded that women did exist— "cannot wait for the leadership in Washington to tell them what to do. In the time it would take, Washington, DC could be wiped from the face of the earth."

"Secretary Perry?" Grant raised his ample frame in his chair with the same leisure as he voiced his question.

"Yes, Senator."

"You've come here to advise us of your plans for the new, improved military, and that's good. But something about this concerns me. It appears you've mistaken whose role it is to advise, here. I believe the way the Constitution puts it, Congress is supposed to advise you."

Perry raised his hands in a deferential and, Raybelle thought, rather fey gesture. "Well, not me, Senator Rivers. The president. Or, as it's more appropriate to call him in this context, the commander-in-chief."

"Right, right." Grant's face took on an expression that Raybelle was coming to recognize as predatory. "That's another statement you made that's bothering me a little bit. You said something about—help me out here—not waiting for the leadership in Washington to tell the military what to do?" Perry nodded. "So what you're saying is that the commander-in-chief, our president, is not in charge of the military? That his commanders in the field should tell him what to do?"

"The president is in complete control—"

"Now hear me out, Mr. Secretary, hear me out. I just don't much care for the sound of this. Our men and women in uniform do not choose their mission. We send them."

"But the president, as you know, Senator, is a decorated veteran and knows what the generals in the field have to do."

"Before they do, I'm sure." Grant's tone was dry. "You don't have to defend the president's valor; this isn't an election campaign. But if we start letting the military direct the civilian leadership, then we might as well be Turkey."

"Turkey is a great ally of—"

"I yield to my esteemed colleague from the state of Tennessee."

When Grant leaned back, Raybelle was sure she caught a wink meant for her. They were allies; they both loved Congress more than they loved their own parties. She addressed Perry, and felt the red dress as smooth on her as the timbre of her voice. Perry wouldn't even know she was insulting him.

"You know the Constitution well."

"I'm sure I do."

"I'm sure you do too." It was all Raybelle could do not to buff her nails. "And you know that the oath of office of the chief executive, whom you serve, is 'to preserve, protect and defend the Constitution of the United States.'"

Perry smiled, not in a nice way. "The presidential oath becomes you, Senator McKeehan."

"Then you further know," she said, "that 'this august body' is responsible for whatever authority the president has to wage war. You come to Congress to ask, Secretary Perry. Not to tell."

She paused for an instant, and in that instant Raybelle and Perry locked eyes. A draw, then. She'd take it.

***

"Oh, you did great in there, Senator!" Melody was walking faster and talking with more enthusiasm than she had that morning. Truth was, in the course of the exchange with Perry, Raybelle had forgotten that Melody—or anyone else—was there. Their confrontation had been as intimate as if they were the only ones in the senate chamber.

"Thanks." She could use the tuning-out process now, as the bustle around her seemed to be unceasing.

"He's right, you know," Melody went on. "You sounded like a president."

"Every senator wants to be president."

When they reached the office, Melody said, "Do you need something for lunch?"

Raybelle looked at her. "Lunch? Oh, I don't keep a regular lunch hour." Before Melody could reply, she said, "But you go right ahead and eat. Just—if you don't mind staying nearby, for today. I have some papers you can help me with this afternoon."

"I've got my lunch right here." Melody pulled a paper bag from a tiny refrigerator near her desk that Raybelle had forgotten was there.

A few minutes later she was ready to cuss the computer when she smelled a strong and unfamiliar aroma coming from Melody's work area. "Lord, what are you eating?"

"Kimchi," Melody said, a forkful of it halfway to her mouth.

"And what might that be?"

"Fermented cabbage." Melody's shrug was meant to seem apologetic, but wasn't at all; Raybelle knew that shrug from her colleagues. "It's Korean."

Raybelle figured a day would come when she'd be eating popcorn or some odoriferous takeout and nobody would dare complain then.

"So, Senator. That Doctor Jefferson called again about your brother. Thought I'd draw up the paperwork she needs this afternoon and you could sign it."

That was just what Raybelle had planned to have her do. Was it possible that she was "proactive," as all job applicants claimed to be these days? "You can tell her, if she calls again, that you'll fax it to her later today."

"Oh, I already did."

That was two ways in as many minutes that Melody had impressed Raybelle with her Washington insouciance. "Did you really just graduate from college?"

"Mmmhmm. Just moved here."

"And you're from Chicago."

"No, Naperville. Third largest city in Illinois. Were you going to tell me what kind of delusions your brother has?"

And persistent as hell. That's three. Raybelle looked at the ballsy assistant, who had finished her kimchi and was waiting for all the world as if she were owed an answer.

"My brother thinks he's Jesus."

CHAPTER TWO

Tomas threw her things in the locker, not bothering to tie a towel around her waist. No one was around; she must have stopped between the start and finish times of whatever cardio class women took who didn't work during the day.

In the shower, she indulged in a bit of narcissism, enjoying the feel of pumped arm muscles and taut abs under her own soapy hands. No one else would be appreciating her for a while. Of all her reasons not to date, one of them was that it just took so much *time*. She couldn't, like a gay guy, just go to a bathhouse and get blown on her lunch hour, no matter how often she might be in the mood for that. Women, under the most casual circumstances, required too much attention. She'd have to take them out to dinner, and Tomas didn't do dinner very well, as Alicia would have told anybody (and no doubt had, by this point). If Tomas wasn't bolting Chinese takeout or, worst of all, french fries in the basement of the hospital, she was distracted by her pager or going on and on about something gross she'd cut into that day. She had the sensitivity of silicone, according to Alicia. And less emotional availability.

It wasn't like Tomas to pine after a lover. As if she'd never had another, or as if Alicia had been the love of her life. She was pretty sure she'd loved her but, as Alicia had often complained, it didn't "translate into action." Unlike Tomas, Alicia had never worried about using, let alone counting, unnecessary words.

***

The first time Tomas had seen Dennis McKeehan, the senator's brother, she was working her Wednesday shift at the street clinic on Roosevelt Road. She usually worked in the shiny environment of the University of Chicago Hospitals, where her patients could pay. It was a laboratory of humanity. But once a week she did her pro bono work, and this was an entirely different laboratory and a South Side entirely different from Hyde Park.

That day, a white man had walked in wearing shabby clothes and a green canvas backpack, on top of which rode a serene black-and-white cat. Tomas was called to reception because Dennis X, as he identified himself, had to be persuaded to leave the cat there. At a regular clinic, a pet would never be allowed into the lobby, but this place had its own rules.

The cat's name was Friesian—"after the pattern of the cow," Dennis said. Friesian looked to be in better health than his owner, who was decked out in old camouflage gear and boots with the soles coming loose. The man's beard and hair were wild and knotted, with little seeds in them, and Tomas had a vision of a tree growing there.

When she got Mr. X back to the bare-walled examining room, she asked him to sit down in a chair adjacent to her own. She preferred to face patients, and their problems, head-on, but at the clinic it was suggested that the patients (Tomas refused to call them clients) would be more at ease sitting in this friendly, side-by-side way.

But Dennis wouldn't have it. "Prefer to stand, ma'am." Then he looked at her for the first time. "Is Friesian all right out there? I'm worried about him. I just started looking after him; a friend of mine—"

"Your cat will be fine," Tomas said. "Now, is it Mr. X or—"

"X, like Malcolm! Do I look Muslim to you, Doctor?" He laughed, and the laughter reached his blue eyes. "I have the beard, eh?"

She looked back at him.

"Sorry, ma'am. Got no problem with black folks. Believe me."

"It doesn't matter to me whether you do or you don't." She articulated extra clearly, tongue on polished teeth. "What matters to me is your health problem. You've been found to have a rare disease called the Chikungunya virus. Any idea where you picked it up?"

He did sit down then, and she expected him to smell but it was no worse than when she rode the el every day. He folded his hands in his lap like a Christian child, and his nails were incongruously trimmed and clean.

"I know where I got it," he said. "I went to Mauritius, and when I got back home, I came down with something. They told me nobody in this part of the world ever catches it. Guess that's why you want to study me."

"Treat you," Tomas said. "I'm here to treat you, Dennis."

He looked up at the name. "Whatever. We don't get doctors like you down here. You're here to study me, but that's okay. All I want to do is help."

She phrased her next question with care. "If you're living 'down here,' as you say, may I ask how you could afford to travel halfway around the world?"

Dennis crossed his feet on the floor. He breathed so deeply it reminded Tomas of yoga.

"Am I not here to give stool samples or something?" he said. "Do you want to hear the story of my life? I didn't think you were that kind of doctor."

"It's customary to start with your history," she said. "Not least because you've contracted a very unusual disease that's only present in a few parts of the world. I'm curious as to what you were doing in Mauritius."

"You recording this?" He nodded to her visible recording device. "Is this going to some kind of government grant-making body? Because I've done enough for national security. I don't even have an address."

Tomas pushed the stop button, leaned back, and crossed her ankles. Not her arms. Administrators hated crossed arms; the psychological people said that was a sign of confrontation, and she didn't want a confrontation with this patient, at least not yet. "No recording."

"Voluntary poverty." Dennis enunciated each T.

"What does that mean?"

"What it sounds like it means. I've taken a vow of poverty."

"Like a monk?" Her words sounded mocking in the stark interior of the room.

"Sort of. My trip to Mauritius was a mission. Paid for by people who believe in what we're doing. We go places where people are living in poverty, and we live among them, as they do."

"What. Just for the experience?"

"As witnesses." Dennis rolled his eyes, and Tomas observed that they were a dark blue, not that steely shade more common in blue-eyed people. "I went to Mauritius to live in solidarity with slum dwellers," he said. "There are people there who were forced from their homes in the Chagos Islands. Tricked by the British government, all so the US could build an air base on one of the islands. Maybe you've heard of it. Diego Garcia." Tomas didn't respond. "Anyway. Ever since then, they've lived in these appalling conditions but it takes more than that to bring attention to what they're going through; it's been decades. Some of these folks are trying to get some kind of justice, and I was there as a witness with them."

"A witness." Tomas resisted reaching for her pen, but she longed to clutch some kind of object: a stethoscope, a syringe. "You mean like in a court case."

"No." Dennis turned those clear eyes to her, and she felt as if he were evaluating her. "Like, *witnessing*. 'Can I get a witness?' Don't you know this stuff?"

"I don't have a religious background," Tomas said in a crisper tone. "Whatever you may have assumed."

"Huh. Well, we've both done some assuming, I'd say." He stood, palms flat to his thighs. "So can we get this exam over with now?"

***

"He thinks he's Jesus?" Melody said to Raybelle. "You mean, literally? The Son of God on earth?"

"I'd feel better if he did. Crazy people you can treat. At least he'd have an excuse, if he was sick. No, my brother knows who he is, as far as I know. What he thinks is he's on a mission from God, so he goes around acting like a bum and sponging off people."

"He embarrasses you."

She should never have started this conversation, not with so many people around. "You know what, Melody, I am hungry. If you could get me a sandwich, I'll change out of this horrible dress. Turkey with provolone cheese."

"I think you look nice in that dress."

"Thanks, so do I. It doesn't look horrible, but it feels that way." It was all she could do not to start scratching herself, and she wasn't that big a hayseed. "I'd appreciate it if you could get Doctor Jefferson off my butt today."

"Consider it done." Melody swept up her jar and napkin and went back to work.

***

Henry Perry turned up the CD player on the shelf next to his polished oak desk. "Riders On The Storm." It was his favorite Doors song because it reminded him of Kelly. No one could hear his music except right in front of the desk, and no one entered his office without permission. It was a sacred space, wood-paneled and priestly. Perry answered only to the president, and if the president needed to see his Secretary of Defense, they would meet at the White House, not here.

Perry's wasn't a big office, considering all the communications and electronics he needed access to and all his responsibilities. "Defense" was such a namby-pamby word; Perry wished his agency were still called the Department of War. When terrorists had first struck the homeland, some of the president's pussy advisers, whom Perry was reluctant to call his colleagues, had tried to persuade the commander-in-chief that the terrorist attacks were crimes, rather than acts of war. Their argument was that terrorists were murderers, albeit on a massive scale, and shouldn't be given the dignity of calling them warriors, or "enemy combatants."

That was a phrase Perry was proud of. It did away with whatever dignity the law of war might entail, because, in fact, the rules had changed. War was lawless now, and if there were no longer laws, there could be no crimes. There were only combatants, ours and the enemy, riding the wild frontier. If it hadn't been for the seriousness of the "war on terror," and the deadly consequences if he lost, Perry would be quite excited about it.

But he would not lose. He had won the battle to define the terms of the war, and he would win every subsequent one. It was not about him, but about America, and the lives of her sons and daughters. Perry felt as if the weight of fatherhood of the entire nation rested on his strong shoulders. Sure, George Washington was supposed to be the father of his country. But Washington was dead.

When the buzzer sounded he turned down the CD player to an imperceptible level. "Send him in, Dick," he instructed his secretary.

Perry did not stand to greet his visitor—remaining seated, in a relaxed posture, sent a message of power and control, and he never missed an opportunity to send those messages. "Sit down." He didn't offer coffee, either; Dick would have seen to that.

"Now don't worry." Grant Rivers smoothed his suit jacket and adjusted his tie. "I've got everything under control."

Perry fixed him with a stare. "Care to rephrase that?"

Rivers cleared his throat. "Everything is under control. Thanks to you, Henry."

"Please, no names." Perry glared around the office, as if a bug or some kind of recording device might be hidden in the cabinetry. Which was not possible. Only his enemies had reason to be paranoid.

"Right." Rivers seemed less sure of what to say, which was what Perry wanted.

"Things today did not go exactly as I planned," Perry said. "Or, less exactly than I would have liked." He waited for an explanation.

"I was trying to be the bad cop, like you said. Figured if I stood up right away and put some pressure on you, that would set it up. Then, the rest of the committee would feel like fair attention had been paid, and they'd back you in whatever you want. I'm senior on the Hill. I carry a lot of clout."

Perry shook his head. "I have no issue with that. What about the lady in red?"

Rivers gave a short laugh. "Raybelle?"

"I said no names." What could Perry have been thinking when he went into business with this bumpkin?

"Oh, she's not gonna be any trouble. I know her. She just wore that dress to impress you." Rivers's face took on a sly look. "So? Did it?"

"I wasn't troubled by her dress." Perry's voice was cold.

"No, I bet you weren't. You'd never know that ass was fifty years old."

Perry brought his hands down on the desk, his voice pitching higher in a way he'd tried to train out of it for years. "I don't care how old the bitch is or what she wears. I want her sitting down and shutting up. You're supposed to be asking questions out there. Not her."

"She follows my lead," Rivers said. "Now, I've known her for a lot of years, and she may be a bitch, but people respect her. You go pissing her off and she'll find a way of making us look bad. Just answer her questions nicely, and I'll make sure she's out of our way when it counts."

Perry made notes in pencil. Always best to be able to erase. "We should start collecting the dirt on her. Like we do on anyone who's not on our side."

Rivers had a pork belly laugh. "Oh, I don't know that there's any dirt to speak of."

"Find some."

"We can't point out anything money-wise that looks any

worse than what other members of Congress are doing. *Looks* any worse," he emphasized.

"Then find something else. Fifty and never been married? It's a wonder she got elected. There must be a string of dicks, or pussies, in her past."

"That's why she did get elected," Rivers said. "We can't connect her to anybody. The woman is married to Washington."

"Washington's dead," Perry said, too softly for Rivers to hear.

CHAPTER THREE

Tomas wasn't really treating Dennis. He'd been right about that. Her case report on the Chikungunya virus was almost written, and would surely be accepted by one of the medical journals. A nice notch on her *curriculum vitae*. But since Wednesday was her regular volunteer day at the street clinic, it was natural for her to keep seeing Dennis as long as he kept coming in.

"How are you doing?" she asked him. "Looks like your viral symptoms are all clear."

He looked at her with that earnest, clear-eyed gaze. "I hear things, Doc."

As a doctor, she shouldn't be surprised by anything. She would have to work on that. "What things do you hear?"

"You know, voices. People that aren't there." He leaned forward on his elbows; they were scabbed, but he didn't smell as if he'd missed more than one shower. "I know they're not there, though. That means I'm not crazy, right?"

"I would never call you crazy, Dennis." Tomas took a deep, slow breath, so he wouldn't notice. She wasn't a psychiatrist, but that didn't matter here; she might be the only physician he would ever see, and all she had to do was listen. "Do you recognize the voices?"

He broke eye contact. "I know them. They're dead."

Listen to what the patient is saying. "Who are they?"

"I remember hearing them. I remember the people. What they sounded like."

"You must be concerned about them."

"I keep telling you, they're *dead.* I'm not concerned about them now."

"Concerned about the voices," she said. "What you're hearing. Does it disturb you? Are they telling you to do things?"

He looked up, but didn't answer. She should be more sure of herself; this shouldn't be such hard work. She'd had patients who argued with every word she said, patients who wouldn't do anything, and she'd found none of them as challenging as Dennis McKeehan.

"How old are you, Doctor Jefferson?"

Ah, this she had been trained to answer. "Why is that important to you?"

"It's a simple question." He slapped his hands on his knees and stood up, as if to leave the room. "You know how old I am. You can ask me anything. You can make me pee in a cup, or go up my ass—"

"Dennis," she said, in a soft tone intended to calm him down. She didn't want to have to call security. "I'm thirty-five."

"You don't look it, Doctor Jefferson." He put his palms up, smiled. "Hey, that's a compliment to a lady. Or meant to be."

Tomas slid one file folder over another. Time to get this back on a professional level. "What have you been doing since I saw you last?"

"You mean during the day? I was selling *StreetWise* for a while, but I wasn't very good at it." He tapped his chin and Tomas had a vision of him as St. Nick. "It's the beard."

"What about your beard?"

"Puts people off."

She wanted to ask why he didn't shave it then, but he probably didn't have a razor, and it might not be a good idea to suggest one, since he was having hallucinations. "Is there a particular reason you grow a beard?"

He harrumphed a laugh. "I'm growing it till Jesus Christ comes back to the earth," he said. "I'm growing it till the Cubs win the World Series again."

Tomas recognized that he wasn't answering her questions, but she let him talk. Dennis wasn't the only one who had to listen to what wasn't being said out loud. "And where have you been staying at night?"

"Lower Wacker Drive," he said. "When the shelters are full."

***

"Melody, I know it's Friday evening." Raybelle's voice echoed around her large living room, which had been decorated twelve years ago by a total stranger. She tried to wedge the cell phone to her ear, like she would a regular receiver, and almost dropped it on the floor.

"What do you need, Senator?"

"I went to this…blog, that you set up, and now I'm not sure what to do with it."

"Oh. Well, just go to your first post, and start typing away. We don't have to publish it until you're ready. Just save it as a draft, come back and we'll edit it later."

Raybelle was frustrated by her inability to reach the keyboard. "Listen, I'm not sure this is a good idea. Blogs may be cutting edge this year but by next year, they could be old news. Like e-mail."

"People still use e-mail, Senator. All the time."

"I know that." Raybelle leaned back in her uncomfortable swivel chair and adjusted the gooseneck lamp, the only light in the room. "But young people—and that's who we're trying to reach here—you're all, what is it, 'texting' now? And by 2010 it will be something else again."

"It doesn't matter what happens in 2010," Melody said. "The election is in 2008."

Raybelle chuckled. "I knew I liked you, Melody."

"What? What's funny?"

"You are. For a second there, you sounded like you were running for office."

"Thank you, Senator. I think."

Raybelle lost it then, a great laugh she hadn't shared with anyone in years. For a moment, she felt less alone.

She reached for her pad of paper and a cheap ballpoint pen. "I'm no good at drafting on a computer. Help me out with some talking points, or writing points or whatever you call them. What are we trying to accomplish?"

Melody had taken to this use of *we*. "We want to target the younger group of voters, eighteen to twenty-five, who have grown up with the Internet and expect to go there for our news and information." She never had any hesitation; always so well prepared. "We want to present 'Raybelle,' your cyber-persona—"

"English, please."

"—as someone comfortable, someone they can have in their living rooms, talk to on their cell phones. Beyond that, we want to appeal directly to voters, over the heads of the usual party functions. This is grassroots, from the bottom up—"

"This is nuts."

"I don't think it is, Senator," Melody said, as if she'd already considered, and dismissed, that possibility. "I think this is very much in step with your new—or rather, distinctive—brand of politics. Young people aren't interested in labels anymore. We don't like to think of ourselves as just Korean or Baptist or straight or—"

"*We* young people?"

"Are you trying to limit me?" Melody's tone was taunting now. "Set boundaries to my discursive voice?"

"Shut up."

"Sorry, I went to the University of Chicago. I'm not used to making much sense."

"Yeah, well, I'll keep that in mind when you proof this later." Raybelle turned back to her monitor. "So here's my first topic: Washington, hypocrisy, and Islamophobia."

"Wow, that's going to make you popular."

Although Melody couldn't see her, Raybelle put a hand to her ear. "I missed the part where I was asking you for political advice."

"I wouldn't dream of it, Senator."

"You already have." Raybelle scribbled another note. "I thought I'd title the post *Inshallah*."

"Arabic? For?"

"'God willing.'"

CHAPTER FOUR

Tomas started her mornings early at the hospital, grabbing a quick sandwich for "lunch" at ten or ten thirty. Younger doctors and nursing staff trailed in the white wake of hospital surroundings: white coats, white walls, floors and bedding. Recently there had been the excitement of an MRSA scare in area hospitals, so even white masks had come out. If there were any more barriers between Tomas and her patients, they wouldn't even breathe the same air.

By March, she had found herself looking forward to Wednesday afternoons at the clinic. This day Dennis said, "My sister's running for president."

Tomas was getting good at not letting anything register on her face. "Oh?"

"Not officially. I mean she doesn't have her name out there, like Barack Obama. That's a name, hey? Barack *Hussein* Obama."

"Please continue."

"But she wants to be president. Has, ever since she was a little kid." A time Tomas couldn't imagine.

"Why are we talking about your sister?"

He gripped the sides of his chair. "Because I'm sick of talking about me."

Tomas rolled her pen between her fingers, reached for his file to make a note of his belligerence today, thought better of it. "The Chikungunya case report's been accepted for publication. Should be out in August or September."

"I don't care."

And she didn't care to talk about Raybelle McKeehan. But she couldn't examine the reasons why she didn't, and it was too early to let Dennis go for the week. "What makes you think your sister will run for president?"

He leaned forward; Tomas could see more dirt than usual under his nails. "All senators want to be president. They're evil that way. Besides, she's on the Internet now. Not her official website, but her 'blog.' My sister the campaigner." He sounded sarcastic, but there was an edge of pride in his voice.

"Where do you use the Internet, Dennis?"

"At the public library. All the street people do."

"Which library?"

"Why'd you need to know anything else about me? Report's finished." He sat back, smiled. "Harold Washington, right downtown."

"That's a beautiful building." She remembered when it opened.

"Yeah. Anyway, I Googled her and you wouldn't believe the shit that comes up. Sorry." Tomas didn't know why he apologized for language; he swore less than she did. "Everybody wants a piece of her. Left wing thinks she's going to save them, be the first woman president; right wing wants to claim her as one of their racist own."

"Is she?"

"Nah. She thinks racists are as nuts as I am."

"You mean, as you think they are?"

"No, as she thinks I am! She thinks I'm nuts. Don't you?" He laughed when she didn't respond. "The right-wingers like her because she opposes state interference in general, and they don't want any interference when they shoot or pollute or express their crazy views. 'He who is not against us is for us,' and all that."

"I'm not familiar with that saying."

"Jesus." At her look of surprise, Dennis said, "Oh, never mind, Doctor. Why am I here?"

"You were talking about your sister's blog."

"What about it? Look it up." He cleared his throat, twice. "I'd e-mail her, but she'd never respond."

"How do you know?" Tomas could have wrapped the session up, but she'd noticed his thinness and was waiting to see if he would cough.

"Raybelle McKeehan knows that winning any election, or reelection, depends on me not being there. All she needs is for someone to find out there's madness in the family."

"You're not 'mad,' Dennis. You had a virus. Do you mind if we do another radiograph?"

"What?"

"I'm sorry, X-ray." Tomas smiled. "I've been reading proofs of my article."

Dennis shook his head. "No proofs, Doctor. There's no proof of anything."

***

Raybelle could walk into her office every day, past armies of staffers, say "Good morning" to them all and stop to interact with some along the way, without ever noticing how many people were actually there. All bustling in that post-typewriter way they did, with new beeps and buzzes and phones that no longer sounded like phones. And Raybelle's path through the maze, a thread running true, led to her own desk area, with its windows, where she could be alone.

Except for Melody. "Grant Rivers is on the line."

"Raybelle, how're you doing?" he mumbled when she picked up.

Why did he always have to be eating something? "I'm just fine, Grant. What do you on the dark side need from me this morning?" She stood as close to her office window as possible, admiring the dark clouds and the jagged lightning streaking through them. The window might not be the safest place to be in these conditions, but she loved storms. They were apocalyptic, cleansing.

"There's a storm coming, Ray. This news about the military hospitals."

"What news, Grant? And get that muffin out of your mouth."

He stopped chewing. "Haven't you been on the Internet?" Pause. "Okay, the radio then?"

"Melody has me waking up to some kind of calming CD, whales' blow-holes or something. Just tell me what I need to know, I need breakfast too."

"Soldiers getting sick, remember? That hospital bug? It's all over the headlines today. Some patients and their families have complained, and the latest is allegations of systemic neglect. It looks bad for the president." He sounded pleased about this. "Though he's blaming it on the Veterans Administration, naturally. Not the Department of Defense."

"Don't they all work for him anyway?"

"Don't you mean 'us,' Raybelle? You're a Republican too."

"I never mean 'us.'"

"I hear you. So, as reluctant as I am to help Republicans, the fact is we need to pin this tail on some ass as much as the president does."

"Sounds so productive."

He missed, or chose to ignore, her sarcasm. "You and I need to push a bipartisan investigation into this mess. If it's VA bureaucrats, fine. And if it's Defense, well. You, of all my colleagues, won't mind holding Henry Perry's feet to the fire."

"Flattery will get you nowhere, Senator Rivers." She smiled as she said it.

They spoke for a few minutes, setting up the details, which as usual involved Grant making any calls or public announcements, and Raybelle doing "research." Raybelle summarized their conversation for Melody. "Got all that?"

"Sure." Melody looked up from pushing the stylus on her handheld, and her eyes looked troubled. "Senator, is this really what you want to be doing?"

"What? Sticking it to the president, or Secretary Perry?"

"Veterans' issues." Melody set the device down. "Specifically health care. I know you and Senator Rivers co-chair this committee, but—" the corner of her mouth quirked—"how is it that you're the one behind the scenes, while Senator Rivers gets to be in front of a microphone all the time? Don't you want the attention?"

"First of all I want the facts. Grant is a blowhard, like those whales you put on that CD for me—awful sounding, by the way."

"You're welcome."

"He can get out there and blame the administration or the VA or whomever he cares to, but I'm more interested in what's happening to these veterans." Melody didn't need to know how false this was. Raybelle's own brother was a veteran, and a troubled one, and he was the last person she was interested in learning about.

***

Tomas had gotten to this stage in her medical career without having made any serious mistakes. She suspected she was overdue for one, but that was too superstitious for a physician.

Not having a PhD hardly counted as a serious mistake. She had an MD, and no one else but her would regard not having both as a disappointment. She had envisioned doing research, being Virologist of the Year, but had surprised herself by being drawn to patients, to the point of continuing her weekly sessions at the street clinic. She'd never in her life had to worry about money, and had taken her place at the upper end of the black middle class. When she did take time away, she indulged her one (expensive) hobby: scuba diving in exotic locations. Since Alicia, she'd had flings on vacation, but that's where they remained.

Dennis's appearance had changed over the months. His skin was pallid, and not because he continued to cover it with layers of clothing, no matter the weather. His beard was scraggly and wild, and his eyes looked like sleep was a distant memory. And the pang of concern Tomas felt was for a person more than just a case study.

"What's the matter?"

He took a moment to register.

"Dennis?" she said. "Have you been sleeping on Lower Wacker again?"

"Not sleeping."

She wanted to ask him why. To ask if this experiment in poverty had not gone on too long, and gone too far. Voluntary poverty was his business, but how could people on some distant island be helped by Dennis sleeping on the street? He was only hurting himself.

"You think I'm crazy too. Don't you?"

"I want to help you. I don't know about anyone else. Do you talk to someone?" The boundaries, of her profession and her soul, were loosening, but Tomas was less attached to them than she had once been.

"What do you want from me, Doc?" His voice held an immense weariness, as if he had lived a hundred years.

"I don't want anything," she said in a gentle tone, knowing somehow it wasn't true. "Will you let me help you? You never seem to tell me when something's wrong."

"You know viruses, don't you?" he said. "Viruses. Not even living things. At least, from what I've read, scientists can't agree on whether they're living or not."

"Where'd you read that?"

He smirked. "On the Internet, where else?"

"Go on."

"Well, I am a living thing, Doctor Jefferson. I'm—" He coughed, shuddered—"I'm a man, a living being. Like a tree or, or a dog."

"Why compare yourself to a tree or a dog?"

"Stop the shrink routine, okay? Looks bad on you." He coughed again, into a cloth of some kind. Tomas thought it must hold a rich collection of specimens.

"What you want to know is why I'm not desperate. Why I'm not calling in friends, anybody, to help me." There was no sarcasm in his voice. "Why I'm not at the VA with my old buddies, sucking through a straw."

"You're a veteran?"

He put his palms to his cheeks, closed his eyes for a minute. "You know how this whole thing started. When I went to Mauritius."

"Yes."

"It wasn't the first time I'd been," Dennis said. "And I didn't just go back to express solidarity. I went for repentance."

"Repentance?"

"I forgot, you don't use words like that. It means turning back from your sins," he said. "Your crimes."

***

Raybelle's Blog
March 11, 2007
Crimes and Misnomers

Dear People,

Does the term "war crime" sound redundant to any of you?

A crime is the breaking of a law. War is supposed to be governed by the laws of war. That's where the term war crime comes from.

Lately, I don't know about you all, but I don't see the laws of war carrying any more weight than some flower child on the side-lines, chanting "Make love, not war."

Raybelle stopped typing her draft post long enough to wonder if the phrase "make love" would trigger any sexually-based Web searches, and if that would be a good or a bad thing.

We, the citizens of the United States, are no longer protected by privacy laws from "unreasonable searches and seizures," as the Fourth Amendment to the Constitution requires. A search of our phone or Web records is unreasonable. And we no longer capture "prisoners of war," although we're supposed to be at "war" on terror. A war Congress never declared.

A war that should never have been authorized, because what happened to our country on September 11, 2001 was no act of war. It was a crime, a mass murder, and should have been treated like one.

When the Irish Republican Army launched terrorist attacks in the

United Kingdom, they called those acts of war, and themselves "freedom fighters." But they didn't deserve that dignity. They were lawbreaking thugs.

***

"I don't know about the comparison with the IRA, Senator." Melody handed Raybelle one of two cups of coffee. "That's going to yank a lot of people's chains."

"I sure hope so," Raybelle said. "I'm being provocative." She looked at the mess on her desk and, with one sweep of her forearm, dumped everything onto the floor.

Melody sighed. "I wish you'd quit doing that."

"Organizing experts say you should touch every piece of paper only once." Raybelle set her coffee on the clean desktop. "You were saying?"

"The British Army was in Northern Ireland for over thirty years." Melody brushed one delicate hand along her delicate skirt. "That makes it seem like a war."

"Just because troops are sent someplace doesn't make it a war." Raybelle's hair was getting stringy. Like Navratilova's at Wimbledon, she thought irrelevantly. She pushed it out of her eyes. "Look at Iraq. The last time this country declared war was 1941."

"Which Americans no longer remember." Melody sat on the edge of her desk, sipped from a green eco-friendly mug. "Face it, boss, you're going to lose support with this kind of thing."

"What 'kind of thing'? The last act of US belligerence that can be justified?"

Melody blinked. "Are you saying the Vietnam War can't be justified? I always thought you supported it. You've taken a lot of flak for that."

"Don't ever use *flak* as a figure of speech," Raybelle said. "Not when you're talking about Vietnam." She poured coffee down her throat, winced when it scalded.

"I'm just playing devil's advocate before you post something that isn't well thought through."

"Why? This Web of yours is so much trash," Raybelle said.

"Everything's 'beta' and 'citation needed.' And if I do choose to show stuff to anybody, why should it be you?"

Melody's look turned from apologetic to smug. "You've been reading your own Wikipedia entry, haven't you?"

Raybelle stared hard at her, but was the first to blink. "Ah, Melody, is it really that bad? You said there's been a lot of traffic to my site."

"And a lot of hate mail. Some comments call for the judgment of God on your head—"

"Can't we turn those things off?"

"—others are more, ah, graphic in nature."

Raybelle laughed. "More graphic than the Last Judgment? Didn't you study art at the U-ni-ver-si-ty of Chicago?"

She was pleased to see she'd at last succeeded in irritating Melody, who scooped up the papers off the floor and dropped them in the confidential recycling bin. "Fine, Senator," Melody said. "Clean up your own mess. But I'm telling you, veterans aren't going to appreciate your saying their war didn't count. That their sacrifice was in vain."

"It always is," Raybelle said. "And don't talk to me about vets right now. Thanks to Grant Rivers, that's all we'll be dealing with for the next I don't know how long."

CHAPTER FIVE

It was an unusually warm spring day in Chicago, and the emergency rooms would be filling with asthma attacks and gunshot wounds. Tomas sweated on her walk to the Dan Ryan el. It was just as uncomfortable in the clinic on Roosevelt Road, although she'd shed her white coat.

"I dream about fire," Dennis said.

"Where's the fire?" Tomas said. "In your dream."

"In the tunnels," he said, "in the camp. Garbage cans, paper— always lots of garbage where we live. You touch flame to it, like from somebody's cigarette, everybody's cardboard box could go up in flames." He turned bleary eyes on her. "Like hell."

Tomas knew that this man needed more help than she could

give. She wasn't a priest, to whom confessions of sin or fear of hell might mean something. But Dennis didn't want, or intend to seek, anyone else's help, because he didn't believe there was anything wrong with him. It was what he had done, his "cross to bear." His religious terms made her edgy; she sat stiff in her chair.

"Was it like that in Mauritius?" she said. "In their slum?"

She had never seen him hide his face in his hands before. She could feel, although she was several feet away, the scratchy material of his old clothes, and a darkness passed into the room, eclipsing her papers, examination table, the wall bare of framed diplomas. When he looked up, his words came in a whisper. "I made that slum."

She waited for him to go on.

"We did. The United States Marines, proud and brave, did that to those people. We took their land and put them on a garbage scow to nowhere, Doctor Jefferson. It was no different than the American Indians, but a hundred years later. We should have known better."

"You know better now." She wanted to say, *Look at you, you're wasting away, because of people you can't help.*

"But nobody cares," Dennis said. "Nobody gives a damn. Excuse me again for swearing."

It was hard for Tomas to imagine him as a marine, killing enemies or rounding up civilians, any of the things he'd done that he now felt so terrible about. His hands were covered with nicotine stains and what she'd determined were old blisters. He smelled of the outdoors, not in a pleasant way, but because he slept and did everything else outside. Looking from his hands to his gaunt body to his haunted eyes, Tomas no longer saw a subject who had come to her with a bloodstream full of exciting learning material. She saw a man, incapable of any but the gentlest actions, with a cat named Friesian being looked after in the lobby.

"You had to do some tough things over there," she tried again.

"I didn't have to," he said. "I followed orders. I could have chosen to do what was right."

"It must have been hard for you, to be so rough with people."

"People." Dennis gazed at her. Something fierce in his eyes. "I haven't told you the half of it, Doctor. I haven't told you about the dogs."

***

"I'm not doing it, Mel."

"Don't call me that." Melody's tone was mild, but her shoes clicked next to the desk, like Dorothy's in *The Wizard of Oz*. "Please."

Raybelle looked up, hoping the respect showed in her face. Respect, like other feelings, was not something Raybelle expressed often, or well. "Sorry. You can call me Ray next time, if you want."

"How did you get your name? If I may be so bold."

Raybelle picked up the memo impaler and balanced it in her hand. "My parents, of course. My daddy was Ray and my mama, Belle."

"Do you miss them?"

"I'm not 'blogging' about my family, okay? What might serve a male politician is a liability in my case. Put out one piece of information, and people will just go poking into what isn't there. No respect for privacy. My political philosophy is built on privacy."

"I know," Melody said, as if she'd written a dissertation on the subject.

But Melody didn't know. She, and the rest of America, probably thought that Raybelle had a private life that was just more private than most. In fact, there was no life. There was nothing to reveal and nothing to hide. Except Dennis, her mad brother, who had been doing a good enough job of hiding himself until that doctor came along.

"What's 'driving traffic' to my website, anyway?"

For once, Melody looked hesitant. "The fact that you're a woman, I think. A woman with ambition," she amended. "I think people see you as the next woman president, and there you are, posting controversy in the first person. It's like a car wreck; they have to stop and stare."

"Do they care what the subject is?" Raybelle tried not to betray hope.

"With all due respect, Senator—"

"Oh, don't give me that, Melody. Nobody says that phrase and follows it with words of respect."

Melody sank into her chair on the opposite side of the office. In her matching navy jacket and skirt, her silk blouse, she was dressed to kill, which in her case meant kill Raybelle's ego. "Senator, you do go on and on about the Constitution."

"What about the Constitution?"

"It's not sexy."

Raybelle's fingers clenched, and the membranes behind her eyes clenched at the same time. "I don't do 'sexy,' Ms. Park."

"I didn't mean literally."

So Melody thought *sexy* was a preposterous word to associate with her. Raybelle was somehow offended. She walked to the window and fingered the ancient, dust-patterned curtain. Unbelievable how seventies these senate offices were. So stuck in time, it was a wonder she'd been elected to this place.

Melody said, "And I wouldn't have recommended tearing into the 'enemy combatants' controversy right now. It's the president's pet term, and most of the country is on his side."

"Nope." She turned from the window. "It's Secretary Perry's pet term. And I wrote that just to make him mad."

***

Raybelle's Blog
March 21, 2007
Crimes and Misnomers, Part 2

Dear People,

Why did the US have to invent a special term for the "enemy combatants" we captured in Afghanistan after September 11? Why don't we take prisoners of war? Is it because the war is undeclared?

The last century had lots of bad men. It would be hard to find somebody with more blood on his hands than Stalin, or Pol Pot. But even by those standards, I think you would agree there was something uniquely evil about the Nazis. The mechanized killing. The industrial machinery of mass murder.

What did the Allies do with our Nazi prisoners, though? We know what the Japanese Empire did with their Allied prisoners of war. They tortured and starved them. We, the Allies, could face ourselves at the end of World War II, because we did not do this. We gave those war criminals a fair and open trial.

Can somebody please explain to me why, because some terrorists have no use for the rules of humanity, we should dispense with ours? We tried Nazis at Nuremberg. Are today's "bad guys" worse? Or are we worse than we were in 1945?

Perry hated that bitch. He hated her, and he hated the fact that he had to read her rants, her online ramblings, that he had to waste his time. Other points of view made him feel soiled.

He wiped the crown of his head with a white handkerchief that had been crisp this morning. Prisoners of war. What century did McKeehan think they were living in? The Greatest Generation was toothless now; the country required leadership too clever to have actually fought in any war. Perry's peers might have been grunts in the Vietnamese jungle, but not him. "Prisoners of war" made McKeehan sound like one of those bleating vendors in front of the monuments, with their POW stickers and their eyes that Perry never met.

Grant Rivers looked uncomfortable seated across from him, but Perry was in no hurry to speak. He glanced toward the bookshelf, straightened his sleeves. He would let the tension build until Rivers lost control, but he himself never would. The only sign of his own discomfort was this unaccountable sweat.

Rivers held a printout of McKeehan's blog. Perry refused to look things up on the Internet; a lackey printed out anything he needed to read. He'd handed the paper to Rivers the moment the senator entered his office. He enjoyed the feeling that gave him, that Rivers was just another lackey.

The senator couldn't keep himself from speaking. "She has pretty strong feelings about this."

"I want to know why."

"Well." Rivers shifted his bulk in the chair. "She has pretty strong feelings about everything. I mean, that's Raybelle."

"I want to know why this, in particular. 'Prisoners of war' evokes the Vietnam era. Everyone has an opinion about Vietnam."

"I can tell you hers. We shouldn't have lost."

"We didn't lose." Perry wiped his scalp again. "The US does not 'lose' wars."

"Okay, we didn't win." Rivers spread his hands in a conciliatory manner. "I'm not here to invent new words, Henry. That's your area of expertise."

"Jesus, you sound like her." Perry reached over the desk, snatched the printout, and scanned the first sentence again before crumpling the paper into a ball. "I want her *out*."

He would never admit this to Rivers, but the woman made him uncomfortable. All women did. He couldn't even face his own wife, not since the day they'd learned their daughter was dead, that she would never be a woman herself. Raybelle McKeehan was worse than other women, though, because she carried power with her. And everywhere Perry saw power, he wanted it.

***

Melody had recommended the *1812 Overture* for Raybelle's ring tone, and Raybelle agreed, though it sounded tinny and Russian. "Get that, will you please?"

"Senator McKeehan's office. Yes. Yes. I'll get her."

Melody put a hand on her arm. "I think you'd better take this. It's Doctor Jefferson."

Raybelle did not expect Melody's touch, and her tone, when she answered, was more cross than she felt. "McKeehan."

"Senator, it's Doctor Jefferson. I'm afraid I don't have good news for you—"

"You never do." Raybelle looked for Melody but she had moved a discreet distance away.

Dr. Jefferson paused, as if considering how many words she could spare. "Dennis is dead. I'm sorry."

Raybelle tried to draw strength into her voice. "What happened?"

***

The clinic had had the hospital page Tomas to give her the

news. She'd awakened on the couch, but had no memory of falling asleep, though it should have been memorable; she did it so seldom. The vibration at her hip wasn't the sensation she'd prefer to wake up to, but it was all she could expect.

"This is Doctor Jefferson," she said when the receptionist picked up. Three words more than necessary.

"Oh, Doctor Jefferson. I'm sorry to disturb you at home, but I'm afraid one of your patients—"

"It's Dennis, isn't it?"

She almost wondered why they'd called; she wasn't the coroner. She hadn't been much help when he was alive. You could do so much for a patient, but you couldn't live his life for him. Still, this loss was harder than most.

It seemed Tomas's had been the only contact information anyone could find in Dennis's abandoned backpack, on which Friesian still sat. His remaining possessions in the world. Was Friesian a possession? "I'll pick up the cat," she said.

People who saw it said that when Dennis set himself on fire, he twirled, hands spread out, like a pinwheel in flames. He'd been staying on Lower Wacker again. A lot of homeless people slept on grates, for the heat. The city of Chicago was always trying to "clean things up."

What stood out, in the reports, was that Dennis was standing when he self-immolated, on his feet. He'd been lying on that grate for days, fighting to keep warm. But when warmth was no longer enough, he went out in a pillar of fire.

Now, after a very busy Tuesday and the obligatory phone call to Raybelle McKeehan, Tomas stroked Friesian's fur as he purred in her lap, oblivious to everything. Cats didn't care. Friesian could have slept through Dennis's whole hideous self-sacrifice and now couldn't tell the difference between one owner and the next—between a homeless white man of unknown preferences and a lonely black lesbian physician. All Friesian cared about was his next meal and where he would sleep. It was so simple, like the kind of ideal Christianity Dennis had described.

Like Friesian, Tomas knew where she would sleep next, but not when. She decided to concentrate on the meal part. It had been some time since she'd bought herself a good sit-down dinner.

When there had been reason to celebrate, and Tomas had taken the time to do so, she and Alicia used to go to the Berghoff. She missed the Berghoff. Missed its décor, German beer, fabulous beef roulade. She could get a good dinner anywhere, but the loss of her favorite restaurant, its beautiful turn of the century interior, as well as the woman she took there, drove her to drink.

Over a solitary steak and a very good bottle of red wine, which Tomas could too easily finish off herself, she thought about Dennis McKeehan. When she'd awakened early that morning, she had been Dr. Jefferson to any number of patients over the years, some of whom had died. But now she was just Tomas, a human being, who could die or, for that matter, kill in the performance of her profession. Now she was just a woman with a lost friend, and no other friend to call and tell because she hadn't realized until she looked behind her that no one else was there.

CHAPTER SIX

All her life Raybelle had looked forward. At the age of ten her bedroom was full of books about the presidents, and decked out with the American and Tennessee flags. She'd planned her law career in Poudre Valley, her eventual election to the state legislature in Nashville, her friendship with Lamar Alexander and even Al Gore. Every step had taken her closer to Constitution Avenue and the US Capitol.

Mama had always believed in Raybelle's ambitions, while Daddy had been gone too soon to see her fulfill any of them. With the passage of years, she'd had less and less occasion to look back, especially at the men in her life from whom she'd gained nothing. But now, with the weight of Dennis on her mind, she found she had no choice but to go home.

She approached her house in Tennessee driving with caution, more than was needed to get around the curves in the road, which everyone else took too fast. Most places she went, she was accompanied by a bevy of hangers-on and "helpers." Other than Melody, they weren't very helpful. She preferred to travel this way, driving her own cheap Ford, with just another staff member or two riding along. If it was good enough for Russ Feingold of Wisconsin, then certainly a Republican could make a no-frills trip.

Home looked like a farmhouse, white siding and green trim, and there was the barnyard next to it, but most of the two acres hadn't grown anything but grass for decades. When Mama was alive, she'd had her small garden near the kitchen window, with a few vegetables and a little strawberry patch.

Mama would have been at the window now, waiting for Raybelle. She wouldn't recognize the car—it was always a different car—but she would listen for the slowing of wheels around that last curve, the tumble of gravel down her steep driveway. She would dry one last dish, though it wouldn't need the extra polish, and put it away in the cupboard. Then she would be at the door, hand on the knob, smile on her face.

Raybelle stared at the grass Dennis had once cut, the old tree where the tire swing had hung. With every mile closer to the McKeehan house, she'd felt herself grow younger, until by the time she got to the door she was a girl again, coming home from school to report that Dennis was in trouble. Worse than trouble. The worst he'd ever been in.

"Come on in, girl," Mama would have said today, as she always did, and wrapped her floury arms around Raybelle's taller frame. "When was the last time I saw you except on TV?"

"Too long, Mama," was what Raybelle always said.

Every visit, Mama behaved as if Raybelle was from the long-ago past, and might never visit again. Mama watched too much international news, and when she saw something unpleasant, from Sarajevo or somewhere, she worried that Raybelle would be attacked. But that was just the usual maternal exaggeration of her daughter's importance. Raybelle used to almost wish she had such power and influence to be the target of assassination.

In this Southern house, there had always been an escalating rivalry between the amount of food they could place in their mouths and the conversation that came out. Raybelle could see and smell and taste it all, and it almost surprised her when the door was locked and she had to open it herself. It was her house now, had been for years, but Mama still floated through it like a hint of old perfume. The house had the feel of a place no longer lived in. It wasn't as simple as the fact that Raybelle wasn't home that much. Mama had been a person so alive, she filled the house with her cooking and caring.

A picture of Belle Garfield (Mama's birth name) stood on the mantelpiece. It was from Belle's final year of high school. Raybelle was proud of her mother for graduating from high school in the midst of a cruel Depression that had deprived so many American girls and boys of the most basic opportunities. In turn, Raybelle's college education had always seemed a matter of more pride to Belle Garfield McKeehan than anything else, including her daughter's advancement in politics. Raybelle couldn't blame her for that.

"Hello, Mama." She picked up the frame and held it with reverence.

She was in the habit, on her private trips home, of talking to her mother's picture, and thus with her spirit, though not in an ethereal sense. Holding this photo in her hand also meant she could avoid the other pictures on the mantelpiece. Dennis, so young in his dress uniform, and their parents' wedding day. Mama had kept these pictures out, along with one of graduation that Raybelle had since put away in the attic, because they all showed young people on the cusp of their potential, with hope-filled eyes and faces not lined by subsequent tragedy. Only Raybelle knew that, even at that age, Dennis was shadowed by grief. Not by the loss of their father, who had been cut down by a heart attack at forty, silently, the way he had moved through life, working and watching television every night. Never raising his voice, let alone a hand, to his wife or his children. No picture of Ray McKeehan on his own stood in this living room, just the wedding photo in which his shy figure was outshone, as always, by Belle's exuberant one.

"Hello, Daddy." She nodded to that picture.

It was cruel of her to remember Daddy as an afterthought just because he had never imposed himself on her memory with any act of violence. He had lived in the shadow of his wife and it had worked for the two of them; they had shared a happy life. Holding the picture of Mama, Raybelle had intended to explain, in her mother's presence, what had happened to Dennis. But now, she replaced the photo and addressed the one with Daddy in it instead.

"This concerns both of you."

***

Two days later Raybelle was meeting Grant Rivers for breakfast back in Washington, DC. It was later than she would usually eat breakfast, if she remembered to eat at all. But being home had shaken her up, and she needed to talk to someone. She couldn't keep the life and death of Dennis to herself for long. Grant was one of the few people on Capitol Hill, or in Washington for that matter, who knew Raybelle had a brother.

The moment she walked into the dark and dated senate cafeteria, Grant rose from the table. Looking at him, you'd think he was here every morning of his life for all you can eat. His girth spread out in the booth from the confines of his tailored jacket. Raybelle happened to know that he'd been a football star in high school, a powerful tackle, but the athletic aspects to his great size and weight had disappeared with the years.

"So," Grant said, "what can I do for you?"

"Lord, Grant," she said, "let's get in line, get something to eat. Can't talk business just on coffee. What am I, a Yankee?"

He laughed at that. North and South was a running joke between Raybelle and Grant, on account of his name. The Civil War (as Yankees called it) had not only divided the states from each other, but people within the states. East Tennessee was hillbilly country and had no use for the economics of slavery, so crucial to the cotton plantations further south. Which didn't make her or Grant's ancestors any less racist toward the blacks they did know.

Soon, plates were piled high with eggs, bacon, sausages, biscuits and gravy, and hominy grits. Raybelle always meant to leave

room for some fruit, to cut the grease and salt quotient a little
bit, but it just never happened. She made a point of getting a
large orange juice as well as coffee, though the orange juice was
from concentrate and not the best feature of breakfast. At least
it wasn't Tang.

"Now tell me," Grant said, and plunged a forkful of egg into
his mouth, ensuring that Raybelle had his undivided attention.

She rested her fork in the grits. Good grits could hold a fork.
"I need a little advice from my old mentor," she said. "I believe,
and you've said you believe this too, that I have a real shot at being
a nominee for president—even if it's with the wrong party. But
now there's this hospital investigation. I'm honored to be asked
to undertake it, but it concerns me too. Exposing things that not
everybody may want to come to light could cost me. In the short
or long run."

"Well," Grant said, "surely you're not afraid of a little
controversy. If this thing needs looking into, if it's got to be done,
then you're the one to do it."

Raybelle smiled at the compliment. "You're right, I'm not
afraid. It's more to do with how I feel about the situation."

Grant looked at her with steady eyes; she saw compassion in
them. "It's Dennis, isn't it?"

She nodded.

"Is it because of Dennis being a vet, or because of the
disagreements the two of you had?"

"Both," she said. "I know if I find out those guys have been
mistreated, it's going to upset me, and I don't want to…appear
out of control. Don't have a choice about that, if I'm going to run
for commander-in-chief."

Grant wiped his mouth with the napkin from his lap. "Ray,"
he said, "you've pretty much built your reputation as a straight
shooter who always goes for the truth. I don't see any benefit in
altering that now."

"That's just it, though. I don't know that everybody wants
the truth."

He gazed at her. "You mean Henry Perry?"

"You know I do."

"Well, the secretary's job is only as secure as that of the

president," Grant said. "Less so. He has his interests, but you have the interests of the American people."

"You sound like a speechwriter."

He laughed, a hearty laugh from his gut. "I've been at this job for a long time, Ray. I'm not saying Perry is the enemy. But, in a sense, anything that threatens our troops anywhere is the enemy. Whether it's terrorism or an infection. You keep clear on that, keep saying it out loud, and I guarantee, you'll have all the good people on your side."

"And if I don't?"

His smile was broad and kind. "There's one Major Rivers who'll be more than happy to call in the cavalry."

"Thanks, Grant." For the first time, she thought the rumpled, crusty veteran might fit his namesake, General Grant, after all.

"So Grant, you're heading for my end of the state. Why's that?"

"It's commencement at Herald Aviation," Grant said. "I'm going to speak to the graduates—all three of them."

"Isn't it a little early in the year to be graduating?"

"They don't follow the regular school year. When you finish your course, you're done."

Raybelle felt more than a little miffed that Grant had been asked, instead of her. Herald Aviation was an offshoot of Herald College, an industrial-strength Bible institution—as in "the herald angels sing." The aviation school, which happened to be in her hometown, trained missionary pilots to fly light aircraft into the hearts and souls of the heathen. Hardly Raybelle's cup of secular tea, but at least she was a Republican.

"Isn't having the state's top Democrat speak to the Herald Aviators sort of like inviting Satan?"

Grant dabbed at the corner of his mouth. "They must think they can withstand the temptation. You didn't expect them to invite you?"

"I didn't know it was going on, but it would have been courteous."

"Ray, you know I don't think the way they do about a lot of things. But in their world, leadership is male. A Democrat is better than a woman."

She knew it was that simple, but it still sounded harsh to her ear. "Well," she said, "maybe courtesy isn't the Christian virtue it was when I was growing up. Or treating a lady like a queen."

"No one treats you like a queen."

"I was thinking of how we were raised to treat Mama."

Grant put his hand on hers, and for the first time, she noticed liver spots. Sometimes she forgot just how senior the senior senator was. "How's Jean?"

He drew away at this change of subject. "Why?"

"Why? It's customary to ask after someone's wife."

"You know she's fine," Grant said. "I treat her like a queen."

***

Just the memory of her conversation with the senator made Tomas tense. She knew about being dispassionate, and that politicians were cold-blooded by nature, but still, she had to hand it to McKeehan. Learning of her brother's death, then making an offer in the same phone call. Tomas had been rushing down the corridor to her next patient when McKeehan's office rang, but the senator didn't care that she was busy.

"I just hope we can keep this out of the papers," she'd said, and Tomas wasn't sure how to respond to such callousness. "But I'm glad you called, Tomas—can I call you Tomas?" The senator had not even thanked her for the notification about her brother. "We've got a bit of a problem down here in Washington, and I think you might be able to help us out."

Tomas doubted it. "What's that?" One extra word.

"Seems there's been some issues over at the military hospital, and I'm trying to peel off certain layers of dirt that keep sticking. But I could use an expert. Somebody who sounds like she knows what she's talking about. You follow me?"

"Not yet."

"You're a doctor."

"Yes."

"If you point to a moldy wall and say there's *staphylococcus* growing on it, that will make news." At least she knew the actual term. "It just doesn't carry the same weight for me to point to it and say 'Filth.' Though it should."

"That's a very kind thing to say, Senator," Tomas bullshat, "but I'm a practicing physician. I can't just leave town even if I wanted to. My patients need me."

"You have one less patient now, Doctor Jefferson." McKeehan's tone was ice.

Tomas closed her eyes, took a deep breath. "I'm aware of that, Senator. And I'm sorry."

"Don't be sorry. Come on Thursday. There are flights from Chicago every hour."

"Senator—"

"And don't tell me you can't afford it."

Indeed, that would never have crossed Tomas's mind. "You know what, Senator McKeehan? I only called to tell you about Dennis. I'm sorry I can't be of more help."

"My brother was in the military, Doctor Jefferson." A rare pause. "You know about that, don't you?"

"Some." One word, that was it.

"Then you knew him as well as anyone." From the horn blast in the background, Tomas guessed that McKeehan's driver had pulled into traffic. "How soon can you be here?"

"Senator, I'm sorry—"

"Just be here Thursday evening. There's a reception at the White House."

"Senator McKeehan—"

"Listen, Doctor, I hate to say this," McKeehan said, in that way that meant she couldn't wait to say it. "But the fact is, you owe me. So far all you've given me is bad news."

Tomas wasn't believing this woman. A guilt trip over her own brother's death. "I don't owe you a favor!"

"I'll introduce you to the president." And McKeehan hung up.

Tomas was no fan of the president, but still. When was she going to get a personal invitation to meet him? Back in college, she remembered telling her roommate, Dana, "You have got to seize opportunities when they come along." Dana had always thought it was a sign of the privilege with which Tomas had been raised. To Tomas, it was just instinct. *Carpe diem*, and all that.

She was used to being summoned, but to her patients, not away from them. This white woman—Dennis had mentioned her Web log, but Tomas had never bothered to look at it. She should Google her, just so she wouldn't be the picture of complete ignorance.

When Tomas got home to her laptop, the first link she found was to the official US Senate page of Raybelle McKeehan (R-Tenn.) One of those faces made for politics. Photographed well, conveyed power, and didn't tell you another damn thing. Might as well be printed on a dollar bill.

While she was waiting for a page to load, Tomas called the clinic. With Dennis gone, the clinic felt less important to her. She could leave a day early. She also called her neighbor, Tim, and asked him to take care of Friesian, saying, "I have to go out of town urgently."

Because she was going to Washington. Tomorrow, when the senator wasn't expecting her. Not for Raybelle McKeehan's sake, but for Dennis's. He was a marine, and warfare was all about the element of surprise. Go in fast and hit them hard. Dennis was no longer around to confront his sister, so Tomas would have to do it for him.

She returned to the McKeehan site and scanned it for something worthwhile. The senator was involved in hearings and committees of which Tomas had never heard. There was an address for the senator's office at the Capitol—she made a note of that—and another located in Tennessee, at the Tri-Cities Regional Airport. The Tri-Cities: Bristol, Kingsport and Johnson City, Tennessee. Constituents (no one else, apparently) were welcome to contact Senator McKeehan by any of the following means...There was no mention of any personal history. No spouse, no children, no brothers who'd gone out like Roman candles on Lower Wacker Drive.

Tomas shut down her laptop and tried to remember how she'd managed to get her bachelor's degree without ever using the Internet. She could hardly imagine life without it now, and she wasn't that old. Pretty soon patients would be examined by remote computer-scope, and then medicine could be outsourced to India. Fair was fair.

As a test, she logged back in and searched for "India" on McKeehan's blog. Sure enough, this search turned up a rant, but not the racism, disguised as protectionism, that she'd expected. This one was about the Fourth Amendment and how, thanks to the current administration, Americans no longer had any privacy in international communications, even if it was just to a call center in Bangalore. Tomas spared a thought for remote-control medicine and what that would do for patient–physician confidentiality.

Then she imagined meeting the current president. The president whose administration Senator McKeehan savaged online ("he has betrayed his oath to protect the Constitution of the United States"), and now wanted to introduce her to. The woman had *cojones*.

Tomas would do more research later. Maybe on the flight. She booked it before she could have second thoughts.

She changed into a T-shirt and well-worn boxer shorts and curled up on the black leather couch in front of her television. She reached for the remote, hoping she would sleep, but doubting it somehow. She wondered, too, if she would dream of anyone.

CHAPTER SEVEN

Spring had come fast to the nation's capital. As much as she didn't have time for tourist clichés, Raybelle did enjoy her occasional glimpses of the cherry trees in blossom, from the window of a car that was adding to the pollution that would one day choke the cherry trees… Cycle of life. The trees were a gift from the Japanese, and look at the history America had with Japan. She wondered if sixty years from now, the Mall would be adorned with the legacy of some Arab enemies turned friends.

"I hope I can control how this plays in the press," she said to Melody, in the office at seven a.m.

"Who are you kidding?" Melody's growing insolence contrasted with the ladylike way she peeled the wrapper off her muffin. Looked like raisin bran.

"Well, if they report on my brother, I want the emphasis to be on his service in the Marines. If they have to report on his illness, I want it associated with sick veterans and their neglect. Turn it back on them, not on me for having one crazy relative."

"Aren't all relatives crazy?" Melody waved at the past week's accumulation of newspapers, which Raybelle had piled beside her desk. "Senator, reporters write about your hair, which is always going to look windblown unless you spray-paint it into a helmet shape. Their heads are full of stuff that some staffer younger than I am made up. Somebody went through your trash last week."

"Who?" Raybelle was incredulous. "Here?"

Melody nodded, her mouth full of bran. "I shred everything, as you know, but that doesn't stop the white van crowd. Speaking of crazy people."

Raybelle said, "You know, if I did decide to run for president myself, I might like to keep you around."

Melody laughed, a laugh as sweet as her name. "I think you're going to need a lot more than me, Senator."

"Like what?"

"A personal life."

"Oh, no." Raybelle pulled out her compact and inspected the aforementioned hair. "An earnest young feminist like you, and you're telling me to, what? Find a little woman to make the coffee?"

"No, that's my job." Melody shot her crumpled muffin wrapper, basketball style, into the wastebasket, then pointed to it. "Organic waste only."

"Don't tell me you're a green too. I thought Chicago was the university of free enterprise economics."

***

Tomas had gotten the earliest flight to Washington, only to spend most of the morning waiting in various anterooms of the Dirksen Senate Office Building. It was, from her perspective, a dump. It reminded her of a writ-large version of the county health centers where, as a very young doctor with a coat that didn't fit, she had performed measles, mumps and rubella vaccinations, and asked thirteen-year-old girls if there was any chance they were pregnant.

"I have an appointment," she kept repeating. But since no one, least of all Tomas, could verify an actual time for this supposed appointment, she was kept waiting securely. Not sent away; after all, she might be important, represent a lobby, or have a lot of money to donate.

"I spoke to someone," she said, standing taller than the stringy-haired assistant to the assistant who was the latest white boy blocking her from McKeehan.

"Everyone spoke to someone," a tired black gentleman said from one of the other seats.

"What was it concerning?" Stringy asked, as they all kept asking.

But some ethical tic of Tomas's wouldn't let her reveal McKeehan's private family business, which, as far as she was concerned, was the purpose of her visit.

So she continued waiting until the name McKeehan had given her finally jumped back into her memory. "Melody," she said. "I spoke to someone named Melody. She'll know all about it, just ask her."

***

"Yes." On the phone, Melody always sounded as excited as a girl working her first day at the ice cream parlor. "Yes, all right. We weren't expecting her today, but that's fine." She put the phone down and said, "It's Doctor Jefferson."

"Did she say what it's about?" Raybelle said. "I mean, I know what it's about, but did she say anything to anyone else?"

"No. I suspect that's why she's been kept waiting so long."

Moments later, Melody returned with a tall black woman. Raybelle plastered on her campaign smile and extended her hand. Tomas Jefferson's grip was firm and warm.

"So glad to meet you." Raybelle fought not to appear surprised. "Thought we'd see you tomorrow."

"I got a flight today. Hope you don't mind." Tomas stood very formally, and Raybelle wondered if she had a military background.

Melody would know. Melody had probably researched everything about Tomas Jefferson, but Raybelle hadn't been filled in at all.

"You weren't expecting a black doctor. Is that it?"

Raybelle kept her smile locked in place. "Not at all, Doctor Jefferson." She gestured to a seat.

Tomas set her coat down. She looked unconvinced. This was going to be a harder sell than Raybelle had thought. The office felt warmer with the heat of an extra body, and she wished she were a man or at least wearing a tie; she felt like loosening it.

She eased into her own chair and observed that Tomas didn't look as if she had just tumbled off a plane. She wore viciously creased black pants and a pure white shirt, the type that was styled in the shoulders to look feminine, with no buttons at the collar. A small gold hoop stood out in each earlobe. Tomas's eyes were clear. "I understand I can help you with something."

"Yes—"

"But that's not why I'm here." Tomas enunciated the words as if to emphasize her background and education. "I'm here because I knew your brother, Senator. We were—friends."

Raybelle sat up straighter, bringing herself equal in height—all Tomas's height must be in her legs. Seated, they were eye to eye. She forced a smile. "I'm glad to hear that," she said. "He needed a friend."

"Everybody does."

"Well, I appreciate everything you did to help Dennis," she said, "and now, I'm hoping you can help me."

"Senator—". Tomas was interrupted by Melody bringing the coffee.

"I'm sorry," Raybelle said. "Doctor Jefferson, this is my assistant, Melody Park."

"We've spoken." Tomas shook Melody's hand.

"At any rate, you must know Dennis didn't think highly of me, so I don't expect you to either. What I would like is for you to help other veterans, and the people of the United States, with this investigation at the military hospital."

"As I've explained to you, I have a practice in Chicago." Tomas spoke as if Raybelle were stupid. "And there must be many qualified experts who could do this job better than I could."

"That's exactly it." Raybelle tented her fingers. "They're already in Washington, but you come from outside. You have no interest other than the patients'." Tomas appeared to take this as a compliment. "You don't have an agenda, unlike everybody in this town. They say the best leaders—politicians, generals—are those who don't want to be there."

"Is that true of you?"

"Is what true?"

"I hear you want to be president."

Raybelle shifted in her chair. She would have to tell—no, *ask*—Melody to get a new one ordered. "What makes you think that?"

"Your blog," Tomas said.

"You've read it?" Raybelle was more pleased than she could account for.

"Dennis did."

All pleasure fled. "Dennis and I never agreed about anything in our lives."

"I doubt that's true, but in any case, he read your blog."

The nerve of this woman. "What about you?"

"I don't have time to read blogs."

"I suspect more people write than read them."

"If you want to call it writing." Tomas sounded disdainful. "I'm a scientist. Facts mean something to me, and citations and references."

"Well if you're so fond of footnotes," Raybelle said, now riled up, "you'd know that's all facts are—"

"Politics are long on debate and short on the scientific method. The closest thing you have is precedent. If science worked that way, we'd still believe in spontaneous generation and the sun going around the earth."

"Are you telling me no, Doctor Jefferson?"

Tomas stood up. "It's been a pleasure, Senator. Have a good day."

"Wait, please. Come to the White House with me. I did invite you to meet the president while you're in town."

"Who are you going to say that I am?" Tomas said. "Your housekeeper?"

Raybelle felt her face go hot. "How about sister?" She moved closer to Tomas. "I'm sorry you've got such a chip on your shoulder,

Ms. Yankee MD. But I bet you have somebody cleaning your house. Is she Filipina? Or Eastern European?"

Tomas smiled, a wicked, triumphant smile that made Raybelle hate her. "I believe the chip is on your shoulder, not mine." She gathered her coat from the back of the chair. "Now if you'll excuse me, I'm going back to my hotel."

And how much did Tomas think those hotel workers got paid? Raybelle sat back down and rubbed her temples.

"That went well," Melody said when Tomas Jefferson had left.

"Melody. Please shut up."

***

By the time she got back to the Hessian Hotel Tomas was aching for a workout. Just standing in an office made her so tense, she couldn't imagine just sitting and working in one all day. She would be curious to meet the president, because she'd heard he was a fitness type of guy, jogging daily around the White House grounds. If she had a chance, she'd ask him if it helped. If he got cramped sitting at the Oval Office desk, needed to get up and stretch from time to time.

Tomas tried not to think about what impression she'd made on Raybelle McKeehan. What did she care? If it weren't for her brother, whom the senator didn't seem to like, Tomas would have no reason to meet her at all.

She didn't realize how much the encounter had taken out of her until she took out her room key and saw it shaking in her hand. This never happened. She was a doctor: cool, professional, always in control. She drank coffee all day, but her hands didn't shake.

It was probably lack of sleep, but when had she ever slept much? Could such a short plane journey have messed with her routine? She also hadn't gotten the exercise she was used to. Good thing the Hessian had workout facilities.

She felt much better once she'd put on her Sharm El-Sheikh T-shirt and old sweatpants and was grunting away on a weight bench. With every rep, a little of her irritation seeped away. She couldn't believe McKeehan, talking race and class like she knew anything at all about where Tomas was coming from. Politicians always did that, especially white politicians talking to black people. Always thought they knew where you were coming from.

Tomas ran on the treadmill for forty-five minutes, had a shower, and stretched her plane-cramped muscles in the whirlpool. Then she dressed and went back to her room, where she'd left the cell phone because damn it, she was on vacation. Not working, just because McKeehan had asked her—to do what? Whitewash some hospital scandal?

There were no messages on her cell phone, but there was one at the hotel extension, from Melody Park. Melody apologized, without saying it was her fault, for how the meeting had gone with her boss, thanked Tomas for showing up on such short notice, and gave details of when and where she would be picked up for the president's reception, and what sort of attire she should wear. The consummate assistant. Maybe Tomas could steal her away from McKeehan.

***

Melody paused before leaving the office. "You coming? Everybody's gone for the night."

"I know what time it is." Raybelle's eyes did not leave the screen, and she gripped the mouse hard enough to give herself carpal tunnel syndrome right then and there.

"I know you're still upset about earlier," Melody said, "but you have no reason to take it out on me."

Raybelle released the mouse, feeling the ache in her hand. "I'm not—" Try again. "I'm sorry, Melody, but I'm not upset."

"Uh-huh. Well, don't forget the 'clear desk' policy, Senator. I hate to complain about the cleaners losing some valuable documents, if it's you."

"Who are the cleaners?"

"What?"

"Do you know them? Have you ever seen them?" Melody shook her head. "Maybe we should check on that. Wouldn't do to have subcontracting and immigration status become an issue next year, would it?"

"I'll make a note. But I thought you told Doctor Jefferson you weren't running for president."

"Who said anything about—"

"In fact," Melody raised a forefinger, as if testing the direction of the wind, "you didn't say that you weren't. You just parried the question. If that's not proof you are interested, I don't know what is!"

"Go on, get out of here." Raybelle brandished her memo impaler.

"Goodnight, Senator. I wasn't invited to the White House, and I have a date with my DVD player."

After Melody left, Raybelle shut the computer down. She'd been trying to research Tomas Jefferson, hadn't asked Melody to do it because she didn't want to have to explain herself. But Raybelle could only find a handful of medical articles, and those she couldn't be sure were coauthored by the same "T. Jefferson." She didn't know how old Tomas was.

With a name like Jefferson, she should have guessed the doctor was black. She'd known Park was a Korean name. Not that it mattered. Try telling her some multimillionaire quarterback driving a Hummer with a movie screen in it had anything to complain about. No, it was the worse-off folks, black or white or whatever, whose kids were defending this country and its Constitution. Not their wayward commander-in-chief with his violated oath. It occurred to Raybelle that the president's puppet master, Henry Perry, might be at the White House tomorrow. She didn't know whether or not to hope so.

***

Tomas couldn't sleep. This wasn't in itself unusual, but it was agitating her tonight. She sat on the made-up hotel bed in boxer shorts, having removed her T-shirt because the room was stuffy and overheated. Goddamn forced air. Normally, just messing around with the TV remote long enough would put her to sleep, and failing that, there was nothing stopping her from taking matters into her own hands. But she didn't feel like having sex with herself tonight, and no one else was there.

She thought she could dull her senses with a sports broadcast, and found a channel showing what purported to be football, but turned out to be a talk show about that talented quarterback who had decided to get involved in a dogfighting ring. Why was this not on the news network instead? Dog killing—an all-American blood sport, direct line to the hearts of the people. Tomas wished this fool was on the other channel, if only because she made a point of never watching television news.

She was nervous about meeting the president. That was understandable enough. Politicians themselves didn't sound smooth when they hadn't rehearsed what they were going to say. Look at the stuff that was pouring onto the Internet like maple syrup every morning. Make the most obscure slur at the most obscure event, and the next day it's all over YouTube and you're all over.

CHAPTER EIGHT

Tomas was surprised not to be frisked at the White House, considering someone had flown a human bomb into the Pentagon a few years back. She'd left her phone at the hotel, although, incredibly, phones with cameras were allowed in the White House, since she couldn't actually use it without confiscation by the Secret Service. Playing the doctor card wouldn't help.

Being a doctor didn't mean anything. She could still be car-bombing Glasgow airport, or force-feeding prisoners in Guantánamo Bay.

She would have to be her own camera. In fact, Tomas preferred to be without one. If she'd had a camera, she would have felt obligated to take pictures of everything, as if to prove she'd been here, at this ultimate work-from-home spot. Instead, her mind recorded every detail of the admittedly impressive State Dining Room, from the shining gold sconces (Hillary Clinton's era) to that "thinker" portrait of Abraham Lincoln, chin in hand.

What was he thinking? Tomas thought. Whether it was really worth freeing the slaves in the South, or whether they were better left alone? Did he know what would become of his party, and his successors?

Tomas knew the president didn't drink, which wasn't an excuse for serving his guests what she considered inferior wine. "Quit looking like such a martyr," McKeehan said, and made some reference that Tomas would have to look up later, something about wine in new wineskins. The two women had greeted each other with cool civility.

***

Tomas Jefferson was, in fact, driving Raybelle nuts. Insolent as Melody, like overeducated people always were; and Raybelle couldn't say a thing about it because it would be interpreted as some kind of racial remark. You had to watch your mouth in politics. The press—and there was press everywhere, if not someone legitimate then a "blogger" like herself—would love nothing better than to pit the woman card against the black card, or some other divided-they-fall strategy. A strategy as old as Lincoln, that overrated opportunist, older than the white suffragettes back in the nineteenth century, who'd been persuaded not to stick with freed slaves against The Man. Just scratch and claw for their one little bit of liberation and forget everybody else. Well, that's what happened when you started splitting people into groups. People whose ancestors had been slaves versus people whose ancestors were too poor to own slaves. People with penises versus people with indoor plumbing. People who got excited about books and art galleries versus people who got excited by "reality" television shows…

"Senator McKeehan!" The hand of a latecomer landed on her upper back, and Raybelle snapped back to focus on ice-blue eyes, which clashed with the powder blue of his shirt. "I haven't had the pleasure of meeting your…escort."

Raybelle didn't like the way Perry said that, and from the slight narrowing of Tomas's eyes, she didn't either. "Mr. Secretary," Raybelle said, thinking that although he had the same title as an administrative assistant, he probably knew less. "Doctor Tomas Jefferson, from Chicago. Doctor Jefferson, this is Secretary Henry Perry."

"A medical doctor?" Perry said.

"Yes." Tomas shook his hand.

"Why then, we're both in the business of saving lives."

"I'm familiar with your work."

Perry smiled, but his eyes were cold, whereas Tomas looked about to burst into flames. "Well, I'll let you ladies finish your meal," he said. "Save room for the strawberry shortcake; it's excellent."

"I'll consider that an order," Raybelle said.

As Perry moved away, she studied her dinner companion. Tomas wore red, which stood out in a sea of black, white and the occasional beige. Hers was also one of the only dark faces in the room, if you didn't count the serving staff, which, of course, Raybelle did. The red was a little much. Tomas didn't need to impress anybody tonight. Then again, maybe she did. The silk sleeves hugged Tomas's arms and did nothing to disguise her powerful shoulders. Weightlifting, maybe?

"Don't stare, Senator." Tomas popped a stuffed mushroom into her mouth, and Raybelle forced herself to look away. Henry Perry's wife was attached to a wineglass, and in need of attention.

"Senator McKeehan," Barbara Perry said, "I haven't seen you since my annual ice cream party for children's literacy."

"Barbara, of course." Barbara had been drunk then too. "I'd like you to meet Doctor Tomas Jefferson. Doctor Jefferson, this is Secretary Perry's wife." She set her hand in the small of Tomas's back. Tense as steel.

"Charmed." Barbara extended her hand, floppy wrist down. Tomas took it, in a gesture so courtly she looked about to touch it to her lips.

"Barbara's cause is children's literacy in DC," Raybelle explained.

"I've always wondered," Tomas said, still holding Barbara's hand. "When I hear about government business, on the news, people always say Washington. But when you talk about the city and its problems—say, children and illiteracy—I tend to hear DC. Are they two different places?"

"Well, no." Barbara didn't sound at all sure. "Not that I'm the person to ask. You should ask someone from the area, Doctor Jefferson. Someone—"

"Black?" Tomas suggested. Barbara looked like she'd swallowed a jalapeño.

"Why," Raybelle interposed, "your glass is nearly empty, Barbara. Let me take care of that for you." She took the glass and handed it to a nearby server, mouthing "Coffee." Barbara, having nothing to hold on to, made her unsteady way back to her seat.

"What the hell are you doing?" Raybelle whispered to Tomas.

"Don't worry, she won't remember anything we said." Raybelle couldn't dispute this. "I'm only here because of Dennis. The least I can do is be as irreverent and aggravating as you'd expect him to be."

Tomas's eyes swept the room, practiced and diagnostic. She took in every detail: the president in his thick-soled shoes, which were shined to leather-boy quality and designed to make him appear taller. Perry, the brain behind a defense department that drove men like Dennis McKeehan mad but could not keep kamikaze pilots from crashing into their own offices. And Dennis's sister, the senator, decked out in a black dress and pearls that were all the sexier for being understated.

She'd expected silence and for the president to dominate the dinner conversation, but everyone talked all the time, which was how she ended up sniping at McKeehan. "These strawberries come from your small family farm, Senator?" She sucked one clean off the too-firmly-attached stem. "All picked by white legal residents, no doubt?"

The strawberry shortcake was as excellent as promised. Afterward, Raybelle and Tomas joined a long line of people waiting for their fifteen seconds with the President of the United States. Raybelle had a vision of her fellow members of Congress kicking up their heels to absurd music, and a phrase came to mind that she'd heard from a politician in Australia, where folks were a little more forthcoming: "a conga line of suckholes." To her horror, she started laughing at her own interior joke.

"What's funny?" Tomas's arms were rigid at her sides.

Raybelle fanned in front of her rapidly flushing face.

"For chrissakes, it's the *president*," Tomas said, as the conga line snaked nearer.

Oh, so now Tomas was embarrassed by her? That was a rich thought, which caused Raybelle to recover just in time. "Mr. President."

"Raybelle, how are ya?" He said it in that gum-snapping way he had.

"May I present Doctor Tomas Jefferson." She pressed her hand to Tomas's back again.

Tomas shook hands. "A pleasure to meet you, sir."

"Nice to meet you," he said, already looking past them to the next suckhole. He reminded Raybelle of the minister at her last church, the Episcopal cathedral in Knoxville, back before she represented Tennessee's First Congressional District in the House. The minister had shaken her hand like this every Sunday morning she attended, but she was sure he'd never remembered her from one week to the next. No wonder she'd stopped going to church.

"I can't believe I was nervous about meeting him," Tomas said, once they'd left the conga line.

"Were you?"

"Thanks for the invitation," Tomas said. "Will you excuse me for a moment?" She glided away.

Raybelle felt the space between them, uncomfortable. What was it specifically that had not impressed Dr. Jefferson about this president? He wasn't a tall or physically imposing man, for all the power he had. Aging Ken doll looks and nearly-blank eyes. Contrast those with the square-framed glasses and shaved scalp of Henry Perry, who radiated power. Raybelle was conscious of that power and the receding energy of Tomas Jefferson, two magnetic poles at either end of the State Dining Room.

***

Tomas went over the evening in her mind later, her second all-but-sleepless night at the Hessian Hotel. When she'd looked at Perry, from a distance, she'd felt his coldness. And she'd been offended by the way the president had looked at her, but thinking about it now, she was ashamed to have directed that same look at more than a few people in her life. Alicia, for example. Some of her patients. It was a look that said, Words are coming out of your mouth, but I'm not listening to you. It said, How can I treat whatever small and relatively insignificant part of you is causing trouble, so I can go on to the important part of my own life? It said, Next!

Tomas was brought down by that look, like she didn't matter except as a vote, or a kidney stone. She didn't want to look or be looked at that way, ever again. She didn't know what Raybelle McKeehan wanted her to do or if she could do it, but she would try. Otherwise what made her different from all the president's men? Men who knew nothing about the casualties of war, whether on the battlefield today or on Lower Wacker Drive, forty years after they, these men in power, had been deferred from the service they'd grown up to extol.

She opened her computer, found the senator's website, and looked through the photos of McKeehan. The best one showed her in three-quarters profile, laughing at something someone else had said. Who knew if the laugh was genuine, but it looked good to Tomas. She'd searched the senator's eyes for that coldness, the look she'd seen on the president's and Perry's faces. McKeehan's face was all smile, and Tomas wished she had been the one to put that smile there. She couldn't account for this, nor did she know what it would be like to work with a person whose public image was so important that she couldn't grieve her own brother. That she could laugh like this should be Tomas's warning that Raybelle was mentally ill, at least as much as Dennis had been.

Tomas stared at the image. There was indeed something real there, or as real as it could be in two dimensions. If she wasn't going to sleep tonight anyway, she could at least plan leave from the hospital. She'd call in the morning.

CHAPTER NINE

The hotel phone jangled Tomas awake from a raunchy dream. "Jefferson," she said.

"Hey."

It was Raybelle, and Tomas didn't know which surprised her more: that the greeting was so informal, or that she immediately recognized the voice. "Senator, good morning."

"Listen, I'm sorry about last night."

Tomas had already started thinking of McKeehan as Raybelle, despite her exalted office. "What happened? Did we drink too much? Did you take advantage of me?"

"Very funny," Raybelle said, in that tone people used when they didn't find it funny at all. "I meant, we didn't have a chance to discuss your helping me. Now, I know you already said you wouldn't do it, but hear—"

"I'll do it."

On the other end of the phone, Tomas swore she could hear Raybelle blink. "I haven't told you what I need yet."

"I'll stay in Washington." Tomas sat up in bed, drew one finger up her torso from the waistband of her boxer shorts. Hmm, abdominals needed some work.

"Very well. How about we talk about it over lunch?"

"Somewhere less formal than the White House?"

This time, Raybelle laughed. "You better believe it."

***

Lunch was at a Middle Eastern hole in the wall, one of dozens in Adams–Morgan. These restaurants were called different names depending on the ancestry of the owners, though the same coffee was served from Turkey to North Africa. This particular restaurant was Syrian.

When she got there Raybelle was seated with two other people she didn't introduce. Tomas tried to act natural with this, and agreed on the appetizer plate. "One of the great ironies of Washington," Raybelle said. "The capital of the Great Satan, and more Arab restaurateurs than you can shake a stick at. All living the American dream."

"That was Iran," Tomas said.

"Beg pardon?" Raybelle paused, hand in the bread basket.

"Iran's leader called America the Great Satan. Iranians aren't Arab."

"I know that, *Doctor* Jefferson. But you have to admit, that whole part of the world has been a mess since the turn of the century."

"You mean the twentieth century."

Raybelle tore off a chunk of bread with her teeth, then spoke through it. "You know, this isn't going to work real well if you're going to spend every minute pulling intellectual rank. So let's both agree that you're smarter than I am, and move on with our lives."

"I don't think I'm smarter."

"Different smarts, then. You're a respected professional, while I'm a used-car salesman."

Tomas was spared having to guess at the sincerity of this self-deprecation, because the waiter, a bearded twenty-year-old of startling handsomeness, had returned. "Welcome to Little Damascus, Senator," he said. He had a flat Midwestern accent, like a generic American on TV.

"Hi," Tomas said. "I'll have the falafel plate, with hot sauce on the side. Please."

"How you doing, Yusuf?" The southerner proceeded with conversation, none of which involved an order, then saying, "You know what I'm having!" and motioning as if to swat Yusuf with the menu. If Tomas didn't know Raybelle was an ass-kissing politician, she'd swear she was flirting with him. An idea she didn't much like.

"Good choice," Raybelle told her when Yusuf had left. "They have the best falafel in town."

"I'm glad to hear that. It's too early in the day for sheep brains."

Raybelle almost spat out her drink.

Tomas went on, "When you've dissected something, you know, eating it isn't necessarily the first thing you want to do."

"Enough." But if Tomas wasn't mistaken, Raybelle seemed to be enjoying herself. "Mealtime with you must be hard to get used to."

"Don't worry, you won't have to."

The falafel was the best Tomas had ever tasted. She enjoyed it so much she almost forgot this was a business lunch, and a weird one, with guests who didn't speak. Unfortunately, Raybelle remembered.

"So listen, Doctor Jefferson. I need you to go with me to inspect the veterans' treatment wards, 'cause we've had some complaints. And no representative wants to let wounded soldiers down, especially during wartime. People may have differing views about the war, but everybody supports the troops. Right?"

Tomas did not answer the rhetorical question. "What am I doing there?"

"You're a medical doctor. A researcher. You study viruses, yes?" Tomas nodded; Melody had come through again with her background checking. "You're there to validate what I'm doing, to give it the seal of scientific approval. The soldiers deserve no less."

"Isn't this kind of informal? I haven't been appointed—"

"I'm asking you. As a friend."

"I'm not your friend, Senator. I was your brother's friend."

"I don't want to drag him into this."

"You mean, you don't want to be reminded that he died on the streets."

Raybelle clenched her jaw. "I didn't realize he meant so much to you."

"Neither did I," Tomas said. "But we need to talk about Dennis."

Raybelle fixed the smile in place and turned left and right, like a flight attendant. "Okay, are we on camera? Because this sounds like one of those afternoon shows. *Doctor Tomas.*"

"I know what your brother did in the Chagos Islands." Tomas regarded her with a fierce, but calm, stare. "Ever hear of them?"

"Is that where he picked up that bug you were studying?"

"No, the 'bug' he picked up on Mauritius," she said. "Which is closer to Africa. The Chagos Archipelago is closer to India, and that's where your brother was in the early seventies. Serving his country."

She almost spat the last phrase, and Raybelle chose to fasten all her resentment on that. "Whatever he did, I'm sure someone ordered him to."

"And I'm sure the September eleventh bombers were following orders from God."

Raybelle's hands bunched into fists. "God shouldn't be mentioned in the same sentence as terrorists."

"You think so?" Tomas folded her hands across one blue-skirted knee. "I've always had a problem with the idea of a god, so let me tell you what's sacred to me. Human life. And the oath I took to protect it. That's sacred to me. When you have doctors assisting at executions, or monitoring interrogation procedures—we're in the realm of Doctor Mengele, then." She paused. "You do know who I'm talking about."

"The Nazi physician."

"Yeah, but he wasn't the only one. There were all kinds of doctors who signed up for these shit kinds of experiments. Eugenics, whatever."

"Lots of people went along with the Nazis, including ministers of the church." Raybelle knew what Tomas would make of that. "And of course, all those soldiers. If it hadn't been for regular Germans, none of Hitler's schemes could have ever gotten off the ground. Why are we discussing this now? Are you calling Dennis a Nazi?"

"Damn, Senator, you can say the most ignorant things. He was your brother. He was my patient, but he mattered to me." She looked surprised to be saying this. "He did things he regretted, so he spent the rest of his life trying to make up for them. Maybe I don't have the capacity to appreciate his faith, but I respect him for trying."

"And you're saying I didn't?"

"This is not about you!" Tomas closed her eyes and spoke in a softer voice. "This is not about you, Senator McKeehan. I'm not here because you asked me. I'm here for Dennis."

For once, Raybelle couldn't argue. Because, if the military was letting its people down now, it wasn't the first time. They'd let her brother down too. Almost as much as she had.

***

When he put the headphones on, Perry felt as if he were sealing himself into another world. They were big, earmuff-style headphones, like those with which he'd listened to 8-tracks in the seventies. It was a decade he preferred not to think about often. You had to shed those early credits on your résumé, no matter how hard won. Had to stay one step ahead of the past.

"Ready, sir?" the young woman beside him said.

"Yes. Go ahead, Captain."

Captain Wyatt, who wore head-to-toe camouflage and army boots despite working indoors, launched the computer console. At once, Perry was lost in a "virtual reality" so graphically vivid that he felt dizzy. It was better than an IMAX film, not that he'd been to one since… He became aware, over the rat-tat-tat of simulated machine gun fire, of Wyatt narrating the episode in his head.

"The TRAX system simulates urban warfare," she seemed to shout from inside the program. "Something we don't get a chance to practice at home. In wars of the near future, we will increasingly be battling street to street, as we have in Baghdad. Soldiers of the United States and our coalition allies must train to fight block by block, in close quarters, with civilians everywhere who may be innocent, or may be bearing improvised explosive devices."

"IEDs."

"Yes, sir. The only way to rehearse these situations is with virtual reality software, such as TRAX."

Perry could think of another way than games to rehearse.

"War games have been a part of US military training for a long time," Wyatt continued. "We've come a long way from the beginning of World War II, when soldiers trained with boxes and rifles made of wood."

Perry wasn't interested in World War II—we won; game over. He was much more engaged by the din from the simulator. Arab-appearing figures, including children and women veiled in black, appeared in doorways. Some waved; sometimes the wave was the prelude to something being thrown. He toyed with a joystick that connected him to his "avatar," the soldier he was playing on the 3-D screen. His avatar walked quickly and led a dog on a short choke chain.

"Why's it called an avatar?" he asked Wyatt.

"The avatar refers to your computer representation of yourself, or your on-screen personality—a pseudo-identity, if you will, sir. It's the 'you' other computer users can see. The word is Sanskrit. In Hindu scripture, an avatar is the incarnation of a god."

Perry found the god notion interesting. But Wyatt didn't need to know that, only the personality he chose to present. "What's this?" He indicated a blinking signal in the corner of the screen.

"That's a CII, Cultural Insensitivity Indicator, sir," Wyatt said. "When you approached a doorway with your search dog, the CII lit up because dogs offend Muslim sensibilities. They're considered unclean."

"Dogs? Or Muslim sensibilities? And how do I know these characters are Muslim?" Before she could answer, he said, "This isn't very realistic, is it, Captain? We wouldn't have a CII going off in the middle of a war zone."

"Sir—"

"Scrap that feature." Perry straightened up and removed his thick goggles. "By order of the president."

"Yes, sir."

Perry would fill the president in on this later—maybe. The commander-in-chief was kept informed on a need-to-know basis, and both he and his Secretary of Defense agreed that his need to know was...limited. One of the great innovations of this administration had been the ceding of military expertise to commanding officers, whom Perry knew better than the president did. In the twenty-first century, it didn't make sense for a president to think of what he might want the armed forces to do, and then ask for the impossible. That had caused the mistakes of the past. Better to put men, and women like Wyatt, on the ground and have them figure it out, then tailor policy to match practical reality.

As opposed to virtual.

CHAPTER TEN

Normally, Tomas slept better in hotels than she did at home. In Chicago, the smells of the hospital and the sound of patients' fear would hover around her like a rain cloud over a cartoon character. She almost always woke up in the night, her brain processing, and there was nothing to do but shift positions, unless she gave up altogether and watched television or read. She hadn't been able to do this while living with a lover. She always had to lie very still and not get up, for fear of disturbing Alicia. It may have been a holdover from this habit that kept Tomas awake in her apartment.

But tonight, hundreds of miles away in Washington, she was doing no better. Someone a floor away could flush the toilet and

Tomas heard it as if they were having sex in the next bed. She felt herself awake every hour and should have just given up, but she didn't want to dress and watch whatever was on at two thirty a.m. She wished she could work, but they hadn't been to the military hospital yet and she didn't know what she could expect to see there.

The mattress was big and comfortable, as you'd expect in a hotel. Tomas had read in some journal that housekeeping staff had started complaining that mattresses were now too heavy for them to turn without injury. She should ask Raybelle McKeehan what she thought about that. Raybelle professed such concern about workers and women of color, as if she, or any of her ilk, had ever been a friend to labor or blacks.

Raybelle McKeehan was a goddamn problem. Why was it that the charming women were always impossible? Tall, blond, and handsome besides. Tomas hated the inconvenience of sexuality, how it got under her skin and how it was attracting her to the most difficult person on the planet. Like she was being punished for letting her last lover down.

In addition to the fact that Tomas didn't like Raybelle that much, there was no reason to imagine the attraction could be mutual. The senator had always, as far as Tomas could determine, deflected attention from her personal life, making clear that she didn't think the public interest coincided with anyone's private relationships, and she appeared to have none. Sure, there were rumors that she must be a lesbian, but all that meant was that she was a forceful woman who sometimes got on men's nerves. No one had managed to link her romantically to anyone, male or female. An elected Janet Reno. If America could handle that, could the presidency be far behind?

Which meant Dennis had been right about his sister. Tomas pushed the pillows up behind her bare back, let out a deep groan. Raybelle was a woman of single-minded ambition who would not let even her own flesh and blood get in the way. Doubtless, this whole inspect-the-hospital scheme was just one more publicity stunt. Raybelle could show her concern for veterans, whom everyone supported, and distance herself from the lame duck administration's military plans at the same time. If her brother's death came to light, she could say, "Why, he was a veteran!" and that she was honoring his memory, which meant turning the attention back on herself. She could, if necessary, point out that was how she'd become acquainted with Tomas Jefferson, research virologist... Tomas saw where all this was going. Raybelle was a rural, white southerner. If she was campaigning—and did members of Congress ever stop?—it would not hurt to be seen in the professional company of a black doctor from Chicago.

Against her better judgment, which usually spent the night elsewhere, Tomas allowed herself to imagine Raybelle in a less professional context. She'd glimpsed a fire in Raybelle's eyes that she didn't think was just related to wanting to be president or the next chair of some committee. No matter how cynical politics had made Raybelle, Tomas could just about believe that she'd gone into public service out of some noble desire to right wrongs, make the world better.

Which was more than Tomas could say. She'd been ambitious, sure, and medical school seemed an accomplishment no one could argue with; only she had the secret feeling that stopping at an MD degree and dealing with patients all day was somehow short of her true worth. Had she ever, even at the beginning, been focused more on others than herself?

But questioning her own values and motives was not an exercise Tomas felt comfortable with. She was only justifying Raybelle because she was horny. Three in the morning. Maybe if she just stretched out and closed her eyes.

***

Across town, in her apartment near the cathedral, Raybelle hunched in front of her open laptop and rubbed her eyes. The amount of time that could be wasted at a computer was astounding. Like this blog of hers. Melody thought it was a good idea, sure, but who read it?

The sense that she might be wasting her time was unfamiliar and unwelcome. There was only one area—her private life— where she had no confidence at all, and that was just because she'd never taken the trouble to cultivate one. She didn't need a private life to interfere with her public ambitions, and so she had sacrificed it, along with the demands any type of romantic relationship would place on her. She knew how to take care of her physical needs. That was efficient, like everything else in her life.

Well, it hadn't worked tonight. If she couldn't sleep, as she so often couldn't, she should be making notes, reading the news or some official report that would cure her insomnia. She didn't meditate or do any kind of purposeless exercise, and she didn't normally stare for hours at a Web page, wondering what she could post that would impress not just the public, not voters in general, but one in particular.

Raybelle shoved her hand through her hair for the hundredth time this early morning. Why did it bother her that Tomas seemed to regard her, and everything she stood for, with contempt? Wouldn't they work better together if they didn't like each other? Raybelle had seen that all her working life. The people she could strike deals with were, more often than not, people she'd barely have a word to say to over a casual lunch; they shared none of her beliefs or her interests other than getting things done. Someone like Grant Rivers, on the other hand, was a friend and mentor, but she couldn't just sit around waiting for him to take the lead. She had to do things herself.

Good thing Grant was a showman. He liked to talk on television, but it was all right with him to let a woman do all the work, whether that meant his wife Jean, or his secretary, or the junior senator from Tennessee. It was the kind of working partnership that suited Raybelle too.

She turned the laptop off, her writer's mind still as blank as the screen. She would call Grant, see if he wanted to talk. His candid approach would soothe her, as it soothed the people when he chose to address them. The US could have had a President Rivers by now, if he weren't so lazy.

Raybelle wasn't lazy. A lazy person would get more sleep.

***

Tomas didn't know Washington well, but there had to be someplace to go out on a Sunday night and have a drink. She wasn't much for dancing or clubbing, but she had a certain amount of energy and needed to take the edge off. A beer would do it. Maybe two.

She found a sports bar around the corner from the hotel, and slid onto a bar stool next to two black men who were absorbed by a game on TV. Chicago basketball. A team she'd heard of, at least.

"Get you something to drink?" the bartender said.

"Yes." She glanced at the taps. "Bass Ale, please. And can I get a menu, or do I have to sit at a table to eat?"

"You can sit wherever you like." He was a little too solicitous, but Tomas was used to this. She didn't seek the attention of men, but she was aware enough of her own attractiveness to know she was going to get it.

The men watching the game, on the other hand, ignored her at first. Men watching ballgames always assumed that women weren't interested. Tomas wasn't a sports fan, but she could talk about the Bulls enough to earn these men's attention, and she enjoyed a challenge. There was a special kind of camaraderie that came of not knowing anybody, just exchanging "Yeah!" and forgettable pleasantries with strangers at a bar.

By the time she left at the end of the night, Tomas had two new best friends and had drunk four more beers.

When she crossed the street, she saw a homeless man stretched out in a sleeping bag. His eyes startled her, open, gazing into hers. She could discern nothing menacing in them, just the acknowledgment of mutual humanity. His features were softened by a beard and, though he bore no resemblance to Dennis McKeehan other than white skin, she sensed the effort being made to sustain dignity in the horizontal plane. Tomas had seen it in the eyes of patients too, stretched out on examining tables, stripped, only their gaze dignified. It struck her as the ultimate trust, like trust in the eyes of a lover, naked and vulnerable.

And Tomas was aware, as she had never before been aware, that a person could put a foot wrong, slip, and just a few precipitous stumbling steps later fall into homelessness. The way she'd been brought up, lacking for nothing and with talent matched only by her expectations, hadn't prepared her for empathy. She now looked through the display window separating her privilege from this man who'd lost it, and saw how thin the glass was, as slippery as ice.

She dropped a five-dollar bill in the man's cap. But he didn't move, not even his eyes, and she hoped the money would still be there when he got up. His sleeping bag was army green and she wondered if he, like Dennis, had participated in dubious military missions. She'd heard that many of the street people in America were veterans, but as with so many other things, she'd never paid attention to this until she tripped over it.

She continued walking until she saw the illuminated dome of the Capitol. Hard to imagine working there. She'd expected Washington to be locked down, security on every corner, but instead the openness of its democracy touched her cynical heart. The only guards she'd seen were a type of park ranger who guarded the national monuments, and they looked about as fierce as Smokey Bear. The first free time she had, she would come down here to see the Mall: go into a Smithsonian museum or two, check out the Lincoln and Jefferson memorials, visit the Wall.

There were any number of people sleeping on the streets within walking distance of the Capitol, where people like Raybelle, who probably had never known a moment's want, made laws that affected their lives. But it was this particular homeless man's eyes that had bored into Tomas, as if he saw through to the emptiness inside. His eyes reminded her of Alicia's the last time they had parted. Alicia at the door, her eyes holding a pain gone cold and dead, a pain that said: I have nothing to offer you anymore, and it is all your fault. At that moment, Tomas could have denied her nothing, but it was far too late.

Tomas's breath came out in a cloud of steam; the temperature must be dropping. She felt her sigh coming from deep in a place that someone religious would call the soul. Tomas was too rational to believe in signs and symbols, but something was chewing on her insides tonight, and she didn't think it was the five pints of ale, though her normal limit was three. She felt there was something misaligned, something wrong between the people out here in the cities and the streets, and those they'd chosen to govern them. Everyone else must come to Washington with this same notion, but she hadn't thought of it at all till she'd arrived.

CHAPTER ELEVEN

Tomas had expected paparazzi, but the senator felt it was important for them to arrive unannounced, and so they entered Walter Reed Army Medical Center via a back door. "Preemptive strike," she said, and her teeth showed in a feral grin. Tomas couldn't bear the use of the president's phrase. Raybelle McKeehan must grandstand in her own shower.

The party turned down a corridor, but a whiff of gangrene stopped Tomas. That smell was unmistakable, like death. She ducked into the room and saw a young male patient with several days of beard who looked pale and emaciated. Tomas approached the bed and clasped his hand. "I'm Doctor Jefferson."

"Private Jefferson, ma'am." He attempted a smile. "Same name."

"You don't have to 'ma'am' me, I'm a civilian." She smiled at him, though anger rose in her throat. "What happened?"

The soldier glanced down at the lower half of his body as though it no longer belonged to him. "IED," he said. "Paralyzed from the waist down."

She leaned in closer, put a hand on his shoulder. "What do you feel?"

"Wish I was dead."

"No, Private—"

"Wish I was with my buddies in the morgue," he said, and there was a quality of despair in his voice that Tomas felt nothing could console.

She turned to Raybelle, who had followed her into the room. "I'm going to talk to a nurse."

Raybelle looked around as if she expected women in white caps to come racing down the hall. Tomas walked toward the nursing station. She introduced herself to the tall man in charge, and watched him puzzle over whether she was any kin to Private Jefferson.

"I'm pretty sure I smelled gangrene," Tomas said, though she was more than sure. "I think Private Jefferson needs to be examined by a doctor."

"The doctor's already been on his rounds," the nurse said. "Early tomorrow morning, though."

"I'd say the sooner the better," Tomas said, still trying to sound conversational. There wasn't much time. "The patient is paraplegic."

"I know that."

"So he can't *feel* it." She knew her anger was misdirected at a fellow professional, but she was running out of places to put it. She turned and walked swiftly back down the hall toward Raybelle.

"You want some sound bites, Senator? This stinks. Stinks! Who's in charge of cleaning this place?" When Tomas reached a janitorial closet she flung the door open, half expecting a sex scene. There was mold growing between the tiles. "You were right. Somebody needs to clean up this mess."

"You sound like you care." There was a note of uncertainty Tomas had not heard in Raybelle's voice before. Had anyone ever heard it?

CHAPTER TWELVE

In the ladies' room adjacent to the senate chamber, Raybelle found the soap dispenser empty. Maybe the same cleaning contractors who were letting down the veterans were also at work in the Capitol. Could they not even refill the soap?

She and Barbara Mikulski reached the one full dispenser at the same time. Raybelle exchanged smiles with her colleague from Maryland. You had to respect a woman who'd been in the Senate that long. Mikulski had been there when the ladies' room was quieter than the reading room, even emptier than it was today.

Raybelle dried her hands and walked, without eagerness, back to the chamber for the latest round of confirmation hearings. She'd still been in the House of Representatives during the hearings for Clarence Thomas, when Anita Hill's sexual harassment allegations had drawn attention to the almost total absence of women from the Senate. Mikulski had been there, of course, and Nancy Landon Kassebaum who was at least a Republican. Raybelle had maintained throughout her career that it didn't matter whether you were a woman or a man, that was no reason to vote for someone, but she too had grown uncomfortable as Howell Heflin, Bob Packwood, Strom Thurmond and their ilk had sat there on a confirmation panel representing America opposite one black woman and her version of events.

And what had come of that? Justice Thomas had a seat for life on the Supreme Court. The "year of the woman" saw five (out of a hundred!) elected to the Senate, and the new ladies' room installed. Much to the envy of Congresswomen like Raybelle, who still had to wander all the way over to the reading room just to use the bathroom. Even with a woman as Speaker of the House.

Raybelle returned to the senate chamber and took a more comfortable seat. This was a room of power, and yet, the rumor was that deals were still often worked out in the men's room, as was true in every other sector. The men's rooms must hum with influence and renovated plumbing. There were more women in Congress now, but sometimes Raybelle thought things were still as segregated as old Strom would have wanted them to stay.

***

Within an hour after Melody got to the office, she'd drafted a new blog entry that would send a "live feed" to everyone who was connected to the senator's website.

"So that means, what?" Raybelle said when she remembered she could call Melody on her cell phone. "Everybody on the mailing list will know about it instantly?"

"Right, and it's flagged URGENT, so they'll see right away it's breaking news." Melody's fingers flew across the keyboard; somewhere along the line, she'd been taught to touch type. "We are the media now."

"I hope that's not the title of the post," Raybelle said. She was standing outside the Capitol, making a motion with her middle and index fingers like she was one of the smokers, and staring out at the rain.

"No, I was thinking something less self-referential," Melody said. "Such as, 'Who Let Down Our Men and Women in Uniform'? And lead with a graphic of Doctor Jefferson holding a piece of crumbling tile."

"Right. But I think we should allude more to the 'rubble' theme. You know, young soldier's been in the rubble of Baghdad or wherever. Then he comes back—"

"Only to find," Melody said, tapping away, "that Washington is in ruins too. At least as far as these veterans are concerned. And Doctor Jefferson is the face of outrage on this. The picture of righteous indignation."

"That she is." Raybelle was in one place, Melody another, and Tomas existed only on the screen.

***

In fact, Tomas was back in her empty hotel room, looking at the prints on the wall that matched the carpet. In two dimensions she may have been the picture of burning moral outrage, but she felt so lonely she could have curled up on a grate with one of Dennis's comrades. It was a warm spring day outside, but at her core, she could not get warm.

Companionship, for its own sake, had never been all that important to Tomas. She'd loved Alicia—God, she still did—but it felt like luck that she'd ever had a long-term relationship, and when it was over she was sure that she would never love again. She hated to admit it—and never had, to her lover—but Alicia was right, about everything. She'd never given Alicia the time that she needed. Her work was important, and dates were unnecessary; they weren't teenagers. When they had gone out anywhere Alicia complained that Tomas was always taking calls, or fidgeting, as if the last person on earth she wanted to talk to, or see, was the one sitting right there next to her, or across from her at the table, begging to be taken care of, to be paid attention to.

After Alicia was gone, Tomas realized the truth of all this, that she actually had wanted to go places with her lover, make her feel special and wanted. She'd made belated (Alicia would say halfhearted) efforts to convey this, but by then there was no convincing the woman she loved that she was capable of change. In her darker moments—like now, in the Hessian Hotel room, turning down air-conditioned sheets to slip her hot and lonely body between—Tomas had suspected there was someone waiting in the wings, that Alicia had lined up another lover already. But even if that were true, there was no one else to blame. Who wanted to be Tomas Jefferson's other half?

She switched off the bedside lamp. There was nowhere else on earth she wanted less to be than right here, now. Very un-Buddhist of her, but then she never had gone in for spirituality. She would rather be someplace coastal, on a dive boat with polyglot strangers, or "hooking up" (as the young folks were saying these days) with some pretty thing in a dance club, any color of skin or hair or eyes. She wished she at least had something to drink. She'd never carry around a flask in her black bag or anything, but a glass of wine or a beer was very good for unwinding at the end of a tense day.

And it had been a very tense day. But at that moment Tomas realized that it was not nighttime at all. No doubt Raybelle was busy denying funding to someone. She herself should be having dinner somewhere, should at least order something. She shouldn't be thinking about drinking, as if it were an activity in itself; that was the way of substance abuse. And she shouldn't be in bed, restless, chafing her warm skin against cool bedclothes, wishing for the capable hands of an arrogant senator.

Tomas closed her eyes, though it made no difference in a room so darkened by the heavy hotel room drapes. She thought of those hands, every inch of that woman's body, and how Raybelle radiated arrogance the way Tomas's own skin had radiated heat when once, as a child, she'd been out in the sun too long. Her parents had taken her to their family doctor, whose skin was as dark as hers, and he had laughed—laughed!—at her peeling blisters because she was indeed sunburned, something she'd thought a black girl couldn't be.

Tomas had long thought she was—prided herself on being—

the most arrogant person she knew. She had a terrific opinion of her own competence and was unwilling to suffer fools, gladly or otherwise. A quality she admired in those who could carry it off. But she had resented that doctor's laughter, and in all her years as a physician, had made a point of never laughing at a patient's discomfort, at least out loud.

***

Raybelle didn't have to wait long for a response to her blog. Her direct line rang and, because she could see it was Senator Rivers, she leaned over to answer it herself. "Grant! What're you up to?"

"What the fuck did you just do?"

The voice was not Grant Rivers's. "Excuse me?" She wiped at the corner of her mouth, as if making up for the indelicacy of the man on the phone.

"This is Henry Perry. US Secretary of Defense." He spoke as if barking orders; if the call hadn't been placed from Grant's office, she would have recognized him at once. "I repeat. What the fuck did you just do?"

"Could you be a little less rude, Mr. Secretary?" She leaned back in her chair, more relaxed than she felt. She would not become the monster.

"This uncensored bullshit you see fit to spew across the, I don't know what you call it, *cyberspace*. This *blog*." He said these words as if they were the names of terrorists, or unfamiliar vegetables. "When did you become your own press corps, Senator?"

"Well actually, Henry," she said, trying informality to throw him off, "we are the media now." She winked at Melody.

A sharp sucking of air through the teeth. "This is not a joke, Senator McKeehan."

"Oh, stop being so pompous. Against whom are you conducting your fabulous Defense? You couldn't block a tackle by a high school football team."

His voice dripped acid. "We are at war on terror, Senator. As you very well know."

"Yeah, I was just at the airport, I know all about your red and orange alerts. I'm surprised you didn't go for more patriotic colors. But I try to be in Congress for every vote, and I'm sure I would recollect if we'd issued a declaration of war."

"Your quaint—and, if I may say so, treasonous—views on war powers are well known—"

"No, you may not say so." Raybelle was hot again. "Didn't you ever hear of checks and balances? The executive overreaching the legislature? Or did they rip Article I out of your copy of the Constitution?"

"I have no time to debate this with you. I'm far too busy with the war. What I called to tell you was to stop using that black woman as a human shield."

Raybelle bit into a potato chip and crunched into the phone. "You'd know all about human shields, wouldn't you? What is it you say? Collateral damage?"

"Now you listen to me," Perry said. "You conduct your investigation with the dignity becoming your office—"

"Speaking of which," she said, mouth still full, "why are you calling me from Senator Rivers's office? Pentagon not pay the phone bill this month?"

"That woman is not a member of Congress. She doesn't work for you, she isn't in Washington. She has no place on whatever crusade you think you're on."

It was a marvel how almost every sentence of Perry's was fraught with military terms. Or obscenities. "Why are you so concerned about this?" she said. "Or rather, why aren't you concerned? These hospital patients are members of our military. Shouldn't you be concerned about them?"

"Unlike you, Senator McKeehan, I don't take things so personally." He was baiting her again, about family. Sweat started to bead under Raybelle's collar, but she would not rise to the bait.

"I'll see you in the Senate," she said. "My house. My rules."

His voice was quiet and razor-edged. "You don't know how wrong you are."

She hung up, not waiting for him to do so. Lousy appointee of a lame-duck president.

***

"I can't fucking find shit." The guy on the phone had vocabulary challenges, but that wasn't Grant's concern now.

"Paperwork. Don't worry about reading it. Just grab some files and get out of there."

"Files? Shit, man. Ain't no files in here, just clothes and shit. Pigsty. Matter of fact the fire department ought to get in here, they'd fucking shit themselves."

"Get off the phone," Grant said, "and get to work."

He set down his cell phone—disposable and untraceable—and leaned back into the pillows against the headboard of his hotel bed. A United States senator was above direct coordination of a project like this, but Grant didn't trust anyone else with this. Period. How could he? He knew how deceptive people were; it was a way of life for him, as natural as breathing.

All he'd needed to do was hire someone who could dress up enough to convince a doorman he was Dr. Jefferson's gentleman caller. A couple of fifties must have done the job, because this goon sure didn't sound like somebody who would date a doctor.

But Grant could afford any amount it took. It was all going on Perry's bill, the sucker. Grant always threw in a hefty amount for his own expenses, because Perry wouldn't notice. Everyone knew the outrageous prices the Pentagon was said to pay. They could all line their pockets for ages without anyone noticing, and besides, there were new contracts in the pipeline. If they got the bid on the new secret prison—and they would, because Grant's committee was approving it—he might have to buy some new pants with bigger pockets. And a looser waistband.

Grant hated trying on clothes. He'd never been slim, but all this working and no working out was taking a toll on his weight. Barbara didn't seem to mind. He could lie here, gray hair poking between the buttons on his pajamas, and Barbara still looked at him like he was the young stallion every man is in his own imagination. For him, that was her principal attraction.

Grant switched the phone to silent mode, and Barbara padded back into the bedroom. Her hair was up and she wore red silk pajamas. She was not young either, but that didn't bother him. The women he went for were tough, a little weather-beaten, and he liked them in red. He would have long since made a pass at

Raybelle, but by the time she got to the age he liked, he already
knew her too well.

"Still working, honey?" Barbara said.

He loved the way she called him "honey" in a southern tone,
though she wasn't southern. It made him feel comfortable, and
he adjusted the pillows behind him on the bed. "Not anymore."

She undid the clips in her hair. "Does Henry know what
you're doing?"

He looked up at her, surprised. "What?"

"Not us, silly." She climbed on top of him and nuzzled his
forehead. "This 'home inspection' you're doing."

He always fed her some detail to keep her interested and at
the same time unaware. "Henry told me to dig up some dirt," he
said. "He didn't tell me how to do it. It's my job to figure that
out."

"That's because you're smarter than he is."

"Damn right." Grant felt himself swell to meet her. "Why
else would I be sleeping with his wife?"

***

Tomas's left hamstring ached from her workout in the gym.
With difficulty, she negotiated the uneven hallways of what had
to be the oldest and most character-filled hotel left in Washington.
How could they get away with it in these days of accessibility for
all? Tomas had always been able-bodied, but she'd experienced
enough athletic injuries to know what it was like to struggle with
steps.

Her doorknob was askew, but this in itself didn't merit
attention, because everything in the Hessian was askew. It was
when she saw that the pin on the lock was popped that she knew
something was off. The lock was old, metal, part of the actual
doorknob. With the pin popped, she couldn't open it with her
key. Someone else had unlocked it, and been too careful to lock
it behind.

At the front desk she found Bernice, an elderly woman who
came up to unlock the door with her master key. Bernice found
the hallway more of a challenge than Tomas had. She clucked in

shock when she saw the state of Tomas's room. "Lord, girl, I am so sorry," she said. "Television's busted too."

Tomas decided now was not the time to point out that the TV hadn't worked since she got there. "Somebody broke in? Shouldn't we be careful to—"

"Not broke in, sweetie. Somebody had your key." Bernice reproached her as if Tomas were a teenaged girl who'd passed out her keys at the high school dance.

"I didn't give it to anyone. Look, this doesn't make me feel safe," Tomas said, urging Bernice to come away with her and call security.

But there wasn't much that could be done. Nothing was missing, and the hotel furnishings hadn't been damaged. The "change these sheets" sign had been placed back on the bed, though at a slight angle, to go with everything else in the room. Tomas's clothes and suitcase had been tossed about, but everything was still there. Either the intruders had been looking for something that they didn't find, or they had just meant to intimidate her.

It had worked. She didn't need any more of DC. First thing tomorrow, she was heading back to Chicago, which felt safe. Familiar, anyway.

CHAPTER THIRTEEN

When the plane touched down at O'Hare Tomas sighed with blessed relief. An hour later she dropped her bags in her own apartment before going to pick up Friesian at Tim's place. Tomas had asked her neighbor to look after the cat because she knew Tim, had always chatted to him outside when he walked his elderly dog. The dog had died in the spring and, knowing Tim was good with animals, she'd had no hesitation in entrusting Dennis's cat to his large, gentle hands. She thought he dated men, but she wasn't certain.

At the doorway, Tim said "Hey" in that southern way, dragging it out over more than one syllable. Friesian snaked around his calf with obvious adoration. The cat had never responded to her this way and, although he'd lived at her place no longer than she'd been away, Tomas felt a bizarre twinge of jealousy. "Come on in, I was just throwing together a stir-fry. Stay for dinner."

She was about to refuse, but her body moved into the apartment, drawn by hospitality. She'd never been inside Tim's place, within the gentle recessed lighting of his living room. Garlic and ginger beckoned.

"So how was DC?" he said. Tomas had exchanged far more words with Dennis McKeehan, but Tim's accent was not dissimilar.

She didn't want to bring up her encounters with the senator. "It was all right. Have you been?"

"Once." Tim and Friesian led her toward the kitchen. "To see the Vietnam Memorial."

"Ah. Haven't been to that one yet."

"I know some names on the Wall," Tim said, and though he was looking at his wok, Tomas sensed his eyes hardening, as if he were looking right at her.

"I don't know anybody whose name is on the Wall."

"All the more reason to go."

When they were seated, with steaming bowls of rice and vegetables, Tomas realized she was ravenous. This happened a lot, and couldn't be healthy for her blood sugar.

They ate for a while in silence, something Tomas wasn't used to with another human being. When they had helped themselves to seconds, she said, "I did spend a little time on the National Mall." She'd picked up, from one of the stall vendors, a black-and-white patch, with a stark silhouette of a prisoner and the letters P.O.W.–M.I.A. She'd bought it not knowing where she would put such a thing. Maybe in the shoebox in the back of the closet, where she kept sentimental items that Alicia hadn't wanted returned, but that Tomas was still unable to get rid of.

She took the patch from her purse now and showed Tim. She was a bit nervous about his reaction. If he had served in one of those undeclared and unending wars, would he think she was just into paraphernalia that had nothing to do with her life, the way other people collected Chicago police jackets or Russian bear-skin hats? "Tell me about Vietnam," she said.

He looked at her and laughed. "Tell me about being black."

"I didn't mean to offend—"

"Neither did I," he said. "But where I come from—Mississippi, like all the great quarterbacks, since you didn't ask—we believe in a little small talk before plunging right into it. How are you, how was your trip, et cetera."

"I'm not much for small talk. *Nonversation*," she added, a disparaging word she'd read in a business magazine on the plane.

"Well." He took a sip of hot sake. "I prefer not to think of conversation, or anything, in such negative terms. You asked how 'Nam was, and let me tell you, when you're tied up or in a cage for months at a time, hearing nothing but screaming in a language you don't understand—well, you'd be glad for a little small talk."

Images of torture weren't helping her relax into it, but she'd try. "This stir-fry is delicious, Tim. Thank you."

"You're most welcome." He smiled. "Vietnam, since you asked, was an opportunity for me. If it weren't for the United States Army, I'd never have gone overseas. Hell, I'd probably never have left the state of Mississippi."

"So the war gave you advantages."

"Sure it did. If wars had no advantages for anybody, they wouldn't be fought. Would they?"

She wasn't in the habit of answering rhetorical questions—that fell into the "nonversation" category. "I'm interested that you see the army as a way out of the place you were raised."

"Why?"

"Because many people of...disadvantaged backgrounds—for example black folks here in Chicago—sign up for the army, or the guard or whatever, as a way to go to college, make a better life for themselves. And then they end up in a war, and maybe they end up with no life at all."

He was starting to unnerve her with that look. "Tomas, you're used to being an expert, aren't you? Knowing what you're talking about?"

"Yes. Why?"

"'Cause right now you don't," he said, "and it shows."

Tomas tried to take a yoga breath without Tim noticing, but it didn't help. He was right, in one sense. She needed to get back to where she was an expert. This personal stuff was not for her. Tim, Private Jefferson, Dennis—she couldn't relate to these men. She concentrated on infection patterns: it was clear that sanitation was at the root of the veterans getting sick.

"I wasn't raised to say 'black folks'," Tim was saying, "and I sure wasn't raised to have you in my home. I've knocked my accent down several notches, or I'd sound more like the cracker I am. But now, how do you suppose I became an ever so slightly less ignorant cracker? It was through meeting people. Black men I served with, Vietnamese I met over there. Once I got outside my hometown, where everybody already knew how they were supposed to think about everybody else, then my mind opened." He emphasized this by opening his hands, like the blooming of a flower.

The Allen Ginsberg gesture added to her sense that this gentle man had suffered a deep grief. "You must miss him," she said.

"Yes, I do," Tim said. "But if he were still here, I wouldn't have been able to look after Friesian."

"Oh? Was he allergic to cats?"

Tim looked puzzled. "Who are we talking about?"

Tomas had a moment of sinking horror. What if her assumption had been wrong? "Your lover?"

He laughed, the kind of laugh that forced his eyes to shut and water. "I thought you were talking about my dog! No, my boyfriend's fine, he's just overseas at the moment, unfortunately. You'll have to meet him next time," Tim added, as if certain that Tomas would come again and would want to meet them both.

CHAPTER FOURTEEN

Whenever Grant was summoned by the Secretary of Defense, he felt a bit like an unruly student called to the principal's office. Never mind who was really in charge. Grant could arrange raids on Tomas Jefferson's room, pry into Dennis McKeehan's military record, and all Henry Perry did was snivel and jump up and down, like a puppet angry with the person pulling its strings.

Perry spoke in that calm voice that meant he was angrier than usual. "I said I wanted her out."

Grant spread his large hands across his knees, affecting a relaxed posture. "And I heard you, Henry. I want what you want." Perry had no idea how true that was.

"So what's taking so long?" Perry kept his eyes away from

the picture on the shelf, but Grant had noticed. He was thinking about Kelly again. Grant would use this.

"Family matters are delicate, Henry. You know that."

"*The target* does not have family matters," Perry said through his perfectly-aligned teeth.

"Except her crazy brother," Grant said, stretching his legs and brushing imaginary dust from one crease of his trousers. "And maybe more than that, but you have to trust me on this, Henry. No foaming at the mouth."

For an instant, Perry looked about to do just that. Maybe Grant had gone too far. Then, as if a dial had been turned, Perry sat back, hands behind his head. Almost unheard of. "All right," he said. "I trust you. With the 'family' matters."

"With everything," Grant said. "The committee, the investigation. She won't get anything past me, I promise. You concentrate on what you do best."

An appeal to his savior complex put Perry in his place.

"You know how it is, Henry," Grant went on. "You never have just one weapon, or just one plan of attack. You hit them with one thing, and if they come back for more, hit them with another."

"Your weapons are metaphorical." Perry tried to sound superior. "Mine are real."

Grant thought this was funny. "You want to unload on 'the target' personally, then you go right ahead. You be the bad cop. Now, if you'll excuse me, I've got to get back to the wife."

He didn't say whose wife.

***

After Tomas returned to Chicago, Raybelle called several times and attempted to talk her into coming back to Washington. Tomas reiterated that she wasn't interested in returning, especially after the ham-fisted break-in, but Raybelle saw this as a challenge. The more Tomas refused to come back south, the more convinced Raybelle was that she needed her as the face of the hospital investigation.

"I'd be happy to have you accompany me for a private visit to my constituency in Tennessee. I'll be staying at my family home, but of course you can make any arrangements that suit you." She added, "Melody. Melody can book you anywhere you like. There are some decent hotels in the area now."

"Thanks." Raybelle expected Tomas to stop at one word, but she carried on talking. "So what kind of place is your 'family home'? Is that where you scattered Dennis's ashes?"

"Ah—well, I haven't gotten a chance to take them down yet," Raybelle said. "I was planning to take them along."

"Where are they now?"

"In my office," Raybelle said. Through the phone, she sensed Tomas's disapproval, and fought the desire to squirm. "They came by courier, I guess. Melody must have signed for them."

She didn't know why she wanted to explain herself to Tomas, but she did. "Listen. I'm from a very modest background. No doctors in my family. We don't live on plantations in my part of the south. Though my mama did have quite a kitchen. You should see it."

"Should I?"

For the rest of the day, Raybelle somehow could not shake the notion that Tomas Jefferson found her endearing.

***

At Dulles Airport, the metal detector went off and a TSA staffer ran an inspecting wand up Tomas's body, stopping at her ears, which were pierced a couple more times than necessary. But Tomas wasn't working, and saw no reason to dress up. Having her ears inspected en route to the south did remind her of the auction block, but she decided to save her first cutting remark at least until she was on the connecting flight with Raybelle.

It turned out coffee was not available on the plane because this was labeled an "express" flight. There were only a few places from which you could fly to the Tri-Cities, Tennessee. None of them could be much of a city if it took all three for an airport. She put her hands to her temples; they throbbed from lack of caffeine.

Raybelle, who sat on the aisle opposite her two staffers, was wearing a bright blue pantsuit. She had an orange juice—the only drink available, though they were in first class—and yukked it up with the flight attendant, whom she must have known from previous flights.

"Well, Senator, and how're you today?" the flight attendant said, leaning with his hand on the seat in front, pinkie ring flashing. Tomas's gaydar was going off so powerfully she feared it would disrupt the operation of the aircraft.

"I'm fine, Geoffrey." Raybelle ripped a packet of peanuts open with her teeth. "How you been?"

"Fine, ma'am, just fine."

"Family well?"

"Oh yes, everybody's doing just fine." Geoffrey started enumerating news of his "family." Tomas didn't believe in gods, but she wished someone would deliver her from southern conversations. She could have diagnosed Chikungunya virus in the time it took these two to say hi.

"Geoffrey, this is my friend Doctor Jefferson from Chicago," Raybelle was saying. Tomas extended her hand.

"A pleasure, Doctor Jefferson."

She looked into his hazel eyes and knew she'd been clocked. Not that she gave a damn. She just wondered how many minority groups she wanted to openly belong to before touching down in Cowtown, USA.

"We're hoping to get to the basketball game tonight," said Raybelle, who hadn't mentioned anything about this to Tomas.

"Mmm, I haven't been all season. Shame, too. You know what a fan I've always been!" They both laughed like it was the funniest thing ever said, and it was, unless Geoffrey was referring to how good the guys looked in their uniforms.

"I'll have a popcorn and Coke for you," Raybelle said. The ice sloshed out of her juice onto the tray table as the plane hit sudden turbulence.

"I got to get back to the general public." Geoffrey braced his hands on either side of the aisle. "Nice to meet you!" he called over the chime of the seat belt sign coming on.

"Geoffrey's from my hometown," Raybelle explained. "We went to the same high school. Not at the same time, of course." She drank with a steady hand.

After a moment, she asked, "You all right?"

Tomas wanted to ask why she'd been introduced as "my friend," but she figured it was politicians' bullshit for someone they'd just met.

"I prefer my flights smooth," she said.

"Bit of a white-knuckle ride, isn't it?" Raybelle looked at Tomas's hand, clenching the armrest, and her own face went red. "Sorry. Was that inappropriate?"

Tomas laughed, which made her relax despite herself. "I'm not going to believe you thought that was a racial remark."

"I never know what to say to people." Raybelle seemed instantly to regret this confession of vulnerability. Tomas recognized that withdrawal. She performed it every day of her working life.

"You mentioned a basketball game?"

"Yes. Our local team has done really well this season, and I thought I'd try to make it. You can accompany me. If you'd like to," she added, but Tomas caught the note of control.

"I wouldn't know what else to do with myself on a Friday night in the 'Tri-Cities', I'm sure."

Raybelle laughed. "Poudre Valley isn't big enough to be one of the Tri-Cities."

Tomas said, "You're from Poudre Valley?"

"Yes. Why, do you know it?"

"My college roommate was from there."

"No kidding! Well. Six degrees of separation, and all that," Raybelle said, as if it were the most trivial thing in the world.

"Her name was Dana Rignaldi."

"Rignaldi. Now that's not a common name." The plane lurched earthward. "I had a schoolteacher named Mrs. Rignaldi."

"Probably Dana's mom."

Raybelle narrowed her eyes, looked to be doing some kind of calculation. "Would you think me very rude if I asked how old you are, Tomas?"

Dennis had asked, too. "Thirty-five. Why?"

"How about that? Just old enough to be president."

"I'm not running for president," she said. "You are."

"Oh-oh, watch where you say that." Raybelle looked around the half-empty cabin. "The press is everywhere."

"You can stay one step ahead of the press." Tomas nodded toward the laptop, closed on the tray table; amazing that no juice had spilled on it. "You're in the blogosphere."

"Yes." Raybelle ran a finger along the edge of the bouncing computer. Turbulence didn't seem to bother her at all. "I've been trying to think of a topic for my next post. Something to get people talking and set me apart from the competition. Not," she said when Tomas grinned, "that I'm running for president, but a senate seat is never safe, even in Tennessee. Nothing is safe—just ask Al Gore."

The possibility of plunging through the air, and Tomas's irrational sense that her life might end with things unsaid, made her speak without thinking. "How about gay rights?"

She was rewarded with a look of unpreparedness on Raybelle's face. Bet that didn't happen very often. "I don't see how 'gay' rights are different from anybody else's rights. Everybody has a right to a private life, and that's the end of it."

"Forgive me for pointing this out," Tomas said, "but your party hasn't been known for that position in recent years. The right to privacy has just become code for abortion, and abortion's now linked to gay rights. Not that I understand why. How many abortions are the result of gay sex?"

"Would you mind keeping your voice down? You hardly sound dispassionate."

"I'm not." Tomas gritted her teeth against the turbulence. "I'm passionate about my sexuality. People get that way." She couldn't believe the things she was saying, but at thirty thousand feet, what did she have to lose?

"Well." Raybelle looked away. Did Tomas imagine a flush? "It's not the state's business, either way. Only problem for some of my colleagues has been the hypocrisy of it. Why not keep your personal life to yourself and let other people keep theirs? I don't care who anyone…dates; that's celebrity gossip, not the work of the United States government. We have soldiers dying and—"

"Is that what you do?" Tomas felt reckless. "Keep your personal life all to yourself?"

"I don't have one," Raybelle said. "And if I did, you wouldn't hear about it. Which adds up to the same thing." Before Tomas could reply, Raybelle retrieved a *Wall Street Journal* and flipped it open in front of her face.

***

Henry Perry was at his desk at five a.m. An hour earlier than usual, but where else should he be? Still in bed? He didn't sleep much, anyway. Sleeping till four was a luxury. There were troops in the field, and they didn't enjoy deep, uninterrupted sleep. So why should he?

America was at war, and he was in charge. Not that he would ever make the mistake of saying so. Perry did not make mistakes; it was always "mistakes were made." The art of the passive, deflecting any manner of blame onto an imaginary actor. People who were in control never had to point out that they were.

And Perry was always in control. With one hand he worked the strings of his marionette in the Oval Office, and with the other, the purse strings: the power of Congress to finance national defense. A stronger president, or a weaker secretary, would have let generals and admirals report to Congress on the progress of a war, but not Perry. He'd had the sense to defer his own military service until there was no war left to fight, and had more than a little contempt for anyone too thick to do so. He was more useful here than on any battlefield. They—the men (and women; everyone was careful to say that now) in uniform were useful over there. Everyone respected the job they were doing; that was why they were doing it. He would praise them to the skies in committee, or in the halls of Congress. They deserved whatever they needed, the best, and if Congress wouldn't pay for it, the blood was on Congress's hands, not his.

But he saw the big picture. He had been in the Pentagon on September 11. He, personally, had been under attack, on the soil of the fatherland. And America would never suffer an attack like that again. Not on his watch.

His desk held a glass paperweight with nothing under it. There was a single bookshelf above the desk, in matching wood; the dark furniture went with the hush of the office, a sacred space. A busy man needed only the one bookshelf. Perry didn't think he'd read more than a page or two of any title on it, but he kept it full. It gave the impression that he read statesmanlike books, but more subtly, that he gained most of his knowledge from the real world, and not from books at all. Now, more than ever, America needed guidance to separate the real from the virtual. The uniforms would play their virtual-reality war games so that the real war could be won "on the ground." Americans liked to watch the real world on television. They distrusted fiction, as he did, because it was too true. Reality was an unreliable narrative, and he had mastered it. By controlling the story, he controlled the nation's reality.

Below the bookshelf sat a few obligatory knickknacks, diplomatic gifts, a cabinet secretary's equivalent of the shrunken heads Queen Elizabeth was said to have been given in one of her colonies. A few things Barbara insisted he keep here, and Kelly's picture.

He noticed her picture this morning. Every once in awhile that happened, the picture just reached across the room and grabbed him, although it had been sitting in the same spot on his shelf since 1984.

Kelly would have been thirty-five this year.

Perry looked away. He would have to make his own coffee, at this hour. He could go out and buy some but there wasn't time for frivolities like Starbucks. Or a memory. America needed him.

CHAPTER FIFTEEN

"You have got to be kidding me," Tomas said.

"Oh, come on, just for a minute." Raybelle held the blindfold, a swatch of red cotton so old it had MADE IN THE USA printed in the corner. Without warning, the image of a dark silk blindfold came into Raybelle's mind instead. Heat washed over her face, and to keep Tomas from seeing that, she blindfolded her.

The senatorial crew had stopped by a child's birthday party. The father was Poudre Valley's funeral director, and happened to be the biggest local donor to Raybelle's reelection campaign. They did things small-scale back home, and Raybelle couldn't pass up an opportunity to participate, or be photographed. Pinning the tail on the donkey was not that far off from what she did every day.

Grasping Tomas's shoulders, she turned her around three times and put the Wiffle bat in her hands. The piñata was a not particularly well-crafted papier-mâché sheep, and all the kids had had their turn, without good results, by the time Raybelle got there. A Wiffle bat was a poor choice for busting a piñata—not strong enough—but then, maybe it was the children who weren't strong enough. Maybe childhood obesity could be the subject of her next blog post, though it was hard to see what the federal government could do about something like that. In the face of free will and parental rights.

She'd have to ask Dr. Jefferson, who, at that moment, let fly with a terrific crack! The piñata released mini Hershey bars all over the room. Unfit children waddled across the floor, scooping up candies.

Tomas removed the blindfold. "It's been a long time since I did anything like that," she said.

Surely Raybelle was imagining the light in her eyes. "What, swung a bat?"

"Nooo. I don't know that I've ever done that," Tomas said. "I'm not much into sports. Though I did go to a baseball game about fifteen years ago. In college."

Raybelle was aware that this was the second time that day Tomas had alluded to her age, that she was fifteen years younger than Raybelle. She found this irritating.

"Who's playing?" The corners of Tomas's lips quirked upward. "Anybody I'd have heard of?"

"The Poudre Valley High School boys' basketball team. But they play in orange like the University of Tennessee, so you can still wear your Lady Vols stuff." Tomas's face showed no recognition. "Please tell me you've heard of the Tennessee Lady Volunteers."

***

Poudre Valley was playing Sewer City that night. Of course, that's not what the marquee advertised. Sewer City was only called Sewer City by Poudre Valley fans, who regarded Sewer City as their great rival. The much larger town got its water supply, recycled, from Poudre Valley, water that Poudre Valley collected fresh from mountain springs. Hence the nickname.

Raybelle and her entourage were in their seats before the national anthem. It was very important for Raybelle to be present for the national anthem anytime it was played. The gymnasium was a sea of orange. Raybelle felt superior and neutral in blue, coordinating with the orange like a set of bath towels. She represented Sewer City too.

Tomas asked, "So you went to this high school?" in a tone that implied she had trouble believing they had schools that long ago, at least in Tennessee.

"I did."

"And did you play any sports?"

Raybelle hesitated for only a second, but Tomas noticed. "I was a cheerleader."

"You have got to be kidding me," Tomas said, also for the second time that day.

"I know it's hard to believe, but back then, I fit right in. Just about all the cheerleaders were blond like me."

"I'll bet. And none of them looked like me."

Raybelle started to—what—apologize for the south? But Tomas looked at her watch, as if impatient for the game to start. Then she began staring toward the other end of the bleachers.

"I don't believe it."

"What?"

"That's her. Edith Rignaldi. And her friend, what's her name, Linda." To Raybelle's look of confusion, Tomas said, "I've got to say hello to them. Come on."

Raybelle hesitated before taking orders from Tomas, but what the heck. These were constituents. In fact, Raybelle remembered Mrs. Rignaldi as her teacher, and felt an unaccountable hesitation. Which was ridiculous. She was a politician, not an eighth grader.

They made their way along, Raybelle waving and smiling every second or so, to people she recognized or didn't. If she talked to everyone she knew in this building, the game would be over.

"Edith?" Tomas said, and one of two gray-haired ladies put a hand to her mouth in surprise.

"Tomas, what are you doing here?" Edith Rignaldi said, then without waiting for an answer rushed on, "It's nice to see you."

"I'm here with Senator McKeehan." Tomas took Raybelle's arm in a gesture of what felt like pride, and if everything in her life hadn't been so rehearsed, Raybelle might have blushed.

"Why, Senator." Edith shook her hand. "You've done well for yourself."

"Thank you, Mrs. Rignaldi."

"This is Linda Nye," Edith said, introducing her friend, whose handshake was as vigorous as her greeting was warm. "And these are my cousins, Pam and Charlie." A dolled-up woman, who may have been a cheerleader before Raybelle's time, and a stout man with very short hair both expressed their extreme pleasure at meeting someone so eminent.

"You won't remember me," Charlie said, "but you spoke to us once. I'm with the Poudre Valley Police."

"Of course, Officer," Raybelle said, with a genuineness in inverse proportion to her memory of the occasion. "Keep up the good work."

"You should come over to the house after the game, Tomas," Edith was saying. "It's Doctor Jefferson now, isn't it?"

"Yes. But you—"

"Oh, Dana would be so glad to hear how you're doing! But I don't mean to interfere with your plans. I'm sure Senator McKeehan is very busy."

Before Raybelle could say anything, Tomas upstaged her. "Sure, we'll come." She gestured toward the American flag. "Looks like they're getting ready to start. Nice to see you."

"Good to see you. We'll find you after."

As they returned to their seats, Raybelle nudged Tomas. "Do you know all of them? Who's the politician here?"

"Doctors play politics too. And I know Edith and Linda; I never met the straight couple before. Edith, Linda, Edith's daughter, Dana, and I all went on a trip to Africa together, when Dana and I were in college. It was amazing."

"How so?" Raybelle said, still absorbing the words "straight couple."

"Ssh." The high school band was beginning "The Star-Spangled Banner." It always sounded so much better than when they got some karaoke amateur to sing it.

Afterwards, a minister got up in the press box and offered a prayer. Tomas's eyes went so wide with astonishment that Raybelle was embarrassed, although she'd been going to games like this all her life. After the prayer she felt the need to explain.

"I know what you're going to say about church and state, but—"

"I'm just trying to get over what he said, how he asked God or whomever to prevent injury on the court. You know what? Let's just watch the game."

Raybelle expected Tomas to ask what was happening on every play, as people did who weren't accustomed to watching sports, but she didn't. After a while Raybelle started to doubt she was paying attention to the game at all. Maybe this was just a chance for her to zone out and think about whatever she thought about when off duty. Her work? Her friends, Edith and Linda? Raybelle?

Poudre Valley took the game, improbably, to double over-time, and when the home team finally triumphed, much joy rang out from gym to parking lot, in the form of car horns that would continue hooting down the road and into the night.

It took Raybelle quite some time to move from her seat after the game, so many people wanted to shake her hand. Or was it that she wanted to shake theirs? She was never sure, being a politician. It was hard to know the genuine from the insincere, even in herself, because she was trying to guess the difference all the time.

Eventually Edith and Linda made their way over, having taken leave of Charlie and Pam. "Why don't you all just follow us home, when you're through?" Linda said. She pronounced *through* in that regional way, without the *r*.

"I'm up for it," Tomas said, again taking the reins of control.

What was with this woman? Maybe doctors were used to doing that all the time. Raybelle could stop this nonsense now, but she didn't want the evening to end. "Come on, fellas," she said. "Let's find the car."

The senator's party made its way out, stopping every few steps for Raybelle to greet yet another constituent. She'd learned from Grant Rivers that voters could accept a woman in office, as long as she could play good ol' boys with the rest of them. So she smiled at everybody, thanked people for what they said, acted like she agreed with them when she did not. Glad-handing. It was second nature, but tonight, she observed herself doing it, as if from the outside.

***

There were no streetlights once the cars left the "city limits" of Poudre Valley. Rather grandiose, Tomas thought. When they got to the white ranch-style house, Edith welcomed them, saying she was going to heat up some cranberry juice and that would just be a minute. Soon the kitchen began to smell of potpourri. Tomas had never drunk potpourri or anything that smelled like it, but she remembered Dana's family was from a Christian tradition that frowned on drinking alcohol. So this was what they were going to get.

"It's an honor to have you here, Senator." Linda pulled out chairs for everyone. She sat down opposite Tomas and regarded her. "How've you been?"

"Well, thank you. I'm—you know I went on to medical school. I've been practicing in Chicago."

"Still in Chicago." Linda nodded. "You like it up there?"

Tomas was surprised by the question. "I've lived there all my life," she said. "It's home."

"I know Dana found the city very exciting. Me, I'm not sure I could handle that much excitement. This is about as far north as I'd ever care to live."

"You from Georgia?" Raybelle asked.

"Originally, yes. North Georgia. I was a nursery school teacher," Linda said. "Retired now."

"And you do more now than you did when you were working." Edith brought cups of hot cranberry juice to the table.

"How's Dana?" Tomas said.

"Oh, fine. She does something for the government." The uncharacteristic vagueness in Edith's response warned Tomas away from asking further questions.

"I understand you all got to know one another on a trip to Africa," Raybelle said. "I've never been there myself."

"Oh, you should go, Senator," Edith said. "It changed my life." Tomas was sure she wasn't imagining the affectionate glance Edith turned toward Linda, and then back to her. "Well, Tomas." She proceeded to beam at Raybelle, and Tomas felt the need to do some clearing up.

"Senator McKeehan and I are working together. On a medical investigation. I'm a virologist."

"Oh, my," Edith said. "Well, I'd ask you to describe what's involved, but we are at the table!" And she laughed a little.

Linda leaned forward on her elbows, an intent expression on her face. "It's not some national security investigation, is it? Biological warfare?"

Tomas wasn't sure what she should reveal, but Raybelle said, "Oh, no. No. Nothing that should worry the general public."

"So we shouldn't be worried about Ebola virus let loose in Oak Ridge?" Linda spoke in that deadpan way that left Tomas wondering if she were serious.

"No, this investigation is based out of Washington," Raybelle said, as if nothing bad had ever happened there. "Matter of fact, we're just down here for the weekend. I needed to see some people, and Tomas just came along for the ride."

"Oh, Linda," Edith said, "I'm sure these folks have an awful lot to do." And she looked at Tomas, again, in such a warm way that she didn't know where to put herself.

Raybelle set her cup down—she'd managed to empty it—and stood. "You're right. Big day tomorrow, ladies. I do thank you for your hospitality." She grinned, a disarming grin that went to Tomas's heart. It was a not altogether comfortable feeling. "And I haven't even asked if you vote Republican."

Linda looked at Tomas as if to ask, *Is she crazy?* Edith laughed. "You know, Senator, one thing I've always admired about you is how you're your own person. You don't just say whatever it is other folks are saying; you stick up for your principles. That means a lot to me. Much more than whether you're a Republican."

"You didn't answer the question," Tomas pointed out.

"I didn't intend to." Edith smiled, and at that moment, Tomas could see why Linda had fallen in love with her.

Raybelle looked at Edith with respect. "You should be a politician."

"Thank you," she said, "but I'm far too busy cleaning grout out of my eaves troughs."

"It's a thin line," Raybelle said.

Edith opened the door, shook her hand. "Thanks so much for coming by." Then she hugged Tomas, hard. "You take care, Tomas."

"Goodnight, Linda."

Back in the car, Raybelle said, "Whew. She's a piece of work, your friend."

Tomas was thinking of the way Edith kept looking at them, like there was something going on between them. It was pointless to resent this. Just because Edith and Linda appeared blissfully coupled, didn't mean they knew Tomas was gay. It was none of their concern who slept where.

Where Tomas slept that night turned out to be a spacious but not fancy suite at Poudre Valley's only hotel, the Ramada. It had been purpose-built, and not too many years ago, not one of those buildings that had once been something else, like a one of a kind hotel later bought by a chain. Tomas could still smell new carpet. Good thing she wasn't allergic to scents.

***

Raybelle rapped her fingers on Mama's kitchen table. She was booting up her laptop, hoping she could figure out this wireless connection so she could catch up on e-mails. Anything to avoid using that cell phone. So help her, she still wouldn't have one if there was a way to avoid it.

She was used to "multitasking," that hateful word. She was used to typing and jotting and drinking coffee and talking on the phone and in person all at once, but tonight she could barely stand still. She wanted to check in with Melody, maybe update that blog thing, and there were still her brother's ashes to scatter. If she didn't take care of that, Tomas wouldn't speak to her tomorrow.

Without her willing it, an image of Tomas came into her mind, at the Ramada, Tomas stepping from the shower, her dark skin beaded with droplets of water. Rubbing her long body dry with the absurdly thick hotel towel—maybe pausing to read the label, or the little sign asking guests to leave their towels in one

place if they did not require laundering, another if they did.
Tomas at the mirror; leaving the bathroom, maybe wrapped in
the towel, or stark naked, sliding into her own clean sheets. Raybelle
saw all these images in an instant, and she felt something she
hadn't sensed in her body in a long time.

Well, if she could not (and would not) assuage that
particular hunger, she sure could eat. She closed her laptop. The
guys would be up for Denny's, and she craved a Western omelet.

***

Tomas finished showering and went to the queen bed with its
generous coverings and oversized mattress. She rolled back the
covers as if there might be bedbugs among the starched cotton
sheets. None of those developing world concerns would occur
to Raybelle, but Tomas volunteered on the Near South Side of
Chicago.

She had reached that point where she was so tired and burned
out from travel that she no longer cared that she'd had no real
supper. The shower had helped to relax her. She loved traveling
to exotic places, and this corner of East Tennessee qualified. But
she didn't care for air travel, less so since the post-
September 11 security measures had been implemented. Raybelle,
being Republican, probably approved of all this slamming the
barn door after the horses had fled. A metaphor that went with
this redneck place.

Tomas draped the towel, which was not damp enough to
cause damage, across the back of the desk chair, and climbed
under the bedcovers. She'd deal with messages in the morning.
Even with her regular schedule, she was accustomed to waking
at unusual hours of the night, so when sleep was available to her,
she took it. This sounded like something a yoga teacher had
said—"If it's available to you today," and then the teacher would
wrap her thigh around the back of her head or something equally
appalling.

Tomas closed her eyes, but she did not sleep. She wondered
what Raybelle was polluting the blogosphere with, or if she were
coming up with more duties for her. Tomas ran her hand along

her own thigh, making very light contact up her side, and spread her fingers across her breast. The touch didn't excite her, but she appreciated the flesh and muscle she worked so hard to keep toned.

Her thoughts remained with Raybelle. There was no denying some attraction. Tomas remembered that grin, and the note of uncertainty in Raybelle's voice, like a crack in her armor. It wasn't that Tomas hadn't dated white women before, and she had no particular objection to a fifteen-year age difference. But she could not think of a single thing the two of them had in common. Not their politics, their geographic origin, their attitude toward work. At a bare minimum, Tomas required the women she liked to be interested in women themselves.

It was going to be a long night, if she couldn't stop thinking of Raybelle in this way. She was again regretting ever saying yes to the senator in the first place. More disturbing was the fact that she found it so hard to contemplate denying Raybelle anything she asked. If Raybelle had called at that instant, and demanded that Tomas get up and accompany her to an all-night bowling alley for a photo op, Tomas might go.

And that, more than anything else, was the reason she had to squelch any feelings she had for the senator right away. Never would Tomas allow herself to be again besotted with another human being. She hadn't known how much she'd cared for her last lover, until it took years to get over her.

CHAPTER SIXTEEN

The next morning Tomas felt marooned in the Ramada. There wasn't a gym. How was she supposed to work out? Rationally, she knew her muscles wouldn't turn to Jell-O in a single day off, but they felt like it.

She wanted to go for a walk, as it was a bright sunny morning, but there was nowhere she could walk. The Ramada sat just to the side of whatever that interstate was. If it had been a busier highway, she would probably have noticed the noise through the airtight window.

She spent two hours looking up articles about the Chikungunya virus on PubMed. There weren't that many, but she needed something to put in the references for her next study.

She was researching this so she wouldn't be researching Raybelle. Everything official she could find just had the usual politician pictures that made her gag. Senator McKeehan cutting the ribbon on a car dealership, or petting a prizewinning cow. Tomas supposed she had expected shots of Raybelle looking commanding in the company of dignitaries, but no, she was just a perpetual candidate like everybody else. Tomas had never been so close to the American political cycle. One day with it and she felt exhausted.

What was it that pissed Raybelle off so much about her brother? Raybelle didn't seem sad about Dennis, just distracted. It was as if she thought he could come back from the grave and haunt her. Tomas knew better than to judge people's behavior, but it seemed extraordinarily selfish of Raybelle. Wasn't there a saying that you could tell how well a woman would treat a man by the way she treated her little brother?

This was ridiculous. Why was she so preoccupied with this woman, scrolling past screen after screen of text, not reading any of it? The senator was just someone with whom she had a tenuous professional relationship. She wasn't Tomas's type. Tomas liked dark-haired women with angular faces, and Raybelle didn't fit either requirement. And Tomas wasn't crazy about girly girls. She appreciated that suits and heels were expected in Raybelle's line of work, but at the ballgame last night? Tomas preferred a more *ER* kind of look, no matter where the woman in question actually worked. Alicia had been a professor, but in all the years they'd been together Tomas had hardly ever seen her in a skirt.

Alicia, Alicia. Two years and more than a few lovers later, Tomas was still thinking about her. Alicia in that occasional skirt, a pearl necklace at her throat, blowing the rare lipstick kiss; Alicia, straining at free weights, in drawstring pants that she somehow made sexy; Alicia in bed in the early morning, kissing her face. Before it all went wrong. Before Tomas had withdrawn so far up her own ass she'd come out gazing at her own navel and all she saw was lint. That was what Alicia had said, and Tomas had to admit now that it was an accurate, if mixed, metaphor.

And now, of all people to put Alicia out of her mind, a US senator! Unattainable on too many levels to count. Tomas could find nothing in the public record to indicate that Raybelle wasn't straight. Sure, lesbians and homophobes alike shared the fantasy that every powerful woman without a man at her side was a big dyke. But Tomas had made enough mistakes with women in her own profession to know that this was a cruel illusion. And even if Raybelle were so inclined, it was clear she couldn't afford, politically, to be involved with anyone. And if she could, a black, female doctor would scarcely represent the height of discretion.

Tomas reached for the complimentary coffeepot and set it going; there was nothing on the breakfast menu that appealed to her. She had thought she was immune to southern charm, but Raybelle had poured it on, thick as blackstrap molasses. Tomas didn't crave public attention, didn't like to stand up in a roomful of her peers at a medical convention; it felt like a trial by jury. People thought, just because a doctor could meet someone and one minute later have her gloved hand inside him, that she couldn't be shy. Tomas wasn't all that keen on the people part. She preferred the micro level: cells and tiny organisms, structures that were unseen and yet could break down the entire system. A body, or a planet.

Damn, she was too contemplative this morning. First Alicia and now this. She really needed to work out some of this tension. She changed into sweats and was about to head downstairs and ask the teenager at the desk where the hell, please, could a person walk in this town, when Raybelle called. "We're here, you ready?"

"For what?"

"Going for a little drive."

A smile creased Tomas's face, an evil smile. If Raybelle was going to order her around like this, then she deserved to have Tomas show up in sweats. "Be right down."

She didn't see anybody in the lobby. She glanced out front and saw Raybelle at the wheel of the Ford Focus, making a motion as if to honk the horn. This lack of class removed any chance of Tomas being embarrassed by her own attire, or anything else. She climbed in the front, stretched out, and fastened her seat belt as they peeled out of the parking lot.

"I feel like I'm being kidnapped," Tomas said. "Are you taking me to where the black folks live? I've felt very conspicuous since we got into town."

"That's ridiculous," Raybelle said. "Half the basketball team must have been black guys."

"I don't notice guys much."

Raybelle narrowed her eyes, quickly returning them to the rearview mirror. "Someone piss in your Cheerios this morning?"

"I haven't had breakfast."

"Well, that's very unhealthy for a doctor. I figured you got up before dawn and went straight for your petri dish." Raybelle got on the highway in the direction, according to the signs, of Poudre Valley. Tomas had thought this was Poudre Valley. "Why didn't you order breakfast?"

"Frozen tater tots don't do it for me at any hour of the day."

"Lord, you're a snob. Anyway, we don't have time to stop. We have to make the cystic fibrosis bike-a-thon. I'm handing out prizes."

Tomas thought of joking about people with cystic fibrosis riding bikes. But she doubted that would make her sound compassionate, and for some reason, she cared what Raybelle thought. "Just as well I didn't dress up."

"You look fine," Raybelle said, in the exact tone Alicia had used when she hadn't glanced at Tomas. When had Alicia stopped looking at her, really looking? Years before they split up, probably. Tomas wanted to knock these thoughts out of her head.

"Don't suppose there'll be many black faces at a CF bike-a-thon," she said.

Raybelle smacked the steering wheel. "What is your problem?"

"It just so happens that CF overwhelmingly affects white people, which are most of your population."

"And if there was a sickle cell anemia bike-a-thon, I'd be going to that," Raybelle said, with anger or maybe just frustration.

Tomas was certainly frustrated. Raybelle warmed her skin just by sitting next to her. She couldn't explain why. A fifty-year-old blonde who half the time just pissed her off. Granted, Raybelle contained enough controlled energy to set off a reactor, but Tomas wasn't at all prepared for a conflagration.

It was a beautiful day, so she tried to concentrate on that. The sun was bright overhead, and she could think of nothing more appropriate than riding a bicycle around for the benefit of those whose lives were cruelly limited. Sadly, her own thoughts were not limited to the appropriate. She imagined physical activities with the woman beside her, but more disconcertingly, she wanted to do other things first. Get to know Raybelle McKeehan, hear her childhood stories. Tell her things she hadn't told anyone else except Alicia. And things she'd never told Alicia.

"Doctor Jefferson."

Tomas turned so fast she felt a pain in her neck. "Yes?"

"Stop daydreaming. We're here."

***

They stepped into the sunshine and there were enough red, white and blue streamers around the start/finish line that it could have been a used car lot. To Raybelle, it might as well have been. Sometimes all these events seemed to blur together like those little striped pieces of drinking straws that kids attached to their bike spokes. A girl on a pink Schwinn shot in front of Raybelle, causing her to jump back.

"Madison!" someone shouted. "You almost ran over the lady! Get back here!"

Raybelle was amused, and a little disheartened, to find that the little girl had the name of another US president, but who knew? Maybe that's what she would grow up to be.

"I'm really sorry, ma'am," Madison's mother said, clearly not recognizing Raybelle. That wouldn't do.

Raybelle gave a broad, advertising-her-dentist grin, and stuck out her hand. "Hello, I'm Senator Raybelle McKeehan."

"Oh, my God! Well, how do you do! I'm Sheila Odom. And this is Madison." The little girl, helmet askew, screeched to a halt at Raybelle's feet. It took everything in her not to step back in terror again.

"Pleasure to meet you, Ms. Odom." Then Raybelle addressed the girl. "Madison, are you going to ride today and help kids who have cystic fibrosis?"

Madison nodded, with that glazed look all children seemed to have these days. Sugar and attention deficit. "Madison, get on now, the race will be starting soon," Sheila said.

Raybelle decided not to say something to the Odoms about it not being a race, everybody was there to have a good time and help others, there would be no winners and losers today. There were always winners, and Raybelle was always one of them. She didn't believe any of that non-competitive BS.

"Ms. Odom," she said, in case there was a camera around, "I'm here with Doctor Tomas Jefferson—" Raybelle reached to put a comradely arm around Tomas, but she wasn't there. So Raybelle kept smiling until she saw Tomas, then gestured toward her. Trying to save face.

Tomas had crouched down and was inspecting the finger of one of the smaller noncompetitors. Maybe he had some sort of minor injury. Raybelle was struck by two things. First, despite this event taking place on the east side of Poudre Valley, and therefore in the area black residents did live in (there were a few), Tomas's was the only dark face she could pick out of this crowd. And second, Tomas, in her attention to the little boy, was also the most beautiful person present.

Having nothing to use that knowledge for, or to gain from it, Raybelle stuffed it down with all the laundry of her mind. "Doctor Jefferson and I are going back to Washington tomorrow afternoon," she said to Sheila.

"Oh, that's nice. Will she be going to Thankful Baptist?"

Raybelle blinked. "I'm sorry, what?"

"Church tomorrow. Will she go to the black church?"

Sheila looked so twenty-first-century soccer mom that Raybelle had a hard time understanding the question. "I actually don't know her plans."

"What plans?" Tomas stepped up beside her and extended her hand to Sheila, who took it, curiously. Raybelle was mortified to observe Sheila looking at the pale skin between Tomas's knuckles, and her palm. Mortified because she had done that herself, and mortified because she was sure Tomas had noticed, too.

"Doctor Jefferson," she said, "this is Sheila Odom. Ms. Odom was just asking if you were planning to go to church tomorrow." She wanted to mouth "I'm sorry" to Tomas, but could apologize only with her eyes.

"Well," Tomas said, attempting a drawl that horrified Raybelle,

"I was thinking of walking nine holes tomorrow morning, if I can find a golf course that will let me in. Do you golf, Ms. Odom?"

"No, I don't."

"Shame. We're putting together a foursome."

Sheila looked so confused that Raybelle felt a little bit sorry for her. She gestured toward the signs all around. "So, Ms. Odom, does anyone in your life have cystic fibrosis? I understand it's a terrible disease."

"No, ma'am," Sheila said, "matter of fact I never heard of it before. Madison likes to ride her bike, you know, so when she heard about this fundraiser, she just wanted to do it." Soccer-mom poise had returned. "Do you treat cystic fibrosis, Doctor Jefferson?"

"No, I treat patients." Tomas's sarcasm, also, seemed lost on Sheila. "I'm a specialist in viruses that emerge from the tropics, the way AIDS did. For example, right now I'm doing research on the Chikungunya virus. It's found mostly on tropical islands, like Mauritius."

Raybelle didn't enjoy being reminded of her brother, directly or indirectly, and she didn't enjoy Tomas's smirk that said she was sure Sheila had never heard of Mauritius, and had no idea where it was.

"Oh, Africa," Sheila said, right on cue. "So many problems. But, I mean, it's the population, isn't it? Women have so many children over there, there's no birth control. I've heard," she said, like a novice debater.

Raybelle felt the need to step in. "It's true, overpopulation is a big factor. When there're only so many resources to go around."

"Right." Tomas was mad; Raybelle could tell by the way she clipped the *T* at the end of her word. Enunciation spelled anger. "You see, Sheila, the problem is infant mortality. When you see your children die before they can speak, you have a lot of children. And if you look at a demographic curve—" Raybelle could tell that poor Sheila didn't know *demographic* either, but neither of them could stop Tomas now—"if you look at a demographic curve of Europe, in the nineteenth century, you'll see exactly the same as Africa today. If we could wave a magic wand over Africa, and put Western medicine there and clear up child mortality, they'd be thinking about the same things we do. Whether Jennifer Aniston is going to get back together with Brad Pitt!"

"I love Brad Pitt," Sheila said, back on familiar ground.

"Uh-huh," Raybelle said. "Well, it was real nice to meet you. Good luck, Madison!"

She steered Tomas toward the start/finish line, where the noncompetition was about to begin. In a voice too low for the children to hear, she said, "What do you think you're doing?"

"Laying into her ignorance."

Tomas didn't bother to whisper. Why not just borrow the megaphone, and point it right at Sheila Odom?

"She's a constituent. You can't talk that way to—"

Tomas's eyes flashed fire, though her voice was cold. "I can do anything I like, Senator McKeehan. Let's be absolutely clear on that."

"Everybody is a potential voter—"

"And I don't work on your campaign."

The announcements were starting, and Raybelle's instinct was to wave at the herd of children, but Tomas held her attention. How did she do that?

"Look," Tomas said. "Everything may be about votes to you, but you asked me, as a nonpartisan expert, to serve the public interest. I wouldn't appreciate being expected to conceal my knowledge in Washington, and I'm not going to do it here."

"She didn't say anything to you." Raybelle knew, on some level, that Tomas was right, but she resisted this. "Is that what you do? Mouth off to people every time you think they look at you funny?"

"You don't know anything about me."

But I want to. The starting gun went off and Raybelle turned to applaud, but the smile plastered across her face felt unusually fake.

CHAPTER SEVENTEEN

Sheila Odom's remark about Thankful Baptist had bothered Raybelle partly because that's where they were going in the morning. She told Tomas she could sleep in Sunday because she, Raybelle, had an obligation to fulfill. Tomas had reacted when she said this as though nothing was more preposterous than her staying in bed in the morning. Raybelle had to turn away, face flushed. She wished she could persuade Tomas otherwise, but that was impossible.

So it was the white Senator McKeehan who attended services at the mostly black church that Sunday. It wasn't her first time. She liked to make a point of representing all God's children in this part of the world, while simultaneously worshipping him.

The irony was, she stood out in this congregation in a way Tomas wouldn't, yet Tomas probably wouldn't know what to do in a church anywhere. No, Dr. Jefferson would be much more at home in *The Gross Clinic* than at the Last Supper.

Raybelle stood for the appropriate hymns, clapped her hands in that game, white-person way, said "Amen" and the odd "Tell it, brother!" and all the while imagined Tomas's eyes on her, rolling, mocking. Which led back to thoughts of Tomas's eyes on her in other contexts. It sure was hot in this church. How inappropriate could her thoughts get? Tomas was not only godless, but probably a Democrat too.

At the door the preacher greeted Raybelle. "Senator, pleasure to see you again." He pumped her hand with the vigor of the political figure he was too, grasping her hand with both of his.

"Reverend," she said, "it's just Sister Raybelle, here in God's house." To him, it would sound genuine, and she did mean it. Still, always mindful of a photo opportunity, she flashed a camera-ready smile. She pictured Jesus, disgusted, driving merchants out of the temple with his whip of cords. No doubt Tomas wouldn't get an allusion like that.

After Raybelle had finished greeting the other members of the congregation, she headed to the Ramada. When she knocked at Tomas's door, she found her in a pair of gray sweatpants and a BLACK PRIDE T-shirt stained with sweat. Raybelle was assailed by an aroma of warm woman and stronger thoughts of impurity. "What happened to golf?"

"I was shitting that Sheila; I don't know anyone here. Just doing some improvised isometrics." Raybelle saw that Tomas held a book in her hand. Evidently she'd been pumping the Gideon Bible.

"Observing the Lord's Day?"

"Mmm." Tomas turned the Bible over, as if the back cover might contain a helpful blurb. "I've never read much of the Bible, and they always have one in hotel rooms, so thought I'd wound a little eternity. Kill a little time," she clarified.

"I know the quote. Thoreau."

"Yeah." Tomas gave that brilliant grin that was sarcastic at the same time. "Though in this part of the country, it might behoove them to put copies of *The Origin of Species* in the bedside tables."

"That would just encourage reproduction," Raybelle said.

Tomas laughed. "And I suppose you're on board with the 'all abstinence, all the time' crowd?"

"Surely, as a medical professional, you'll concede that abstinence is the only guaranteed method to prevent pregnancy and STDs?"

"I wasn't asking about your position on sex education," Tomas said.

Raybelle, thrown off balance, flushed again. She hated that, how the heat of her feelings just shone through her skin, while Tomas's feelings were opaque to her. Tomas probably thought it was just hot flashes. She couldn't really be interested in Raybelle's own sex life.

Or lack thereof. "I need to change out of these church clothes," she said, hoping that Tomas would feel chastised. "If you could be ready in half an hour, we need to get back to Washington."

A few minutes later, back home and changing her clothes, Raybelle was once more assailed with inappropriate thoughts, this time about what else could be done sitting on the edge of a bed. She needed another shower. A cold one.

She slipped out of her dress, having long since gotten used to unzipping the back herself, and looked down at her breasts. She cupped one experimentally, weighing it in her hand. It had been some time since she'd felt any kind of appreciation for her own body, and she regarded it in the abstract, as if she were a photograph by Annie Leibovitz.

When had she decided to sacrifice any pleasures of the flesh, any desire for family or companionship—anything, in fact, except the goal of higher office? Did this happen to men too? Was it just part of the larger thing that sneaked up on politicians in general? You went in with some kind of sincere goal of public service, you truly did; but then the unending election cycle got you spinning, like an industrial-strength washing machine, and without intending it you were spending more time running for office than you ever spent doing the work.

Raybelle hadn't planned this. And part of it she would defend: she needed to spend time here, with Tennesseans, or how could she effectively represent them there, in Washington? Nobody wanted a senator who was always in Washington and never down home.

She stood up, felt lightheaded, had to sit right back down on the bed. She hadn't had breakfast, just coffee, and after the previous morning's Denny's, her metabolism was protesting for more, like a greedy northern labor union. Was organized labor another issue on which she and Tomas would disagree? Or did the American Medical Association hardly count?

***

Tomas regretted not getting in more of a workout. Her shoulders ached and this airplane seat was only going to make things worse. It was as if they were designed to be uncomfortable, and it wasn't that much flying time, or shouldn't have been. But by the time she'd sat in two airports and waited out the inevitable delays—she had long since stopped asking the "reason" for a delay—she was really starting to be in pain. She would book an appointment with her massage therapist tomorrow, when she was back in Chicago.

Raybelle must have observed her rolling her shoulders from side to side, because she asked, "Are you sore?"

"Oh—yeah. I really need a massage. But I didn't think I could get one in Poudre Valley."

"There's massage places that are open at two in the morning, but I'm afraid I can't recommend them from personal experience."

Tomas started to laugh. "I really didn't have in mind that type of massage," she said. "I'm intrigued, though. Do you mean you have personal experience of massage parlors, but you just can't recommend one?"

She gave an internal laugh of triumph, seeing the blush register on Raybelle's face. She loved being able to do that to her, and tried not to go into too deep an analysis of why.

"You can't stand me, can you?"

Tomas rolled her shoulders again, but it was to get the kinks out, not a response.

CHAPTER EIGHTEEN

It was a truism in American politics that no one liked negative campaigning, but it worked. Voters who were already committed to their candidate were disappointed at the inevitable descent into attack ads and vitriol, which politicians thought were necessary to win over the undecided. Presumably, the undecided were a class of voters to whom nastiness had some special appeal.

Raybelle's fights were within the party, and within her own soul, though to her closest friends she would not admit that she had one. "Closest friends" in Raybelle's world, of course, meant people like Grant Rivers, all of whom she worked with politically. In fact, Grant's being a Democrat helped in the friendship department, because a lot of her fellow Republicans did not like

Raybelle. She wasn't your typical feminist, always going on about Planned Parenthood; but then she wasn't a mother either. And politicians, like most other people who were parents, held an almost pathological suspicion of those without children making decisions affecting "our children's future." Basically, anything worth deciding.

How many people did she have working for her, how big a budget from the good folks of Tennessee, and she could no more rely on the computer equipment than on a comfortable temperature in the Dirksen Senate Office Building. Lord, she was hotter than blazes. She tore at the silk scarf around her throat, wondering what had possessed her to wear it, a so-called accessory. She would have removed her jacket as well, but she had to leave for a meeting in five minutes, and at this point she was afraid of revealing sweat stains.

"You okay in there, boss?" Melody said.

"Told you not to call me that," Raybelle said, but with an undercurrent of affection. Melody had become her rock, her anchor, the one person she could rely on in this turbulent and faithless world. The irony of that. How had this twentysomething become the mother figure?

"Just so you know, we need to get going in four minutes."

Raybelle slapped the monitor, knocking it askew. "Careful," Melody said, "that's glass."

"Do I look like a moron?" Raybelle held her hand up. "Never mind, don't answer that, please."

"*Moron* isn't a nice word, Senator." Melody leaned on the edge of the desk, poking at keys with her manicured fingers. "You might want to curb your terminology, before a clip of you ends up on YouTube." At Raybelle's blank look, she said, "Please don't ask me to explain what YouTube is. By the time I get you comfortable with it, it won't be current anymore." She stepped back from the screen, which had been restored to its condition before it had frozen on Raybelle. "There you go."

"Thanks." Raybelle pushed up her sleeves, hotter than ever.

"Two minutes," Melody said. "And remember, don't say anything to anybody, anywhere, that you wouldn't want broadcast. Everybody's got a camera these days."

"If I went by that rule, I'd never get off the john."

Melody waved a finger. "Exactly the kind of thing I mean."

***

Tim was the first friend Tomas had made, perhaps, since Dana in college. Before, Tomas had colleagues and patients, all in clearly defined roles, but not friends.

She'd edged into friendship almost imperceptibly. First Tim had invited her to dinner, then they'd stopped to talk in the hall and she invited him out the next night—for she didn't cook. Tim declined, pointing out that she could really use some home-cooked food, and why didn't she just come back to his place? Bring the wine. The careful mentioning of his lover, Ephraim, had neatly signposted that the pressure was off.

Soon it became a standing, though unspoken, invitation. Tomas was often not home around other people's dinnertime, but when she was, she was as inclined to call Tim as the Chinese delivery place. His stir-fry was better.

And now here she was with Ephraim, who was again visiting from England. Riding the Ferris wheel on Navy Pier like a goddamn tourist. Tim had called Tomas when he'd been unable to take one more day off work. He and Ephraim hadn't seen each other in months, but Tim was afraid he'd lose his job, and then how could he afford the next plane ticket?

"Why doesn't he come and live with you?" Tomas had asked him.

And Tim had looked at her with a combination of pain and incredulity. "In the US? We're legal strangers, Tomas. I could marry him in Massachusetts, but it wouldn't make any difference at the federal level." She felt his reproach: being gay, too, she should have known.

But all Tomas wanted from Ephraim, as they gazed down upon the modern edge of the city, was to talk about where he was from, the Chagos Islands.

"I had a patient who lived in your part of the world," she said. It was her attempt at "nonversation," but Ephraim's eyes never left the view. Not making eye contact was a bad sign. Dennis McKeehan had looked right at her.

Ephraim was listening, though. "I was able to see out across the ocean, it seemed forever. I do not like these buildings. They are wrong for my eyes."

"How long have you lived in England?"

He spoke with slow deliberation, as if, though his English was perfect, the tongue was unfamiliar to him. "I have been in London now for three years."

"And before that—you lived on Mauritius?" Tomas was aware of taking his history, but Ephraim didn't really seem into small talk either.

"I was there, yes." She observed his avoidance of the word *lived*. "Since the British forced us to leave."

"You blame the British, then? Not the Americans?"

Finally, he turned to her, and half smiled. His teeth matched the whites of his eyes; clearly he had a good dentist. "You are American," he said. "I am only being polite."

"It must bother you, though, being in Britain. When they— or we—are responsible for all your troubles."

He looked out again. "London is a nicer place to be than Mauritius."

"I'm sure you didn't know my patient," Tomas said. "But he went by the name of Brother Dennis."

"I do not know," Ephraim said. "Was he of the church?"

"I didn't understand his religion," she said. "He went there to 'experience poverty.' I met him because he got sick."

"Experience poverty." Ephraim still didn't look at her. "I have done that."

He said it the way she might say she'd ridden this Ferris wheel. "Been there, done that." She didn't enjoy Ferris wheels, or being stuck in a compartment with a stranger. A slightly taller man, with slightly lighter skin than hers. No doubt they looked like a not-very-affectionate British couple. Tomas wore no jewelry. Ephraim had one thin chain around his neck; it looked like gold.

"May I ask you a personal question?" He spoke the words as if he'd learned them from a phrase book.

"Shoot."

He flinched at the word, and Tomas was instantly sorry she'd used it. Clearly that was not in his phrase book. "I don't understand," he said.

How ambiguous her own language was. *No, I don't mind? Go ahead?* She settled for, "What?"

"Are you presently involved in a relationship?"

The cadence of this brother's English! She was so charmed that for a moment, she considered saying no, which would have been the truth. How foolish of her. "I'm not, actually, interested in a relationship right now," she said. This was not the truth, but it saved her the bother of talking about the last person she wanted to talk about—herself.

"Then I will not take it personally." Ephraim emphasized the learned phrase. "The ride is almost over. What do you want?"

She didn't know if he meant what she wanted to do next, or what she wanted from him. Perhaps both. She was not the only one clever enough to use the ambiguity of the language.

They reached the bottom of the ride, and she took his arm. He escorted her gallantly. "Tell me about what you're doing in England."

Ephraim looked directly ahead, and his tone was severe. "I am going to see the British government."

"You?" She added, "Personally?"

"Not for myself," he said. "For my country."

Tomas thought of Raybelle, and without considering her words, she said, "Yeah, we have a lot of people in America who talk about serving their country. They're talking about themselves, though." *All she ever wants to talk about.*

His voice deepened and took on a harder edge. "It becomes more important," he said, "when your country disappears."

They were soon surrounded by the throngs along Navy Pier.

***

Follow the money. Logic dictated that if budget cuts were going on at the military hospitals to save money, then the money saved was going somewhere. Raybelle doubted it was to the American taxpayer. In the history of Washington, there was no evidence that had ever happened.

She had a message to call back the Secretary of Defense. But she'd had enough of phones this week, all that nuance and blathering. She'd go in person. Wearing red again, trousers this time.

She banged into the outer office without announcing herself.

"Senator McKeehan." Perry's aide, Dick, bounded alongside her like the high school athlete he still resembled. "I don't think the Secretary is expecting you—"

"He should be," she said. "He, or should I say you, have called me, or should I say my assistant, six billion times." She paused at the inner door. "One for each person on earth."

"Actually there's more like seven billion now." He placed his hand on her wrist.

She wanted to tell him to shut up and get his hand off her, but why be rude to a perfectly friendly subordinate, just because he worked for the devil? Besides, it was probably bad karma. If Baptists had karma. She'd have to ask Melody.

She rapped on the door, but Dick opened it while blocking her from the view of the office's occupants. "Mr. Secretary, sir, Senator McKeehan—"

"What does that cunt want?"

Dick mouthed "Sorry" and she brushed past him. Like the Queen being ushered into Parliament by Black Rod.

"Hey, Henry, how're you doing?"

The Secretary didn't stand, but he didn't comment on her informality, either. Well, really, how did you follow "cunt"?

"You're a hard man to get hold of." She reached his large oak desk and leaned both hands along the polished edge. Her rings caught the glint of the green banker's lamp. "Which brings me to my question, the reason I came in person."

"I'm afraid you're out of order," he said, with a gleam of the dentition he must be so proud of. So white it had to be bought and paid for. "It's you I called to answer my questions, Senator."

"Oh, Henry." She finally sat, uninvited. She knew his outrage wouldn't be allowed to break through the mask. "Please don't make me have to go through my whole remedial constitutional course again. You know, how I was elected to represent the people, while you were hired by the executive, and so on."

"We've all heard your spiel, Raybelle." His use of Yiddish was ridiculous, but the challenge wasn't lost on her.

"What is going on over at Walter Reed Hospital?"

He blinked at her, calm as a cat.

"Why do we have guys returning from Iraq and Afghanistan, living like barnyard animals?"

"Don't you mean 'guys and gals'?"

She ignored his mocking tone. "Didn't we have enough jollies at Abu Ghraib, without treating our own soldiers like that?"

"Let me tell you about Abu Ghraib. You critics, liberals—and yes, I'm including you, you're as feminist as any Democrat—are utter hypocrites. Those terrorists were fundamentalist Muslims; they were humiliated because they were being ordered around by women. Women soldiers is what you *want*."

"In other words, the prisoners asked for it." Raybelle didn't try to rein in her contempt. "I don't know, Mr. Secretary, if you're aware of anything outside your own hind end, but since our inspection of the hospital we've been getting an awful lot of...*concerned* e-mails. And calls, and press reports. People are wondering why, in this era of perpetual war, we treat like shit the people who fight for us." She smirked. "If you'll excuse my profanity. I'm sure you're used to it."

"Let me ask you something. If you're so sure how wars ought to be fought, and you're just as good as the men, why didn't you serve? Alongside Dennis?"

Raybelle couldn't keep the edge from her voice. "You leave him out of this."

"Oh yes, we know your agenda, commander-in-chief wannabe. You think we're not going to dig up some nutball brother who died on the street?"

"I really thought you'd be above trashing homeless veterans," she said. "I see even that's not beneath you."

"But actually serving, risking your own life in the service of your country was beneath you. Right? Never mind all that equal opportunity shit."

"At least I didn't take deferments up the ass, like you." Raybelle was aware that she had now cussed twice in one meeting. But Perry had made this personal.

He lifted a shoulder, in that maddening way. "Can I help it if I am, quite frankly, smarter than you?" he said. "I wasn't studying at Butt Fuck U."

"Your vocabulary does impress." Raybelle decided to go in low. "What I find interesting is that you can send other people's sons and daughters into 'harm's way,' as the saying goes. But not your own."

For the first time, his eyes glowed incandescent. "Get the fuck out of my office."

Perry had crossed a line, and she knew she could no longer work with him. They were enemies now, much as she hated to make an enemy. This was a war. Look at the depths to which she had already stooped, the language she'd used. He had attacked her family and her education. Raybelle wasn't sure which she valued more.

CHAPTER NINETEEN

Raybelle returned to her office with a BLT and a headache. The latter was not helped by the buzz of fluorescent lights and activity. "Fifteen minutes," she told her staff. She just needed fifteen minutes before she could resume the endless dance of lobbying the lobbyists.

"I can't believe you confronted him," Melody said. "But since you did, might as well use it. Time to go on the offensive, boss. Make this your issue. You're angry about it, and you're going to let everyone know."

"I am?" Raybelle said.

"Sure. This is news. The old media are picking it up and now everyone wants the story of the outraged senator whose brother died with post-traumatic stress disorder."

"What are you talking about?"

Melody wiped her mouth. "I told you we couldn't keep it a secret."

"But it's not true!"

"Ask Doctor Jefferson," Melody said. "She's on the line."

Raybelle snatched the phone and, without waiting for Tomas to say hello, said, "Who cares what my brother did?" She was incensed, and she knew there was no point taking it out on Tomas but she couldn't help it. It was Tomas's fault Dennis was back in her life, more so than he'd been while he was alive. "Since when do you have to have military experience to have an opinion about the armed forces?"

"Calm down, Senator. I called to offer you a deal."

"Oh, a deal." Raybelle plunked down so hard in her chair her vertebrae rattled. "This better be good, Doctor Jefferson. I just got back from Henry Perry's office, and I'm not happy."

"That's what I'm talking about," Tomas said. "This issue you're having, with the military hospital. I can offer you my expertise, if you can try and help a friend of mine."

She has friends? "What's her problem?"

"His. He was removed, by the US military, from his home in the Chagos Islands. Where your brother—"

"I know about Dennis. I asked about your man." Raybelle spoke as if Tomas had a boyfriend. Almost as if she were jealous.

"He's suing the British government."

"Britain? Why?"

"That's where he lives. But his partner lives in Chicago. That's how I know him."

"You want me to help him come here?"

"No," Tomas said. "I want you to be an ally in their case. The Chagossians'. A friend of the court. He's going to try to publicize his case in the US."

"His case of what?" Raybelle felt overwhelmed by the pace of events, as was so often the case when Tomas was involved.

Tomas took over the conversation as effortlessly as she might the care of a patient. "I've spent some time with Ephraim, and told him about the investigation you were running into the hospital scandal. How you aren't afraid to rock the boat, because this is America." Raybelle listened hard for Tomas's usual irony, but she didn't hear it. "I said, sure, our country has problems but at least somebody who criticizes something isn't going to get her bones broken, or worse. How you can get citizens talking about things your enemies would rather you weren't talking about."

"Let me think about it, okay?"

"Senator—"

"I'll call you." She put the phone down, and met Melody's expectant eyes. Raybelle leaned back in her chair, inexplicably relaxed, and at the same time leaned into her native accent, the way she was used to when telling tales of her youth, or speaking to old friends like Grant. "My first campaign, I was a young lawyer— you hadn't been born—running for district attorney in Poudre Valley. A town that had never seen a DA who was young, never mind female."

"What about nonwhite?" Melody said.

"Oh, I would have had no chance then. Anyway, you wouldn't believe the stuff I went through. People calling the radio station, saying I didn't know what I was talking about, because I used the phrase 'human rights' in a speech down by the Monument. I was talking about things like torture, you know, but the reactions I got...and then the Klan came marching. They probably would have marched anyway, but for it to coincide with a woman's campaign for DA..." Raybelle shook her head. "And here I am, a free-speech absolutist. Would have ruled in favor of anyone's right to say anything. Including," she added, "the anti-Klan protesters, who even in Poudre Valley drew a larger crowd than the Ku Kluxers did."

"The Klan marched in Skokie, Illinois," Melody said. "This suburb just full of Holocaust survivors, and neo-Nazis come parading through, just to be evil. They have no shame!"

"On the contrary," Raybelle said in her best Grant Rivers voice, "they're full of shame. Why else would they wear those sheets over their heads? Like those terrorists in Northern Ireland, why did they wear those balaclavas? If people are so proud of what they stand for, and who they hate, let's come right out and see 'em."

"No more blogs on that topic." Melody clicked on what

appeared to be a penlight in her left hand. "But don't worry, I'm recording it all."

"For what? I thought you were terrified of amateur broadcast."

"The record. Someday, when our country lurches back in the direction of civil liberties, there's going to be a need for rhetoric like this."

"Rhetoric? I was just shooting the breeze."

"Same thing."

"You know," Raybelle said, "I kind of like this not running for president. Having everyone speculate about it is much more effective, publicity-wise, than actually paying for a campaign."

"Well," Melody said, "there's a whole line of people waiting to talk to you about that." She looked curious. "Did you win?"

"What? My first campaign?"

"Yeah. Did you win?"

Raybelle cracked her knuckles, to Melody's wince. "No, I lost. To David Payne. We're good friends now, of course."

"Oh. Did he come around to your point of view?"

"No. But he's still a big man in Poudre Valley."

***

Tomas took Ephraim to lunch while Tim was working. He said she didn't need to, but she wanted to spend more time with him. It was an experience unfamiliar to her, with anyone. She drove the car more slowly and carefully than she was used to, as if her cargo was precious.

Ephraim turned impassive eyes to her. He looked like an Egyptian god-king. "About whom are you thinking?"

She noticed he didn't ask "what." "I spoke to the senator," she said, "about your case."

"Did you vote for her?"

"I vote here," Tomas said. "The senator is in another state."

"I cannot vote in my country," Ephraim said quietly. "If I could, I would stand in line for hours."

"There are people in this country who won't so much as get out of bed to vote," Tomas said. "Millions of people don't."

"That is good."

"Why do you say that?"

"If they do not know whom they should vote for," he said in his measured tones, "then you do not want them voting. Do you?"

"I never thought of it that way."

"I think a lot." Ephraim made it sound like suffering.

Tomas didn't have a lot of optimism that Raybelle would help him. To be sure, she didn't have much to offer Raybelle herself, and politics was all about making deals. She shouldn't have mentioned Ephraim's lover; it would muddy the waters, make this a gay issue, not to mention an immigration issue and Raybelle wouldn't want to deal with that—

Ephraim's voice interrupted her thoughts. "You too."

"What?"

"You think a lot. You are not listening to me right now."

"I'm sorry." She slowed for the exit. "I was thinking about what you're going to do." The lie came so easily she didn't think of it as lying. Maybe she should switch jobs with Raybelle.

"I do not see how I have any case in the US. I have no money and no lawyer."

"Well, how'd you do it in Britain?"

"A human rights group is sponsoring me there," he said. "But here, I have no legal standing. If the British government will do nothing for a British resident, what will America do to an alien?"

"You're a foreign visitor, Ephraim. Not an alien."

The corner of his mouth quirked, a first sign of amusement. "That is what American immigration calls us."

"It's rude. It sounds like you're from space."

"I am a stranger," he said. "No one trusts a stranger."

I do, she thought but didn't say. "What are you thinking of doing, since you can't stay in Chicago?"

"I have seen your television," he said, as though referring specifically to the set in Tomas's living room. "A single unknown person, saying one thing, can be everywhere. It is the Internet. Like God."

Sometimes, Ephraim sounded like a psychedelic prophet. She thought of Washington, DC, a suffering black town being drained by its white abscess. Tomas would like to go a whole day without thinking about race, but she didn't have that privilege.

"Ephraim," she said, "do you know what reparations are?"

"I am not familiar with this word."

How to make this simple? "Many years ago, black people were brought to America from Africa, to serve as slaves."

"Yes."

"Now there are some black leaders saying we, meaning the descendants of those black slaves, deserve reparations from the United States government. That we should be paid money, because of what happened to our ancestors."

"What do you think about this?"

Tomas regretted that she'd brought this up on a car ride. "It doesn't matter what I think. What matters is that this idea is out there, in the public consciousness."

Ephraim made a sound that could have been a laugh. "You are a very strange person, Doctor Jefferson."

"Yeah, I get that a lot."

"I beg your pardon?"

"Never mind. Please call me Tomas."

***

Raybelle tried to remember the last meal she'd eaten that hadn't involved toast. "I only have one nerve left, Melody, and you're getting on it. I wish I'd never heard you mention YouTube and Webcasting, and I wish you had never given me that first message from Tomas Jefferson." She deliberately mispronounced "Tomas," like the name of the third president.

"She'd be thrilled to hear that, I'm sure."

"Melody, I trust you to be discreet." Raybelle shoved a piece of toast in her mouth and kept talking. "Heaven knows, I can't rely on any of these other clowns."

Tomas and her Mauritian friend (who wasn't really from Mauritius, but Raybelle had a hard enough time finding that on a globe) had proposed this idea of going on the Web, in a manner clear only to people like Melody, and proclaiming that Ephraim and his people were seeking restitution from the US government for what had happened in the Chagos Islands. "Ephraim and his people" made it sound like one of those old Bible movies. So, for that matter, did "restitution," in whose favor *reparation* had been ditched. As Tomas put it, the originally displaced Chagossians were still alive, and it wasn't money they wanted, but their land and dignity.

Raybelle wasn't clear on what that entailed, but she was certain that it didn't fit into her job description. Nothing about this scheme pointed in the direction she wanted her career heading, which was to 1600 Pennsylvania Avenue.

She'd spent so much time in Washington that she rarely thought, now, about the first time she ever visited, as a student. The numbers of the streets were simple, but not all led in a straight line, and Raybelle had gotten turned around searching for the White House. It felt so ridiculous to ask, "Where is the White House?" But she must have looked lost, because someone had taken pity on her and given directions there. She'd never taken her eyes off the White House since.

It was her first introduction to the kindness of strangers, and Raybelle would need to milk that human kindness dry to get where she wanted to go. Where she needed to go, to serve people. Her people. Whereas Ephraim's people, much as they might make a great human interest story, were not Americans and couldn't vote.

And that wasn't the most pressing concern, if she did run for president. Nor was breakfast deprivation. Money would be. Raybelle had always played up her log-cabin background, evoking Lincoln (heaven help her) and his version of the Republican Party. She knew there was a group called the Log Cabin Republicans who advocated gay emancipation within the party, but Raybelle was all about rights, and didn't think anyone's were "special." The government had no place in people's businesses, doctors' offices, churches, or beds. Or, maybe most importantly, their minds. If people wanted to believe that women were inferior or the world was flat or the moon was made of green cheese, they had every right to say so on talk radio.

But the reality was, you had to raise a ton of money to run for office, and one way to do that was by acquiring a ton of your own. So off she'd gone to become a lawyer, just as Lincoln had and as those wanting to be president would do after her. Would

Melody become the first Asian-American president, or just the first Asian-American woman president? There was no chance at either until the day came when such labels didn't matter anymore. But if she waited for Melody, she'd miss her chance to be the first woman president herself. What that would cost, in terms of the fundraising gang and the endless battle to come out on top...

"Tell me this," she said to Melody. "You're in the blogosphere all the time. What's wrong with me?"

Melody looked tempted to ask where she should begin. "I think you're spending too much time thinking about Doctor Jefferson."

"Lord, you're irritating. I'm talking about public perceptions of me. As, you know, a possible candidate for, ah..." She refused to call the presidency *higher* office, but Melody would know what she meant.

"They say you don't have a chance."

"Well." Raybelle was surprised how relaxed she felt, now that Tomas was no longer the subject of conversation. "If I was interested in playing the victim, which I'm not, I would say I haven't got a chance because I'm a woman. Didn't people dump on Margaret Thatcher when she was British prime minister, saying, 'Ditch the bitch'?"

"That would happen if you weren't white, too."

"Oh, I'm not interested in comparing this to race," Raybelle said. "Far be it from me to decide which of somebody's parents he resembles most. All I'm saying is, they gave Thatcher no quarter for being a woman, but it didn't stop her from changing her country."

"Careful, Senator," Melody said. "You're starting to sound almost feminist."

"Thatcher was no feminist," Raybelle said. "She just won."

***

"Is this very urgent, Doctor Jefferson?" Melody said over the phone. "Senator McKeehan's in the Senate for a vote."

Would she call if it wasn't very urgent? "If you could just have her call me back as soon as she can, Melody, thanks," Tomas said, numerous unnecessary words tumbling out in her haste. "I know she's very busy. You too."

"She has your number, but let me note it just in case," Melody said.

Tomas hung up and exhaled, grateful. How could she explain why she was calling? "I just need to hear the senator's voice?" That wouldn't do. "I need to talk to her about guilt and absolution." Two concepts in which she didn't believe—could not, rationally, afford to believe in—but which, as she had discovered with Dennis and now Ephraim, could prove to be important.

Alicia had often complained that the certainty, not to say arrogance, that so suited Tomas to the practice of medicine was damn nigh unbearable. "I can't live with somebody who's always right and has never made a mistake!" Leaving had been Alicia's choice, but Tomas had not questioned her own choices. Her personality was who she was, and what she needed. If it wasn't what Alicia needed, well, that was Alicia's loss.

Alicia had said that they shouldn't be in touch, so they weren't. Tomas had acceded to her wishes (for the first time, Alicia would say). Still, she was used to the woman crossing her mind at least every day, just as she had on long, busy days when they had been a couple, but hadn't seen each other. Alicia complained that Tomas rarely "saw" her anyway, when she was right there. In fact Alicia's chief function in Tomas's life, then and afterward, seemed to have been as an archive of Tomas's infinite wrongdoings. No wonder Tomas didn't believe in guilt.

She stretched out on her bed although it was the middle of the afternoon. A thing she never did. Even in the years, and it was many years ago now, when she and Alicia had still had a satisfactory love life, Tomas never recalled going to bed in the afternoon. It was something missed out on in her youth, like wild parties or a sophomore slump.

It didn't look like she was ever going to get a chance to make up for that sobriety. Trysts on diving holidays blurred together in her memory like the underwater sights. She hadn't fought for Alicia when she left, because she hadn't thought she should have to; it was beneath her dignity. Another way of saying she had wounds to lick. But no one else had yet uprooted Alicia from her consciousness. When she was kissing another woman, or drowning in another woman's pleasure, it was just bodies slapping together, not something she would remember later as the best this or that she ever had. For all her impatience with Tomas, Alicia had grounded her, and without her, Tomas drifted like the seaweed, free but not belonging anywhere.

She awoke to the ring tone "The Entertainer." She was horrified to have fallen asleep—something else she didn't do in the afternoon; she hadn't drawn the blinds. It took her a moment to clear her throat and focus on answering Raybelle. "Yes, Senator?"

"I am so screwed."

Tomas was instantly much more alert. This didn't sound like something Raybelle would ever say. "Pardon me?"

"They've made me their enemy. The Department of Defense. I don't know who or what's wrong with them, but I'm screwed." Raybelle paused and it sounded like she was chewing something. Didn't she know you could hear everything over a cell phone? Next she'd be on the toilet. Indeed, Tomas did hear the sound of splashing water, and she cringed.

"I'm sorry to hear that, Senator." She'd expected Raybelle to say "I'm returning your call," but as usual she had her own agenda.

"I want you to come back to Washington."

"I'm afraid I can't do that."

"What do you mean, 'can't'?"

"My presence is required here."

"You agreed to help me out," Raybelle said, sounding like a petulant child. God, Tomas hated it when grown women whined.

"Yes, I agreed. I helped you, and then I'd had enough. It's not a crime when you can't stick it out anymore."

There was a pause. Tomas imagined that silence was uncommon in Raybelle McKeehan's life. "Why do I get the feeling I'm not the first woman you've said that to?"

Tomas almost dropped the phone, but instead gripped it more tightly, like the handle on a roller coaster. "Because you're not."

This silence was longer. Without meaning or desiring to, Tomas had waltzed Raybelle into a conversation for which she guessed the senator had no precedent. She was enjoying her discomfort.

"I need to fight this," Raybelle said. "You uncovered some nasty stuff, and I have to pursue it."

"So pursue it." Tomas sat up on the edge of the bed, scratching at her boxer shorts, not that anybody could see. "What do you need me for?"

"Our country needs us."

"Oh, bullshit. You need your country. I've got a man here who doesn't—" Tomas stopped, realizing now that she finally had Raybelle on topic, she wasn't sure what to say.

"Yeah, your friend Ephraim," Raybelle said. "Listen, we can talk about him too. But come to Washington."

The nerve of this bitch. Thought she could just— "Why should I?"

"Because." The parrying tone was gone from Raybelle's voice, and for once, she sounded human. "I need you here."

She couldn't know, or intend, that the words would bore right into Tomas and make her helpless to resist.

CHAPTER TWENTY

Tomas woke sweating in a plane seat. She must have been exhausted; she was seldom able to fall asleep on a plane. The stuffy atmosphere, and her position during sleep, made her cramped and sticky. But it was the content of her dream that disturbed her. Characters in her dreams were always people from her past, usually standing in for some present anxiety. It was hard to ignore the explicitness of this one. She rubbed her cheek, still feeling on it the warmth and moisture of Alicia's inner thigh, the curl of her dark hair. Tomas was struck with a pang of lust, and longing, so powerful she would have doubled over, had her seat permitted it.

She had probably had more sex with women since Alicia than

she had in their relationship. Nothing had come close to theirs, though, in love and intimacy. How had she been so careless of it, neglected Alicia for so long? There was a comfort there, a familiarity, but Tomas had taken it for granted. "Comfort" made love sound like a serving of mashed potatoes.

She needed to clear her head. Not that there was any air on board the plane. Stretching was impossible without getting out of her seat, and she was loath to try this, wedged as she was between unsympathetic sleepy people, but she got up. Her seatmate didn't respond to "Excuse me," so Tomas was forced to slide in front of his knees to get to the aisle, something she suspected few other American passengers were capable of. Then she crunched her head against the overhead bin, and angry tears swam into the corners of her eyes.

To her horror, she couldn't stop them, although she did make it to the bathroom and splashed water on her face. She leaned against it, barely enough room to sit on the toilet never mind move around. Crying wasn't something she was accustomed to. Seeing herself that way in the mirror, all weepy—no, this was not the image Dr. Jefferson projected, either to the world or to herself. She saw patients, dead and dying, horribly disfigured, and was always prepared to show minimal emotion, whether someone lost his limbs in an accident or a child died of a brain tumor.

Now, after a dream of a woman she hadn't seen in years, she was a basket case, falling apart in an airplane john.

Eventually she had to emerge, still not herself, to face a lineup of women for the bathroom. Always women. What was with them? Her face flushed at the memory of Alicia opening her legs—*God*. She had to get it together; she was supposed to meet with Raybelle this afternoon.

She stood in the aisle and stared at Lazy Fucker until he got out of his seat and let her in. This was going to be another turbulent flight.

***

The din was inescapable. In Raybelle's office with its snakes of cubicles and wires, and in her head no matter where she went.

Screens were always on, shouting the latest television news and talk shows, and every pundit sounded shriller than the last. There were always so many people around Raybelle, yet Melody Park would find a way to attract her attention. If Melody couldn't cut through the noise, she would use another sense.

Today it was smell. Melody had opened a jar of those foul pickles she liked, and Raybelle grimaced, but this did not deter Melody. Her grin grew wider before she popped one in her mouth.

Raybelle wandered over and perched, candidate-like, on the edge of a neighboring swivel chair. There was some sense in which Melody's youth and attitude settled her. Maybe she should pick her brain more often.

"I've got ten minutes, Melody," she said. "Tell me something besides 'You're wasting time, Senator. Get on the phone and raise money.'"

Melody looked amused. "Kimchi, boss?"

"No deference, please."

"Well, I've been sending you reminders so I'm sure you know Doctor Jefferson is coming back this morning." Raybelle let her face register nothing. "In preparation for which, I've taken the liberty of drafting some comments from you, acknowledging your brother."

"Melody, when I want anyone to horn in on my personal life, I'll be sure to let you know."

"You said no deference."

Raybelle sighed and reached for the pickle jar. Her sniff brought revulsion.

"Senator, you know it's going to come out eventually. You can't expect people not to find out about your relatives. You don't have a spouse—"

"See, this is why I keep you around. Hey, Bob." Raybelle waved, with practiced enthusiasm, to the third blond staffer to walk by since she'd sat down. "To tell me the confounded obvious."

Melody huddled in, voice lowered. "If you run for president, who's supposed to be First—"

"In the first place, I'm not running for president. Running for the presidency would mean thinking about asking for donations twenty-four hours a day."

"So does running for the Senate."

"In the second place, Melody, being single shouldn't be a bar. We've had a bachelor president."

"Yeah. James Buchanan, and what a success he turned out to be. Lincoln had to come in and straighten his mess."

"Lincoln is overrated."

Melody's eyes widened. "See, there's another one of those kinds of things you should watch yourself saying."

Raybelle was itching something fierce under her pantyhose. "I'm not, nor have I ever been, running for First Lady, Melody."

Melody's smartphone, and face, brightened simultaneously. "Your visitor's here."

Raybelle felt an unexpected delight leap in her chest when Tomas Jefferson appeared, elegant in a gray suit. "Security," Tomas said. "I'm surprised I don't have to submit to a colonoscopy to visit a member of Congress."

"You guys." Melody addressed them like irritating members of her high school class. "You have to stop this."

"Stop what?" Tomas said.

"Making these bold, uncensored statements."

"Why?" Raybelle said, more stridently than she meant to. "Why should we watch what we say? This is the United States of America. Where people are free to say what they want."

"Prudence, Senator," Melody said. "And there's a long tradition of the opposite, too. Censorship, xenophobia. The Alien and Sedition Acts—"

"You mean the Patriot Act?" Tomas said.

"Fuck the Patriot Act."

Both women looked at Raybelle. She was sure neither had ever heard her say *fuck* before, let alone in relation to a law that she herself had voted to reauthorize. Raybelle should have been afraid of this YouTube generation, or what kind of hate mail her next blog post would bring in, with or without the *F* word. But she was not afraid. She wanted to sound brave—wanted to be brave—and knew, somehow, that this had to do with Tomas being present. As a politician, Raybelle had always cared what other people thought of her—voters or subsets of voters: the so-called middle class, veterans. She wasn't used to caring what any one person thought of her, as if this particular individual—not even her constituent!—walking into the office somehow changed everything. Raybelle didn't know how to express this to herself, in words. Thank goodness she had speechwriters to help with that.

"Kimchi?" Melody held a Mason jar out to Tomas, along with an extra pair of chopsticks, still in the paper wrapper.

"No, thanks," Tomas said without disgust. In fact, her smile seemed to suck all the light in the room into it. Raybelle wondered if this might just be in contrast with Tomas's very dark skin, then chided herself for what might be a racial thought. What a minefield.

"Raybelle."

Raybelle blinked, and found Tomas looking at her. She felt, rather than saw, fingers resting on her arm. Electricity. Not the static kind, a shock, but a flow of energy. "What?"

Tomas hesitated, as if checking Raybelle's vital signs. Then she drew her hand away. "You and I should get a cup of coffee," she said, and headed for the door. When Raybelle failed to follow, Tomas looked back. "Senator? Coffee?"

"Where, the cafeteria?"

Tomas's face hardened. "Something wrong with it?"

"Not if you like salt and fat as much as we southerners do," she said. "The House went organic last year, but this is the Senate."

"Still southern, huh? As in, the segregated south?"

Raybelle's fierce self returned. "Yeah, that's right. When Carol Moseley Braun was here, she had to stand up in the back to eat. Right by the 'Colored' water fountain."

The two locked eyes. Raybelle felt Melody looking at her, like a referee trying to decide whether to stop a fight. In her mind she heard a bell clang.

"Take me there," Tomas said.

"Senator," Melody called after them, "what shall I tell Secretary Perry's office if they call back?"

"You got some great quotes from me this morning, Melody. Use one of those."

They walked down the corridor with swift purpose, and Raybelle felt nervous, in a way confronting Perry hadn't made her feel nervous.

"Don't wear heels, huh?" Hers clacked on the floor.

"Not unless I have to," Tomas said. "They go with certain suits. But I'm used to covering everything with a lab coat. I never think of making an impression with my clothes."

"Don't need to."

Tomas looked at her out of the corner of her eye, and Raybelle felt her face grow hot again. Damn hot flashes. She'd have to lose this jacket.

In the dingy cafeteria they pulled up ugly chairs. Tomas didn't seem to notice how bad the coffee was here. Maybe she was used to much worse.

"So what's going on?" Tomas said.

"You know the defense secretary, Henry Perry."

Tomas looked at her over the rim of her coffee cup. "A lot of folks think he's an asshole, don't they?"

"What do you think?" This wasn't how Raybelle had envisioned the conversation, but it seemed important to know.

"Not my area of expertise."

Raybelle smacked her hand down on the table. Her temper was so short around this woman. "Well, what is your area of expertise, Doctor Jefferson? One square inch of the pancreas? Come on."

Tomas didn't reply, and for a moment Raybelle was afraid she was going to get up and leave. So she said, "Tell me about this man of yours. Ephraim."

Tomas leaned in on her elbows. "You're not really interested," she said. "Let's talk about another man. Dennis."

"Why does everybody want to talk about him all the time?"

"Who's 'everybody'?"

"Oh, you. Melody...the women I listen to most." The words left Raybelle's mouth, but she wasn't sure what they meant.

"No." Tomas spoke in a calming tone, as if Raybelle were a very young patient, or otherwise didn't know what the hell was going on. "Don't you know that saying: 'Everybody thought that Somebody should do it. Anybody could have done it, but Nobody did.'"

"Did you come all the way here to recite nursery rhymes? I thought you were a pro."

Tomas glanced around the room, as if to determine whether

someone was listening. "Your brother, with the US Marines after 1967, took over the Chagos Islands and displaced the occupants. It was forcible, not pretty and totally illegal under international law. Not that that's worth much."

"Are you saying the US invaded a sovereign nation?"

"The islands were a 'possession' of Great Britain, which saw fit to sell, or give, them to the United States. Ever hear of Diego Garcia? The base where American planes take off to bomb the Gulf, whenever that needs doing? Evidently Britain thought they could get something out of us in exchange for the islands, or we browbeat them into it."

"It doesn't take much to push Britain into doing something," Raybelle said. "I mean look at Tony Blair."

Tomas ignored Raybelle in a way she found infuriating. "What Dennis participated in haunted him for the rest of his life. He lost faith in what he'd gone there to do—what he'd devoted his career to. What he did toward the end of his life was an attempt to make up for that."

"Well I've devoted my career to serving my country too," Raybelle said, "and I'm not about to repent for that. Maybe we served in different ways, but—"

"Say that again."

"What?"

"'Repent.' That's the same type of language your brother used. A word you wouldn't find in my secular vocabulary," Tomas said.

"I'm nothing like my brother," Raybelle said with disproportionate anger.

"I don't believe it. You sound like him, you look like him. You're as dedicated to the military, in your way, as he was. And as disappointed."

"How can you possibly know a thing like that?"

Tomas folded her arms in what the psychology people would have called a gesture of defiance. "This armed services committee. Your beef with the defense secretary. It's personal, isn't it?"

"He's a misogynist pig," Raybelle said. "He'd be that way with any woman in my position."

"That may be," Tomas said, "but it's personal for you, not

him. You want to be commander-in-chief one day, don't you? The defense secretary's boss."

Raybelle allowed her face to crack into a small smile. "I'm not about to be *accused* of presidential ambitions, Doctor Jefferson. Especially not by you."

"Makes no difference to me," Tomas said. "But something bothers you about the way the military is run in this country."

"Not that it's any of your business, Doctor, but my concerns are well documented. If you'd spent five minutes looking at my congressional record, or that confounded 'blog,' you'd know that I'm a constitutionalist. The power to wage war belongs to the Congress, not the executive. If we in the US government honored our Constitution, who would want to be president? The power shouldn't lie with one man."

"Or woman," Tomas said, in a way that sounded automatic.

"What's your point?"

"What would you change on your first day, if you were commander-in-chief? 'Don't ask, don't tell'?" Tomas fixed dark brown eyes on her, and Raybelle wanted to smack them out of her head.

"I would inform you that that's inappropriate," she said, "but I know you did it on purpose."

She knew the phrase "did it on purpose" sounded petulant, but she couldn't restrain herself from standing up and walking away. This conversation was time she would never get back. Tomas didn't attempt to stop her, and Raybelle was almost sorry about that, although it would have drawn attention to them—and to what she wished they hadn't been talking about.

CHAPTER TWENTY-ONE

Leave from her hospital didn't last long, and Tomas was relieved to be back on her rounds in Chicago. This was something she knew how to do. She had only ever been happy when learning something new. She'd been happy in classrooms and labs, and training in the hospital and on the job. But even in such an exalted field as medicine, once she started working at it, it was amazing how much became routine. She was an infectious diseases specialist, which meant that every day she got to see patients who'd come back from The Gambia, or just a vacation in Mexico, with exotic conditions she'd rack her brain to diagnose in medical exams.

And that was the privilege of it: something she'd wanted to

do since her first picture of DNA, in a seventh-grade science book, she now got to do every day. But by the same token, it was just work now, not scene-stealing excitement like on TV shows about doctors. Even the neurosurgeons probably rolled out of bed some mornings thinking, *Not brain surgery again!*

So she was glad to be back in her routine. And yet, Raybelle McKeehan had disrupted that routine, so that Tomas couldn't settle, as if she were permanently jet lagged. When her long day, divided as it was into fifteen-minute shifts of people's problems and donning masks and gloves, finally wound to an end and Tomas could go home, or go out, she couldn't settle. And so she found herself headed not north but west, to seek out the comfort fast food of her childhood at a suburban shopping mall.

Were they always this crowded? At least the music playing on the loudspeakers was good. Carole King: "I Feel The Earth Move." The *Tapestry* album had always been one of her favorites— not, of course, that Tomas had ever owned the "album." She had a remastered compact disc, with live extras. But thinking of that failed to block, from her mind, the theme song of her only serious long-term relationship: "It's Too Late."

Alicia had always complained, as about so many other facets of Tomas's character, that her mind and heart were never tuned in to what was happening at the time. She was always looking for the bill or feeling for her pager, or lying awake thinking about the next day's work, or listening for the next track on the CD. Alicia said that Tomas lived only in anticipation, and couldn't slow down or relax enough to enjoy what was happening in the moment.

For her part, when Tomas responded to these rants at all, she tended to ridicule Alicia as being full of New Age bullshit. She knew, when performing a medical procedure, how to "be in the moment," but that was no way to actually live. If you didn't anticipate what might be wrong with a patient, he could die. If you didn't plan what to do with your money, the government would come and take it away. Time was precious; you couldn't spend it lingering at a table, just because the waitress was busy tending to other customers.

Now, at a mall in suburban Chicago, Tomas had forgotten

why she was there, and been transported to the past. Yes, she should have lingered over that cup of coffee. She had needed to be there looking at her lover, not her watch. All those moments were gone now, the moments Alicia had urged her to be "in." And she had nothing to show for them.

This realization hit Tomas so hard she almost fell to her knees, felled by her own stupidity, right there in the mall. She felt as if until that very instant she had learned nothing from her relationship with Alicia, not even from its end. Especially not from its end. She had, at least in her own mind (since it was always elsewhere), raged against Alicia for leaving, abandoning her, without warning or good reason, and she had consoled herself in the arms of various vacation lovers. None of whom had made as much of an impression on her, at the height of ecstasy, as Alicia could with one sharp word.

What did this mean? She had loved Alicia. She had said so on many occasions, and remembered having been a generous lover, but she knew now that this had really not been enough. It occurred to Tomas that Alicia's leaving might have been the consequence of something other than caprice. In fact, this might have been the first episode in Tomas's entire life where she'd doubted her own rectitude.

Food courts in malls weren't where she normally wanted to spend moments. Half an hour and her whole body would reek of grease. But there was something about the anonymity of the place that she needed right now, the sense that she could disappear. The streets, with their homeless inhabitants, were too heavy with meaning.

The Orange Julius was refreshing, and Tomas got up off her figurative knees. Who needed somebody else around, expecting favor after favor, none of them reciprocated, all for the price of some fun in bed, which half the time wasn't reciprocated either? She found herself suddenly glad that same-sex marriage was still illegal in Illinois, for the selfish reason that no doubt Alicia would have wanted a wedding, and the last thing on earth Tomas would have wanted was to stand up in front of Alicia's relatives and friends. Somehow they hadn't seemed to have friends as a couple. Tomas had felt deep love, she didn't have to pledge it. Her mind would probably have been elsewhere then too. Alicia would have wanted to plan a honeymoon, not understanding why Tomas just had to get in a diving trip. Or two.

When Tomas's grandmother was still alive, and trying to account for Tomas's lack of boyfriends and inability to settle down, she'd decided that Tomas was "married to her career." And though they'd never met, her grandmother and Alicia would have agreed on this. There was no one in Tomas's life who commanded the attention her ambitions did, first to accomplish what she wanted in school and in college, then medical school, then establishing herself in the profession—however inadequately she felt she'd done that. Like Chekhov, she thought of medicine as her lawful wedded spouse, and so, in the end, had Alicia.

With the frustration of realizing all this came a strange sense of relief, not unlike purging the body of some noxious substance. For Tomas had just learned something new about her life. That was why Dennis had breezed into her clinic so memorably. He was something new and different. She couldn't remember meeting anyone else like him, patient or otherwise. She might not have gotten where he was coming from, but she knew it was a place of his own.

Back out in the mall, she stopped at just the kind of tacky memorabilia shop that would have an outlet in the Washington airport. All kinds of political junk, none of it unfamiliar to someone like Senator Raybelle McKeehan. Raybelle couldn't possibly need, or want, anything sold in this store. Nonetheless Tomas was drawn to a plain white T-shirt, adorned with a rather garish Rosie the Riveter cartoon, and the slogan WE CAN DO IT!

Tomas hesitated. Not because of how cheap the shirt was, the fact that it was made in Guatemala, but because "We can do it" sounded so collectivist. She meant to speak to Raybelle's ambition and desire, woman to woman. That was a stretch: she wasn't a "woman physician" any more than she was an African-American physician. She'd never bought into anyone else's dreams (Alicia would have said "shared"). Still, she walked to the cash register, paying more than the shirt was worth, or perhaps less considering the Guatemalans had probably earned six cents and she was a doctor in America. Who was the shirt for, herself or Raybelle? Would either of them wear it?

She had just put the shirt, neatly folded in its nonenvironmental plastic bag, inside her briefcase when she was annoyed by the ringing of her phone. "Doctor Jefferson."

"It's Tim." His voice sounded strange.

"What's wrong?"

"Ephraim's in the hospital."

***

Raybelle needed to be alone to scatter Dennis's ashes. She'd meant to do it on her last trip to Tennessee. But she was never alone; there were always aides, constituents, and on that trip, Tomas. Whatever Tomas was. A distraction. There had never been a right time for what Raybelle envisioned, which was to drive to the county line, by herself, in a car old enough to have windows she had to roll down manually. That would have suited Dennis.

But she hadn't taken care of it in Tennessee. And by the end of the trip, she was almost panicked by her feelings for Tomas. She couldn't afford them. It wasn't that she'd ever made much effort to act straight, and lots of people probably doubted that she was. But her enemies would say that anyway, just as they would about any powerful woman. Raybelle simply couldn't afford to have that become the focus—a distraction. She couldn't afford anyone in her life, and as long as no one was there, she had no explaining to do.

That didn't just go for a partner, or a husband. It went for a brother who was crazy, and it also went for Tomas and her gay friends. If they were from her state, she'd have to make an effort on their behalf. But they weren't. Ephraim wasn't even American.

So as long as her brother's earthly remains sat in Washington, she would have to deal with them here.

She didn't tell anybody she was walking down to the Potomac River. She would only get stopped, prevented from littering, and she didn't need that hassle. Wouldn't look good on the résumé. If Dennis ended up washed out to sea instead of buried on their ancestral land, well, that was fitting. He'd been lost for years.

She went to the US Marine Corps Memorial. It was a little out of her way, but she relished the freedom to walk, unaccompanied, around the monuments of her country. Politicians always talked about freedom, but Raybelle really appreciated it. That was why she was here, in Washington. She wasn't free to live an ordinary life—whatever that was. She was here so that others could live free, without the government she lived for poking its nose into everybody else's business.

It was another paradox, and looking at the statue of the Marines on Iwo Jima, Raybelle wondered if Dennis had felt it too. That he had to kill, or whatever else he was commanded to do, so that other Americans could sleep in ignorance and peace.

But she didn't have to listen to the ignorance. And she didn't have to listen to Tomas Jefferson, whether she was talking about Diego Garcia, an island that may as well have fallen from the sky for all most Americans cared, or some foreigner about whom they'd care even less.

From across the Potomac she could see the Tidal Basin. Nestled there was her favorite memorial, the one to Thomas Jefferson. Well, Jefferson had been her favorite, before this other Tomas had come into her life and messed things up.

She would not, could not, allow this to happen. She would bury her feelings, and her brother, despite her reluctance to let them go.

It was almost June. No cherry blossoms to cut through the toxic fumes. What did the Marines on the Iwo Jima Memorial think of those Japanese trees? One of the Marines, Raybelle remembered, was an American Indian. He had died in abysmal circumstances back home too.

She took Dennis's ashes from her oversized coat pocket. She felt like an alcoholic, clutching her flask. But instead of trading everything for the contents, she was giving them away.

She walked, and waited, until she was close enough for the ashes to drift onto the surface of the Potomac. In the air, on land and water: a true marine.

CHAPTER TWENTY-TWO

A hospital was an everyday place for Tomas. Its smells and trauma didn't trigger the anxiety in her that they did in people who didn't work there. So she went to work as usual, but the hospital seemed like a different place with Ephraim in it. Even during her day's work, when she was busy seeing other patients, she was thinking about one patient, on another floor, and anxious to visit him when she was finished.

This was a new experience, for the patient to be a friend. Ephraim and Tim offered her simple friendship, uncomplicated and vanilla, and for her it was like some exotic fruit for which she was starving. She might have a boy crush on the handsome island man. She wouldn't rule it out.

That Tim would have a lover of such youth and beauty startled her, though it shouldn't have. Tim had drawn her in with his kindly eyes and his generosity; why shouldn't he do the same for any man who interested him? Tomas found herself in the presence of someone—Ephraim—who drew all the attention, male and female. Including hers. He carried himself regally and there was something in Tomas that responded.

And Tim and Ephraim talked to her. Told her about their lives without expecting her to answer questions in return. Like all lovers still enamored with each other, they were unconscious of this one-sidedness, and she found it a relief. Their story—separation, angst—was a compelling one. Their devotion was obvious. To Tomas, it was like visiting a foreign country every time she opened the door to Tim's apartment.

When she finally got free, she met up with Tim. "How is he?"

"How should he be?" Tim's face was shadowed with anger, and he kept rubbing one side of his stubbly chin. "He was attacked. And he won't call the police."

"Why not?"

"I would love to get your take on that," Tim said. "You can see him."

When they entered the stark room Tomas didn't waste any words on pleasantries. There was nothing pleasant about the way Ephraim looked. "What happened?"

"Hello," he said. His lips were cracked and bloody. She wanted to touch him, but was afraid that every part would hurt.

"What happened, Ephraim?"

He looked away, toward the ceiling; his neck was restrained. "Some men, I do not know who. Their faces were covered. They wore, how do you say—"

"Balaclavas?"

"Yes."

"What did they do?" Tomas said.

"They stole from me," he said. "I thought that's all they wanted, so I gave it to them. But they took me into a van. 'If you want to go back to Diego Garcia,' one of them said, 'we will take you.' I thought then they were kidnapping me. That I would be dead soon."

Tim stepped to the side of the bed and stroked Ephraim's arm. In a tight voice, he said, "This is payback, isn't it, Tomas? You spoke to the senator and look what happens."

Tim's reflexive mistrust of the government was that of a man who had served his country and found it unworthy. That it would not recognize his relationship with Ephraim didn't surprise him. He would have put nothing past America. Tomas regarded this as paranoia, similar to the way members of her own family automatically distrusted any police officer. Still, just because Tim was paranoid didn't mean there wasn't really someone after Ephraim. "Where did they take you?"

Ephraim lifted a shoulder and visibly regretted it. "I do not know. They beat me, punched me in the face. Then they kicked me out of the car. I rolled up against a stop sign." Again, he attempted a smile. "Is that not good? I rolled to a stop."

"Wordplay in English, Ephraim. I'm impressed."

"They could have killed me," he said with neither anger nor fear. As calm as when he'd mentioned the weather. But Tim was upset enough for both of them.

"Does your friend have something to do with this, Tomas? I thought she was supposed to be helping Ephraim. Not scaring him away."

"I am not scared," Ephraim said with quiet dignity.

"I know, honey." Tim's southern endearment was meant for Ephraim, but Tomas felt ambushed by the unexpected tenderness, coming from this immense man.

"I just wish I could stay with you," Ephraim said. "Here, or in England. Anywhere."

Tim bent down and embraced his lover. From where she stood, Tomas could see tears standing in Ephraim's eyes. He didn't let the tears fall, nor did he wipe them away. Neither man looked at her, and she hoped they'd forgotten she was there.

Tim asked Tomas to stay with Ephraim a little longer; he had to get back to work. She felt less than useless in the patient's room. She wasn't Ephraim's doctor, and everything he needed was being done for him.

"Would you like me to turn on the television?" Four words would have done.

"If you like."

Tomas walked to the TV in the corner and switched it on. It was 24-hour news, not her usual choice, but lately half her brain was in Washington.

She didn't pay attention until the headline CONTROVERSIAL POLITICAL AD came up. The background was a map of the state of Tennessee.

"A new attack ad targets Senator Raybelle McKeehan of Tennessee." The announcer was a nondescript white male, like most of Raybelle's colleagues. "Unusual for its ferocity in a non-election year, the ad was shown last night on area television."

"I don't believe it," Tomas said, more to the TV than to Ephraim. "Now they're going to show it nationally, for free."

They did, though not in its entirety—at least Raybelle didn't appear, nor did her opponent, whom Tomas had never heard of. A group of clap-happy young white men, apparently gay clones, were shown screaming, with the caption NATIONAL DEFENSE? An unidentified female voice said, "Raybelle McKeehan has voted to weaken our nation's military. She colludes with Democrats to make our children less safe." This bit was accompanied by the image of a small girl playing on the edge of a playground, watched by a shadowy male figure. "McKeehan—WRONG on national defense, WRONG for our kids, and WRONG for America."

Before the "Paid for by…" credits could roll, the news announcer said, "The ad was criticized for its sexual implications."

"What implications?" Tomas jabbed the remote toward the screen. "The fully clothed men, or the kid on the playground?"

"Excuse me," Ephraim said, "but you are blocking my view."

"Oh, sorry." Tomas stepped to the side just as an obese white woman said, in an accent Tomas recognized as Tennessean, "Well now I just don't think that's appropriate, implying something sexual." (She said *sexual* in a kind of stage whisper, though it was being broadcast on national television.) "While I'm trying to feed my kids."

A faceless baritone voice asked, "Does this ad change your opinion of Senator McKeehan?"

"I'd say yes." The woman nodded. "I'd say yes, because I don't want my children to be exposed to that." She reached down to wipe the runny nose of one of them. "You know."

Tomas said "That doesn't make any sense!" loud enough that people stopped in the hall outside Ephraim's door. Then she remembered why she had come to the hospital. She sat down next to Ephraim, uncertain whether they were supposed to touch. "People are so stupid."

"I do not understand," he said. "What is the purpose of this advertisement?" He stressed the second syllable, reminding her of his foreignness.

Tomas wasn't sure how to explain that sexual minorities were despised in America, to a man who had just been beaten up for totally different reasons. While she, a member of a sexual minority, was a successful, respected physician. "Okay. Nobody in that ad looked like you or me. No people of color."

"Or women," Ephraim said quietly. "Only men and children."

"Yes." Tomas tried to imagine if the ad had characterized the US military as weak and effeminate by depicting a bunch of dykes. She almost laughed. "The malicious person who made this commercial is trying to link two things that aren't related, just by showing them together. One is—they're implying that Raybelle wants to open the armed forces to, ah…"

"Queers?"

"Some would say that."

"I am sorry. Is that not the right word? I have read that you now have 'queer studies' as a university department."

"True. The point is, they want people to think that this weakens the military, that it means Americans aren't protected. Then they show a child, being watched by someone who looks like he might assault the child, sexually. They show these things together, for no reason except they want to link the two in people's minds. Then they show it at dinnertime, and Mrs. Ignorant there can be wiping her own children's faces, and associate these things together, and run screaming back to the nearest candidate who doesn't look like you, or me, or Raybelle."

***

Over coffee in her senate office, Raybelle was saying to Melody, "The worst thing is, now he doesn't have to pay to run the damn ad more than once. Because now it's a 'news story,' and every bozo on TV will do it for him."

"That's why you should ignore it. Don't comment, don't complain."

"They're already saying I complained."

"Your campaign people complained. Your job is to rise above, I'm telling you."

"It's so ridiculous. That vote they're talking about, when I backed gays in the military—that was years ago, and didn't go anywhere. So I co-sponsored a bill. Do you know how many co-sponsors some bills have? Bills that never become law and are never going to. They just kick around Congress for years."

"I know," Melody said.

"Is there anything you don't know?"

"Sorry."

"Clyde Wheatley and my other campaign people are all about 'spin.' How am I going to spin this? I can't play the saxophone or electric guitar."

"I'm just one assistant," Melody said. "Wouldn't dream of telling you what to do."

"Well, right now you're all I've got." It wasn't true—at least half a dozen people had demanded her attention in the past half hour. But perhaps because she was so young and fearless, Melody would tell Raybelle things when no one else would. And this made her closer to Raybelle than anyone else in the Capitol. Or the world outside, if there was one.

Melody hunched forward, thin elbows on thin knees. She looked through the black-framed glasses perched on the end of her nose. "I think you need to do two things. Turn all this attention to your advantage, and focus people on *your* issues. Rather than theirs."

"My issue, Ms. Park, is getting reelected."

"Don't say that in public."

"Of course not. So, what should I talk about? Gays in the military? You think I can win on that? Not unless I put it in the context of my whole career."

"You must have brought that legislation forward for some reason," Melody said.

"Because I thought it was right."

"I wouldn't say that either," Melody said. "People won't believe it. They're not as stupid as they look on TV."

"Fine. Why do you say I did it?"

"Probably because you believe in equal rights for everybody, but unfortunately that isn't enough to win the argument, or gays would have equal rights by now. Frame it in your conservative way: It's none of the government's business. If people are doing their job, you really don't care who's most important in their personal lives. For a lot of people it's a cat or a dog."

"Marrying cats and dogs doesn't sound like a winning argument either."

"Even with the marriage issue," Melody went on undeterred, "what you want to emphasize is keeping the government out of people's private business."

"Marriage *is* government, Melody. The state gives marriage licenses. Nothing is more mixed up between the government and people's private business than marriage, for Pete's sake."

"Well put. But attacking marriage is definitely not going to go over with voters. That'll only focus attention on your not being married yourself."

"I know what I'm good at. Marriage wouldn't be it." Raybelle knew she was snapping at Melody. It wasn't Melody's fault she'd never had a dog or cat that really meant something to her, let alone a human companion. Her aloneness was armor; to lose it would crush the structure, like the exoskeleton of a lobster.

"What about the military?"

"My only association with the military," Raybelle said in a colder tone, "has been working with people across the aisle, not just Senator Rivers. It's not colluding."

"Collaborating."

"Collaborators makes us sound like the Vichy regime."

"That won't resonate." Melody was warming to her new image-manipulation role. "Now, the playground scene is unfortunate, but there, too, what you want to do is focus on the child, not the creepy guy in the shadows."

"Wrong," Raybelle said. "Focusing on children will just remind people that I don't have any myself."

"Okay. Let's concentrate on what you are good at. You're independent-minded, you work with both parties, and now you're under attack. But people say they want Washington politicians to work together. Appeal directly to the voters."

"How?"

"You sound uncertain, Senator."

"No," Raybelle said. "Wrong, maybe, but never uncertain."

"Support the troops," Melody advised. "Everybody agrees with that. Tactics like these only divide and demoralize the military. You're a uniter. That's the angle you want."

"It also happens to be what I believe."

"Don't let on," Melody said.

***

Long after Tomas should have gone home, she sat by the bedside, holding Ephraim's hand. It was a strong hand, but delicate, like the man himself. She didn't remember the last time she'd held anyone's hand, except to take a pulse. She and Alicia must have held hands at the beginning, but for years, even at the movies, it had never occurred to her. This was the way she thought now, blaming herself. In the past she would have found a reason to blame Alicia.

"I will have to go back to England soon," Ephraim said. "Tim will miss me."

She thought that was odd, that he was more concerned with how Tim would feel than missing Tim himself. Maybe that was how relationships were supposed to work. She wouldn't know.

"Why do you care?" He spoke so softly and deliberately that at first she thought she'd imagined the question.

"What?"

"Why do you care? About me?"

"Because this shouldn't have happened."

"No," he said, "but you must see, every day, people to whom things should not have happened. You cannot stay with all of them."

"I will stay with you."

She spoke as quietly as he did, but the words rang in the

room. The TV was off now; there were no witnesses to the closest Tomas had ever come to a vow.

"The patient I had before. Dennis," she said. "He told me about the war against your people, who'd done nothing but live in your own homes. People here—they talk about this 'war on terror,' as if it were Saturday morning cartoons. The Coalition of the Willing versus the Axis of Evil. Good guys and bad guys in two dimensions. But there is no 'war.' Just lots and lots of little wars, mostly being lost."

Although he was in pain, Ephraim sounded amused. "I thought you were not interested in politics, Doctor Jefferson."

"I'm not. Only in casualties."

"Is Senator McKeehan a casualty?"

She looked at him, unblinking. Like Friesian the cat. "Why do you ask?"

"You seem interested in her." He opened his hand, and his smile. "I think maybe it takes you much less time to care about a man than a woman."

"What do you mean?"

"This Dennis, and now us. In a short time, you feel as if you have brothers, yes? But this lady, Dennis's sister, you are all the time fighting. You care so slowly, the lady cannot tell."

"You might have something there," Tomas said, but more to herself.

"I do not understand."

"Neither do I," she said, "but I've got to work in the morning. Goodnight." She stood, hesitated a moment, then kissed his salty lips.

***

Raybelle had been on the phone all morning doing "damage control." She wasn't up for reelection until next year, but with these attack groups, the campaign never really ended. Raybelle had worked hard to be someone the Republican Party, and the people, could handle. She was a conservative woman. She was not running in a rich state, so she hewed toward freedom from government and populist values, either of which could be spun to the advantage of businesses, big or small. She did her job and glad-handed everybody. Where was this coming from? The right?

"It's several things," said Clyde Wheatley, the unfortunate man whose team had the job of managing Raybelle's campaign. "For one thing, you're known for bipartisanship. You've spent a lot of time getting legislation passed, which involves working with Democrats. Now that they're in power, some Republicans think we need someone more combative."

"Am I not combative?" She twisted the phone cord, imagined hanging someone from it. "Have you ever met me, Clyde? Yes, I have a history of reaching across the aisle. That's what people want."

"In a president, ma'am." She hoped she was imagining the mockery in his tone. "That isn't what the party needs, or so I'm hearing from some of the folks on the ground—"

"On the ground? What, are they prostrate?"

"Your friendship with Senator Rivers is well known."

"Grant Rivers is a statesman," she said. "We disagree on some things and agree on other things. We're both in Washington to serve the people."

"Sometimes what seems like an asset can turn into a liability."

Clyde seemed like one right now, but Raybelle didn't say so. She listened to him warn her of the same thing people had said all morning, to expect more media attacks from the family values crowd. In tough times, people looked for security wherever they could find it, and projected their insecurity into other people's homes. "The extent of your family values stump speech is an occasional mention of your mother," Clyde said.

Well she wasn't about to mention Dennis, and she didn't have any other family.

"You know, Clyde," she said, "not having a husband or children is always the thing that's supposedly going to keep me from getting elected. But who has time to do a good job in politics while taking care of a spouse and kids? No wonder most politicians are men. You all don't have to worry about that."

"I'm not a politician," he said.

"Oh, you all are, Clyde. And somebody always takes care of you. Who's looking after me?"

Thinking about that reminded her of Tomas, and that Tomas had asked her for help. The guy was a stranger to her, and a foreigner, but he was a friend of Tomas's. She knew she ought to care, so she placed another call.

***

When Tomas explained what had happened to her friend, Raybelle said, "Sorry to hear that. But what do you want me to do about it?"

"I take it you know nothing about what happened to him."

"Why would I? I'm a Republican, not a fascist."

"Uh-huh," Tomas said. "In any case, I need your help. Ephraim isn't settled here or in the UK. But he needs to stay with his partner."

"Well, can't he get the boyfriend to help him?" Raybelle said. "For crying out loud, the guy's an American citizen."

"And they have no legal relationship under federal law," Tomas said. "Don't you get that? If Tim told immigration that he wants to keep Ephraim in the US, with him, then Ephraim would be suspected of trying to stay here illegally. He could get deported, even banned from visiting the country. Just for being honest about their relationship. In effect, our government punishes gay citizens for telling the truth."

"So why are you telling me? I am the government."

"Because you might be able to make a difference. Isn't that what you politicians are always whacking off about? There's a bill in the House of Representatives that would give us rights under immigration law. We need a corresponding bill in the Senate."

"And don't tell me. You've got Democrats on board, but no Republicans."

"Exactly. So we need you to make it bipartisan."

The *we* grated on Raybelle. "This seems personal for you," she said. "I can't sponsor a law for one person."

"Oh come on!" Tomas said. "The law is for tens of thousands of people. Ephraim's just one example."

The individual underdog did hold some appeal. Maybe Raybelle could file an *amicus curiae* on the guy's behalf...no, better not go down that road. Why should she be a friend of the court when the courts were no friends of hers? "You do realize how unpopular refugees are? If anyone wanted them, they wouldn't be—"

"You always want personal stories," Tomas interrupted. "Every political speech has them. 'Little Scottie who died without health insurance.' Don't help Ephraim; help Tim. He's a citizen, a Vietnam veteran, he's white—"

"He's gay," Raybelle said. "No reason the government should recognize that relationship, more than any other."

"But if Tim was married to a foreign woman, he could sponsor her and she could live here. The government does recognize that."

"Listen, Tomas. Personally, I don't think the state should be marrying people at all. And if someone is enterprising enough to try and make it in a foreign country, I think the border should be open to him. But I can't say that on the floor of the Senate, and I certainly can't say it out on the stump. I represent Tennessee, not Vermont."

"Senator. Be honest. Imagine the impact that honesty would have."

"I resent that." But Raybelle knew what Tomas meant. If she could speak honestly about something this controversial, at least people could believe anything else she said.

"I meant," Tomas said, "be honest about yourself."

This trying-to-care thing didn't last. Raybelle spoke with dry ice in her voice. "This country has been able to handle a lesbian member of the House. This country has a gay senator. But it is not up for a gay president. I can do more for all Americans—and non-Americans—from the White House than I can do for just gays."

"I'm glad you're finally coming out."

"I'm not."

"I meant, as a presidential candidate."

"Well, first I have to do my job in the Senate, or I won't be able to help anybody. I'm sorry, Tomas. Tell your friends to get help somewhere else."

***

Tomas shut her cell phone, then pitched it across the room. It landed in the laundry basket. Friesian bolted from it and looked at her with resentful eyes.

Great, now she'd pissed him off too. At least now she knew where she stood with Raybelle. No reason to call Washington anymore, let alone travel there. One decision made.

CHAPTER TWENTY-THREE

Grant Rivers lit a cigar. Cuban. Behind closed doors he saw no reason to honor the embargo; he was a Democrat. Like Raybelle, and unlike many in each of their respective parties, Grant thought that people in general should be able to do what they liked. In private. He exhaled richly flavored smoke with the satisfaction of being above it all. He picked up the phone.

Perry answered his cell; Grant resisted the impulse, as old as cell phones themselves, to ask where Perry was. "What have you got for me?" Perry said.

"The alien will be on his way back to London soon. Scared shitless. My boys didn't even have to show him a gun. You know in England they're not used to guns. Their cops wear 'stab vests.'" He laughed.

"What about the woman from Chicago?"

"Tough nut," Grant said. "She has it bad for Ray—ah, the target. In other circumstances, that might be useful." He smirked to himself. "Still, she's discouraged. I'd be surprised if she comes back to Washington."

"Not good enough," Perry said. "We can't know where she's going with this. She's out there now. There's nothing to stop her from enjoying her fifteen minutes of fame. She's a private citizen and won't play by political rules."

"I know that." Grant knew better than anyone else that Raybelle had personal reasons to tread softly on the veterans investigation. When the president, in a show of bipartisanship, had asked him for a recommendation, Grant hadn't hesitated to suggest his old friend. The president had to appoint somebody, to get it out of the news. The story was supposed to die, because Raybelle was expected to tread softly. She was ambitious and didn't need to be pissing off the president when he was a Republican too.

But neither Grant nor Perry had anticipated the double complication that was Tomas Jefferson. A political complication because she came from outside Washington. And a personal complication...

"That ad was a gift," Perry was saying.

"Yes, it was." Grant was enjoying his cigar, as he enjoyed most things in his life. "Who would have ever thought we could get people questioning her support for the military? But we can't count on gifts like that."

"So we create another distraction," Perry said. "I can't have that black woman poking around in my business arrangements, no matter how good-looking she is."

Grant chuckled. "You noticed, huh?"

"I don't have time for this."

On the contrary, if anyone in town needed to get laid worse than Perry, Grant didn't know who. "I thought we were in business together," he said, feigning hurt.

"Speaking of which," Perry said, "I don't want any more press on the contract workers. None."

"You're losing focus, Henry." Grant crushed out his cigar. "I'm surprised at that."

"Take care of it," Perry said.

"Give my regards to Barbara."

Perry wouldn't give his wife Grant's regards; he never had. Grant knew this, because he'd asked Barbara himself, on one of the many occasions when he'd comforted her for the loss of her daughter. Henry never would speak of the girl, and her mother did have needs.

So did Grant. He was late for lunch, now.

***

There was no feeling as simultaneously comforting and desperate as lying on a made-up bed, late at night, alone and not expecting anyone. Tomas fondled the remote control as if it might give her sexual pleasure. Lately she didn't have the energy even to take care of that need. She hadn't felt it urgently for a while, just a dull sense of unease.

She didn't intend to leave the news channel on, but pushing more buttons wasn't something she was up for. Instead, she watched the economic news and weather report, equally dire, before it cut to footage of a press conference—and there was Raybelle, in front of Walter Reed Hospital, wearing red and flanked by people Tomas didn't recognize.

"This is a national disgrace." She had a stronger Tennessee accent than Tomas remembered her using in the past.

"Senator, are you referring to the television ad?"

"No, I am not. I'm referring to this." She flung her arm wide, almost knocking a cameraman in the face. "This hospital's standard of care is a disgrace. But that is not the fault of the people who work here. It's the fault of the people who hired them."

"Senator, are you saying that public funds have been misused—" Voices started coming from different directions, and swam in Tomas's head. The TV stereo was too good.

"The problem isn't *public*." Raybelle said the word as if the very thought of public services disgusted her. She was a Republican, after all. "The problem is the folks they hired to do this work aren't public employees at all. Private contractors are doing it, so we've got black mold on the walls and soldiers with bedsores, and we're still paying way too much. It would cost less if we hired registered nurses to go in there and clean the wards!"

Damn. Tomas hadn't expected this.

"Are you suggesting medical personnel should be doing custodial work?"

"I'm not suggesting anything. I am demanding a change. We can't help but ask, can we, where all this money is going. Workers aren't getting rich. Must be somebody else's incentive to cut costs."

"Senator." This voice, wherever it came from, managed to be both gravelly and whiny. "Why are you performing this analysis for the cameras, instead of making your report in committee?"

He had to be a plant. Raybelle put her hands on her hips; Tomas half expected her to start gunslinging. "Because I don't believe in doing deals in smoke-filled rooms, behind closed doors," she said in a pronounced drawl. "You have something you want to say, I believe you say it to my face. Don't go behind my back and then act like you didn't mean it."

She cut off questioning then. Melody must be jumping to attention off camera. Tomas felt vaguely jealous, but it was only a faint emotion, like other sensations she felt. Not enough to do anything about them. On the screen, she saw a tall white man next to Raybelle slowly clapping his hands, an expression on his face that could only be described as a sneer. This press conference must be part of damage control.

The covers on the bed were scratching the backs of Tomas's legs. She thought briefly about seeing if she could take a nap, but she knew she wouldn't sleep. She'd built her life around a single-minded focus on work, at the cost of everything else, and just fit sleeping, eating, making love, whenever and wherever she found the time. And now she had no appetite for any of it.

Maybe a shower would help. If she let the water run on her body hot enough, for long enough, maybe she could get rid of the cold ache inside.

***

Raybelle threw her long blue coat across her desk, sending

papers and empty coffee cups flying. She hated addressing the press. She always rose to the occasion but it sucked the energy right out of her, and all she wanted now was some time by herself, to restore her soul. Unfortunately, that wasn't going to happen. The airwaves were ablaze and suddenly, Raybelle McKeehan was national news. If she didn't seize this moment, she might never get another one.

Melody said, "The good news is, your profile is a lot higher than it was yesterday. We have way more hits on your blog. In fact, if I hadn't set it up on such a good platform—"

"The party platform?"

"—it would have crashed by now. You're welcome. The bad news is that you're getting hate mail, and most of it's from fellow Republicans. It must be your use of the word 'public' without a ritual curse, or spitting. You suggest public employees could do a better job than private, and you're a traitor, you might as well be advocating socialized medicine."

"From their point of view. Heirs of Reagan. Didn't he once say that Medicare represented the end of all freedom?"

"Yeah. These types of conservatives would rather cook their mothers in stew than admit the government could ever run anything."

"Melody, you sound like you've been in this town for years."

In spite of the situation, Raybelle was pleased. The morning had gone well. She twirled a pen for a moment between her fingers. She was the owner of a very fine Montblanc, but insisted on writing with disposable Bics. At least she'd stopped chewing them. "What kind of hate mail?"

For the first time Raybelle could remember, Melody seemed reluctant. "There are rumors circulating," she said, "of a sexual nature."

"An affair?" Raybelle laughed. "You'd think I'd remember that."

"Nothing so specific," Melody said. "You're being linked with Doctor Jefferson—" Raybelle started to interrupt, but Melody held up her hand—"in ways that imply an unprofessional association. But someone's also got wind that you had dinner at the home of a lesbian couple while you were in Tennessee."

"Is that a crime?"

"No, but what you should be asking is, who's tracking this stuff? Who else was there?"

"You don't understand, Melody from Naperville. In a town the size of Poudre Valley, the only way information doesn't get out is if people choose not to talk about it."

"If you don't mind me asking," Melody said, "why did you go to their house? It does seem kind of personal, considering you'd never met them before."

Raybelle sighed. "They're friends of Tomas."

"Forgive the observation, Senator, but you're on a first-name basis with Doctor Jefferson. That alone could start a whispering campaign."

"I don't know anything about her personally. I don't even know where she lives! So far, all Tomas Jefferson has done is blow into town, cause a ruckus on viral video, then retreat the minute things got a little bit tough."

"Cut her some slack, boss. Her friend just got beaten badly enough to be put in the hospital."

Why had Raybelle told Melody that? She'd been trying not to think about Ephraim; it should be easy given all the practice she'd had ignoring her own brother. She knew what Tomas cared about, and why she was no longer speaking to Raybelle. But she couldn't afford to come out on a gay issue now. If she couldn't stay in office, she'd be no good to anybody.

"I think that's where Doctor Jefferson's attention must be now, at any rate." Melody rolled a piece of paper into a ball and tossed it toward the recycling bin. Raybelle hoped it wasn't some important government document.

"So what do you suggest I do? Deny these rumors, or ignore them? Start talking up my veterans credentials again? Lord, I got put on this detail in the first place to take care of veterans, and all I'm getting now is grief about gays in the military and BS. I don't know whether to focus on the military, or walk away."

"I think it's always best to go on the offensive," Melody said. "Say these ads are meaningless, a distraction. Say you're running to represent the people of Tennessee, with their proud tradition of volunteering. That the people of the Volunteer State are brave fighters, and so are you. You're not going to quit because some anonymous jerk thinks a southern lady has no business in Washington."

Raybelle was impressed. "You've been doing your homework. You'll go places, kid, if you stick with me."

Melody grinned. "Like a burr to your backside."

***

Tomas found it unusually hard to get up the next morning. By the time she was ready, there was barely time to stop by Ephraim's room before she got to work. She slammed the taxi door on her trench coat and all the way downtown it dragged through the dirty streets. On her cell phone, Tomas called the hospital, only to be told that Ephraim had been discharged.

"Where did he go?" She traded on her title; she could always count on getting things as "Doctor" that she could never get as Uppity Black Woman.

"Home. To London."

"That's not home," Tomas said, though she knew the receptionist wouldn't understand.

Shit. Why hadn't Tim called her?

It was evening before she caught up with Tim, and her cat. Friesian was always happier over at Tim's, anyway. She was surprised he didn't just stay there all the time. Cats decided with whom they belonged, and it didn't matter who tried to assert ownership, the relationship was always on their terms.

Tim's kitchen was well stocked with chopsticks and square white dishes, but nothing that looked like it had been there very long. When he was finished cooking, he handed her a plate of pad thai and a pronouncement. "You need to go to her."

"You don't waste words, either," Tomas said. They sat at Tim's breakfast bar, and she struggled with chopsticks.

"No need to," he said. "You mention Raybelle McKeehan all the time, although she's no use to either of us. Anyone would think you were having an affair."

Now she wished he'd used fewer words. This last one made her uncomfortable. So she challenged him on another point: "What do you mean, 'use'?"

"I know you're trying to help," he said. "But I don't want you to take our immigration problem any further with this senator. Talk to her because you care about her. Not about us."

Tomas chewed on something vegetarian. "You miss him."

"Like absolute hell."

"Why didn't you call me?" Tomas said. "Tell me he was going."

"I couldn't talk to anyone this morning." Tim's anguish was almost inaudible, but it was palpable. "Do you know what he said? 'Fuck,' he said, 'I don't know how I am going to get through this.'"

"I'm sorry."

"Do you know what that did to me? Ephraim never swears, not ever. He's so proper, he's—"

"Not very much like you."

In spite of things, Tim laughed. "We're nothing alike. And we're perfect for each other. Though how would I know, I hardly get to spend any time with him."

"People don't know how lucky they are." It was a thing Tomas supposed she should say.

"Not lucky. Blessed." Tim stroked his beard. His plate was empty now. "You know what?" he said. "Ephraim has put everything into this case, trying to get his people back to the island. And now we're a case, him and me. Just another binational couple, of the thousands, tens of thousands, split up by American law." He leaned forward. "But I am not a case. Our separation is not to test that law. This is our life."

"I understand."

"I've never been political. I went to Vietnam but not because I was for it, and not because I was against it. It was my life and I offered it up. And me and Ephraim—it was never our desire to be political, to be in conflict with anybody's laws. That's something forced on us. And I don't see any way out of it, or for us to be together."

Tomas wasn't sure how to address despair. Her life was about being competent, and knowing what to do. In the face of Tim's doomed and tragic love, she felt out of place, as if she'd walked onto the stage of some older, grander drama. These were not things that happened in her life.

"You're right, people don't know," he said. "You don't know how blessed you are. To be able to go and see her, whenever you want. To be able to talk to her and try."

"I don't know what you mean."

"Yeah you do, Tomas." He pushed himself away from the table, started to clear it. "Yeah, you do."

***

Clyde Wheatley was giving Raybelle a migraine. "Not a *woman* senator, I'm a senator," she said. "Who am I, Geraldine Ferraro?"

"Let's not be obscene," he said.

"Listen, Clyde. The last thing in the world that's going to help is reminding people that I'm a woman. That needs to not be an issue. I've got my work cut out for me on the other issues. Civil liberties, the military."

"Your poll numbers haven't been good lately," Clyde said, "and if you go out on a limb with any issue, they only drop more. You're the incumbent. You've been there for the people of Tennessee. Remind them of that. They know you."

"Ought to be a positive," Raybelle said.

"Let's come to the point, Raybelle. There are people more conservative than you, that's our problem. What are you going to do when these assholes can make you look like a Democrat? I know you don't want to focus on the 'woman' issue, but that's what it is. Just by being a woman, you're already too liberal for a lot of people."

"Please," Raybelle said. "Only a conservative woman can win. How many times do I have to invoke Margaret Thatcher? Indira Gandhi? Golda Meir?"

"But they had an asset, a crucial asset, that you don't have." Clyde pulled at his tie, as if it were too hot in the room.

"A husband?"

"No," he said. "War."

She let that register for a moment. Well, almost every president in her lifetime had bombed the crap out of somebody. "In case you haven't noticed, Clyde, I'm not president yet. I haven't been in a position to launch any wars."

"But what you have," he said, "is a deeply problematic record on the military. You have a long interest in it, and serve on committees, but you've also supported the gay thing, and questioned the president—"

"And that's illegal now, I suppose?" Raybelle made little effort to hide her disgust. "My record on the armed forces isn't 'problematic,' it's complicated. These aren't simple issues, and I don't treat them as simple. As for 'the gay thing'—I support anybody who's competent and willing to serve the country. If I hadn't voted to include gays in the military, I might as well say women can't fight, and clearly they can, since they're coming back without arms and legs. Americans believe in fair play, Clyde. It's an issue of fair play."

"But this is your president." It was as if she'd said nothing at all. "Your Republican president. Who is conspicuous by his silence on your behalf."

"Why should he care about a fellow Republican when he doesn't care about the Geneva Conventions?"

"Do you care about the party, Raybelle?"

"I'm running on the Constitution." It sure was hot. She was sweating, glad she'd worn blue. "Why can't that be my platform?"

"Because it doesn't mean anything. I know you were joking about a husband, before, but you seriously have to address that."

Melody had said the same thing. And if being single was a problem now, what about when she did run for president? Not that Clyde would think she was a contender for that. She'd be lucky to stay in the Senate.

After she got rid of Clyde, Raybelle could only think of one person far enough away from the whole situation to give perspective, and she had no inkling of why she trusted her. When the voice mail picked up, she forced herself to leave a message: "Tomas, it's Raybelle. Everybody here is insane. I've got something funny to tell you."

CHAPTER TWENTY-FOUR

Raybelle's voice mail made Tomas want to throw her phone across the room again. But she'd already broken one phone that way, when Alicia told her she was leaving. Why did she still think about Alicia so many times in a day, when so much time had passed? It didn't help that Tomas hadn't moved, but she never had made much of a home for herself anywhere. Alicia had taken away whatever homey touches there were.

Tomas knew she had it bad for Raybelle McKeehan. She was hung up on the senator in ways she couldn't recall being hung up on any woman, including Alicia; Alicia had been the one to pursue her. She knew that this was hopeless, that she didn't belong in political life and had been carefully managed out of it. But why the teasing phone calls? If she wasn't to be part of Raybelle's life then she just didn't want to have any part in it. Why should she be teased?

She almost wished, for the first time, that Dennis McKeehan had never walked into her clinic that day. It was easier to care about patients when she looked at them as all the same: the overweight middle-aged man with a heart condition, the child with leukemia, the injecting drug user. She had treated them all, compassionate yet detached, like a god she didn't believe in. Dennis had made a difference, and now Tomas felt different too. Open, raw. Ready to feel friendship, ready to feel brotherly love. She thought of Raybelle in her pumps, those remarkably youthful legs, and bit down on the flesh of her own hand. "Something funny to tell you." What, like one of those Internet jokes?

When she finally got her on the phone, she said, "What do you want, Senator?"

"Well, good morning to you."

"I'm sorry. I didn't mean to be rude." She had, in fact.

"Have you met Clyde Wheatley, my campaign manager?"

Just one word. "No."

"Well, you'll never guess what he recommended today."

"You're right, I never will."

Her tone was now unmistakable. Tomas hated this in herself, but Raybelle must have chosen to ignore it. "He wants me to get married."

Tomas squeezed the phone to her ear, felt a corresponding squeeze on her brain. "What, to him?"

"No, no." Raybelle laughed, a sound Tomas loved. She felt like kicking walls. "Anyway I'm not going to do it. Can you imagine? I could never live with anybody."

Tomas forced herself to take calming breaths. "Why did he suggest marriage?"

"The whole family thing. On the campaign trail. Apparently, stories of my mama's homespun wisdom aren't enough. He wants me to place myself in some all-American context. So people don't link me with prostitutes, I guess."

"There is one way I can think of you placing yourself in a family context."

"What's that?"

"Introduce people to your brother."

Raybelle's tone cooled several degrees. "In case you haven't noticed, my brother's dead."

"I noticed."

The pause felt like a hockey face-off.

"Then what do you mean?" Raybelle said, "Introduce him?"

"Tell people that you had a brother. A family." Tomas couldn't believe she was thinking these things, let alone saying them. "Explain that you've treasured your privacy. People understand about loss and grief. They're universal."

"That doesn't help with the sexuality rumors."

Tomas fought through her reaction to that. "Dennis died very recently. It's not surprising that someone grieving a sibling wouldn't be available for other types of emotional relationships."

"That's an interesting angle," Raybelle said, as if Tomas had suggested she rearrange her living room furniture. Did Raybelle have a living room? "How do I tell people what I don't know myself? Dennis and I hadn't spoken in a long time."

And she wouldn't be sorry now, except she needed him for her fucking career. "Dennis was a marine. With a conscience. That's got to be an 'angle' you can exploit."

"Hey now, no need to get sarcastic. There are big problems with bringing up Dennis at all. For one thing, he was nuts."

"He wasn't 'nuts'," Tomas said.

"That's not your field of medicine."

"I saw him. Talked to him. A lot more recently than you did. He had things to say. You should have listened, Raybelle."

"And you shouldn't be telling me about my brother! What business is it of yours?"

"Then why did you call me?"

Tomas couldn't believe how many words she was wasting, couldn't believe that she was wasting this kind of time with Raybelle. She stared at an old alarm clock that hadn't been wound in years, gathering dust on the shelf.

"I wanted to tell you something."

"What?" If Tomas gripped her phone any tighter, it was going to snap in two.

"About the marriage idea," Raybelle reminded her.

"Oh yeah. Because you thought it was funny."

"Because I wanted your opinion."

"What? Whether you should do it or not? Oh, by all means, Senator McKeehan. Marry whomever you want to. Fuck." Then something occurred to her. "Is this being taped? Am I going to hear about this from some department of spies?"

"Doctor Jefferson—"

"Well hel-lo!" Tomas yelled to an imagined violator of civil liberties. "Yes, sir, Mr. Homeland Security, I said 'fuck' to a member of the United States Senate. Oh, by all means, you can quote me. Put me on the Internet. Put me on YouTube. Publish or perish, you know."

"Will you all please quit talking about YouTube?" Raybelle said.

"Think about what I said, Raybelle." Tomas felt weary, she felt hurt, and she wanted to end this call.

"That I shouldn't consider marriage?"

"Give me a call when you're ready to talk about Dennis." *Otherwise, leave me alone.*

She disconnected. Raybelle must be insane. If she did want to marry anyone, how could she think people would vote for her on the basis of her husband? Surely even a Republican woman couldn't be that sexist.

Tomas was trying to ignore the fact that tomorrow would be her thirty-sixth birthday. Not because age made a difference— only health did—but because everyone else would ignore her birthday, as well. She was careful not to share personal information at work, especially about her birthday, because it only invited comments about astrology, and Tomas was fiercely rational. Now, however, she was only reminded of her isolation.

She decided to devote the next twenty-four hours, minus a few for sleep, to tackling paperwork in her office. But before she could do that, she needed to hit the gym, and sweat women out of her mind.

***

Raybelle hadn't intended to be back in Tennessee for a while. But that was the thing about intention: you could have all the good intentions you wanted, but you knew where they led. Now, at her house, she saw that the lawn needed mowing—well, parts of it did. It had been a dry summer, something else she hadn't been paying attention to. So the parts of the grass that had been in shade were growing wild as weeds, and those that saw the sun were burnt crisp and dry, more the memory of grass that had once been there.

The trees were the same. The lilacs were going crazy, they always did, but the peach tree looked to be in trouble. Well, what did she expect? No one had been around to pick the fruit systematically, so just peach pits and rottenness covered the ground. Raybelle remembered the taste of a fresh peach, picked right from the tree, as the absolute sweetest thing a girl could put in her mouth.

She could never share such a thought in the world she lived in now. Somebody would make a crude remark, and Raybelle would have to laugh. Laughter had become a commodity, a thing owed; she clocked a certain number of jokes, or comments that were supposed to be funny.

She had rarely been this frustrated with the life she'd chosen. She wanted to stand for the same things in every campaign: freedom of thought and individual rights. But from what her staff were telling her, her seat wasn't safe that way. Collective security was paramount, though Americans claimed not to believe in the collective. By staying in one place, Raybelle risked being knocked out of place altogether.

The ditch behind her house was dry, as usual. There were only twigs and rocks to scramble over when she and Dennis used to climb up the forked tree. Every once in a while, after heavy spring rains, there would be a little stream running back there, and Raybelle had found those springtimes magical when she was growing up. Dennis had tied the tire swing up here, and if she could get a turn, the best time to enjoy the swing was after one of those spring rains. Swinging out over the tiny temporary creek, Raybelle could imagine everything was much bigger, that the creek was wide as the Mississippi, and jumping off on the other side was like dropping free into the background of the universe.

There was an old frayed bit of rope still tied to the tree. Raybelle hadn't noticed that before. The knot had bitten into the limb as it had thickened. She empathized with the tree.

She felt the frayed rope between her fingers, like worry beads. Family, everyone said. A politician needs to be able to talk about his family. Family values. Had she valued her family?

Dennis had been crazy, maybe, but he knew where he stood. Before he took that swing, out over oblivion, he knew where he stood. In his own way, he'd been as solid as the tree, rooted, while things around him slowly consumed and cut off life.

Well, she wasn't about to be outdone by her big brother. Even if that meant she could no longer deny him.

She eyed the tree that had held the tire swing, remembered the rush of swinging out over a raging spring creek.

But this was her place. Her people. She would have to fall back on their support, with no safety apparatus.

She felt clean, like after a spring rain, as if someone had just washed the world.

CHAPTER TWENTY-FIVE

"She's onto us."

"Who the fuck cares? We've got her phone calls; doesn't matter what she thinks about it."

"She might stop calling."

Clyde Wheatley shook his head. "I don't think so. She's got it bad. You can just hear it in her voice. Tight with lust."

"Shut up," Henry Perry said.

Obtaining authorization to tap Dr. Jefferson's phones had been simple. No warrant. Perry had asked for, and received, one of hundreds of National Security Letters that were designed to intercept overseas calls. Since medical researchers were on the phone, or e-mail, to other countries all the time, this amounted to carte blanche to listen to anything they said. Dennis McKeehan had provided the catalyst, albeit unwittingly, by making comments critical of his mission while in clinic with Dr. Jefferson, and joking about being a Muslim. Bastard hadn't wanted to serve his country while he was alive, but that was okay. They would make him serve it now that he was dead.

"We need to press the brother angle," Perry said. "The target is desperate to leave her brother out of this, but the doctor is giving us a remarkable amount of help."

"You'd think she was on our side," Clyde said.

"The target isn't lacking in boldness, or what I would prefer to term recklessness. The longer she's out there, fighting, the more likely she is to fight back with something that would not be in our interests. By which I mean our national security interests, always. Remember, politicians running for election care more about themselves than about the country. It's part of their job."

"Which is why governing is done by civil servants like you," Clyde said.

"Exactly. She can't help it. But we have to bring her down and we have to do it soon."

"You mean take her out?"

"Don't be ridiculous," Perry said. "Men have work to do here."

In front of Clyde, or Grant Rivers for that matter, Perry always appeared calm, in control. But he had taken a risk with Grant, and it no longer seemed to be paying off. As long as they were in business together, Perry had put his personal dislike of Grant completely to one side. Security was another matter.

In the privacy of his empty office, he was a bit concerned about Raybelle McKeehan. She'd always been something of a loose cannon, and any absence of control concerned Perry, but if he didn't manage her now she was going to step into something she really should know nothing about.

As a temporary roadblock, Perry would discreetly flag Senator McKeehan as a "no fly" security risk. Of course it would be a mistake, terribly sorry, but just the flex of his muscle could be enough to break her control, make her embarrass herself. She would come out and say the whole security regime was excessive, and most Americans would disagree with her. Just another little show of what he could do. Mistakes were made.

***

Raybelle had been on Grant Rivers, for a while now, to put forward a revised version of the GI Bill that would give veterans something to come home to. She knew a number of other senators, men who had benefited from this very arrangement in their own time, who she knew would support such a bill. But Grant wouldn't commit. Raybelle had always counted on him for bipartisan support and, with his misgivings—never defined—the project hadn't quite gotten off the ground.

With her doubts raised about Grant, Raybelle felt more alone than she usually did in Washington, or anywhere. She couldn't bear any conversation with Tomas Jefferson, who only ever wanted to talk about Dennis. And she couldn't remember now exactly when she and Dennis had stopped communicating. As children, they were as close as a brother and sister who were constantly fighting could be. At the time, fighting back had felt like she was developing an aggressiveness that she would need, as time and again she was told that women couldn't lead, couldn't fight, or wear the pants, or be the president. In boys, this aggressiveness was called "leadership quality."

Adolescence was a period any sensible person would have skipped. Raybelle had spent hers running for, and eventually becoming, president of the high school student body, a position of more worth than being valedictorian. She was the first girl ever to be elected student body president, but she'd never drawn attention to that fact. Merit was her sacred totem, her Holy Grail. She was as faithful to the notion of merit as the sole value in human achievement as she was to personal freedom. The freedom not to be beholden to anyone, not to parade a family in front of the cameras, not to do any of the usual butt-kissing that would have gotten her further, faster, in party politics.

There was, of course, that business about the army. She'd gotten as far as the interview with a military recruiter, a fat-shouldered, square-jawed white guy whose hairstyle made her think of Nazi brownshirts. He asked her if she had a boyfriend. This was a question she'd been answering for years, from older relatives and so-called peers, but there was something grating about being asked by a representative of the United States government in battle fatigues.

"No."

He smiled, not in a nice way. But then, she supposed you turned in your nice smile in boot camp. "Don't have a girlfriend, do you?"

There was something about his question, so at odds with the freedom Raybelle would be defending, as a member of the armed forces. So she said no, which was the truth, and questioned him a little more closely about what "noncombat roles" meant. She determined that women could not shoot at their attackers, but could be shot at, which did little for her notion of justice, another concept she'd wanted to defend. By the close of the interview, she was quite disillusioned with both freedom and justice, as represented by Captain America.

She'd never spoken of this interview again, and had directed her energies—a contemporary word for anger—into a civilian career.

But tonight, in her quiet apartment, she couldn't sleep. She was thinking about men, and more and more women, who had done what the armed forces expected of them, men like her brother but also the thousands now serving in Iraq and Afghanistan, and what were they going to get? The public probably thought veterans went to college for free. If they could still walk and talk.

Grant said you couldn't have a GI Bill because the military had enough problems retaining troops. What was the Pentagon thinking? Weren't servicemen and women enticed and betrayed enough by broken promises about the length of deployment, pay no one could live on, and disgusting hospitals? Good Lord, education would be like offering them the moon!

***

On the Senate floor, Barbara Boxer of California was holding forth about the health effects of asbestos. Raybelle twirled the

Montblanc pen in her hand and baked under the lights. There was a cadence to these speeches, a rhythm people used when they talked about personal tragedy—American deaths. She needed to tell more stories like this. Especially if she was going to run for president.

Patty Murray was speaking now about her bill. Raybelle looked around at her fellow Republicans, then across at the Democrats. It was all too easy to fall in line on an issue like Senator Murray's, resistant to any government interference with industry, seeing it as a restriction on personal freedom. But what if her own brother's death had been caused by mesothelioma? Could Raybelle sit here and vote for Dennis's "freedom" to be poisoned by asbestos? Oh, Jesse Helms had voted for tobacco in his day, but that had been subsidizing industry, not freedom to smoke. How Republican were subsidies? And what did you expect from someone who started off as a segregationist Democrat?

Raybelle thought about those southerners who thought their party had abandoned them. Even lonelier must have been those few who stood for what was right. In the time when Lyndon Johnson was Majority Leader, "the most hated man in Congress" had been Raybelle's predecessor, Estes Kefauver of Tennessee. Kefauver and Johnson had been two of only three southern senators not to sign the manifesto against integration, and the third was Tennessee's other senator, Albert Gore, Sr.

A new GI Bill might not make Raybelle the most hated member of Congress, but she was about to find out. It was her turn at the forest of microphones. With a nod to the C-SPAN cameras and to the late Estes Kefauver of Tennessee, she began.

"Today I am introducing the Service Members' Readjustment Act of 2007."

CHAPTER TWENTY-SIX

That evening, Raybelle was relaxing at a house shared by a few other members of Congress. Maybe she could get one of the freshmen Democrats to put forward a companion bill in the House. One of them, John Scofield of South Carolina, said, "You've got a visitor in the kitchen."

"Oh, Lord. Someone I need to dress up for?"

"Beats me." John sat down beside her on the couch, in front of the baseball game. "Who's winning?"

"The Cubs, can you believe it?" Raybelle decided it didn't matter that she was wearing orange Tennessee sweats. John wasn't an asshole; he'd tell her if it was a photographer or something.

But it was Melody. Raybelle was crestfallen at her loss of authority.

"You weren't answering your phone," Melody said, as if she were irritated at having to track her boss down.

"Oh, I always forget about that thing. What can I do for you?"

Melody glanced around the kitchen, all pizza boxes and Chinese takeout containers. "Is it safe to talk here?"

"Sit down." Raybelle pulled out chairs for both of them. "Since when have you been so paranoid?"

"I take that as affirmative." Melody produced a folder, one of those double-pocketed, school-supply kinds. "My boyfriend just found this in our garbage room. We were on our way out to dinner."

"I didn't realize you had a boyfriend." Raybelle thought she saw Melody color, but couldn't be sure.

"His name's Brian. He's from Chicago."

"Is he a Cubs fan? They're winning."

John came into the kitchen to get a beer from the refrigerator. "Miss Park." He extended his hand. "Pleasure to meet you in person. I'm John Scofield."

"Good to meet you, Congressman."

John seemed to want to linger, so Raybelle asked the score. "Tied now, 4–4."

"Shit."

Melody looked surprised. "Oh, don't be shocked," John said. "Raybelle cusses all the time when she's watching sports."

"John, please get out of here. We're trying to run the country."

"Right into the ground." He laughed, went back into the living room and turned up the TV.

"Democrats," Raybelle said.

"Yes, I'm familiar with him." Melody cleared her throat. "Are you going to look at the documents, or did I postpone my date for nothing?"

Raybelle removed what appeared to be blueprints. They were stamped Department of Defense, but she couldn't tell if they were final and approved, or rejected schematics. "Any idea what these are for?"

"Looks to me like plans for a facility abroad," Melody said.

"'Facility'? What, like a bathroom?"

"Counterterrorism, but that could mean anything." Raybelle

heard the Washington cynicism that had seeped into Melody's voice. It both satisfied and saddened her. "See, here's the location of a security fence, and here's a floor plan for something called the detention and counterterrorism unit. This stuff should be top secret."

"It probably is. What's it doing in your trash?"

"Yeah, you'd think they could at least recycle it." When Raybelle did not respond, Melody continued, "Brian said it was just sitting there by itself—we have a garbage room on our floor, it's just down the hall from my apartment. Really nasty. We get roaches a lot."

"Somebody knew this?" Raybelle said. "Somebody put it there for you to find, on purpose? Who in your building, or who has a key to your building, would want you to find this?"

"Would want *you* to find it. This is a major security breach. You're a known critic of the Pentagon, at least as far as this administration is concerned. And with everything that's going—"

"Hold on, we still don't know what these are," Raybelle said. "A private contractor could have just gotten careless and tossed them out."

"Oh, I'm almost sure of it." Melody looked intent. "In fact, it may not be the blueprints themselves that are important. It may be how carelessly they were disposed of, and by whom."

Raybelle stared at the papers in her hand. They weren't very illuminating, but they were precise: even the locations of disposal units, which she supposed meant trash cans, were clearly drawn. She had a distant memory of a guy she'd known in school, shop class (of course only boys could take that): he'd learned that precise draftsman's lettering. He'd made her a bookshelf in seventh or eighth grade. She'd see it hanging on the wall, still, when she was at the house. Mama's house…

"Senator?"

She focused on Melody's impatient face. "Sorry, yes?"

"Brian's waiting for me in the car."

"Oh, I should have invited him in! We could watch the game together."

Melody touched her hand, and Raybelle felt small and indulged. "Thank you, but we were going out." She said it with emphasis.

"I just wanted to bring these to you right away. Let me know what you want to do about them."

Raybelle rapidly counted twenty-six pages. She stuffed them back into the Mead folder. She would be sleeping with it tonight. First company she'd had in a long time.

Far into the night, long after John had turned off the television and she'd come back to her own apartment, Raybelle sat tucked up in bed with the blueprints. Not sure what else to do with this evidence of contractors' incompetence—or that someone wanted her to pursue it—she'd gone through with yellow sticky notes and carefully labeled the pages A to Z. They were evidence of something, and she wanted to preserve them as evidence.

She carefully slid pages A–Z into Melody's Mead folder. Then she sat up until dawn working on a rough draft. On paper. With her Montblanc pen.

In the morning she called Melody. "Come over," she said. "I'm working at home."

***

The next morning a new blog was posted on Raybelle McKeehan's website. Grant knew this because, as one of her "friends" in cyberspace, he was on a live feed to get her updates as soon as they were made. When he saw her latest on the new GI Bill, his cigar dropped right into his bowl of breakfast grits.

"Ray, what the hell do you think you're doing?" he said to his cell phone, before remembering that he'd have to dial first. Once Raybelle's assistant had answered, he said, "I need to speak to Senator McKeehan."

"She's unavailable at the moment, Senator Rivers."

"Well, make her available."

***

Raybelle was up to her neck in suds when Melody knocked on the door. She groaned. "Please go away."

"It's Grant Rivers, Senator."

"Doesn't he know it's dangerous to have an appliance in the

tub?" But Melody was already in the bathroom, handing her the phone. Raybelle felt momentarily shy about her fifty-year-old body, but Melody was talking, not looking.

"I didn't tell him."

"What?" Raybelle said.

"Anything."

Raybelle put the phone to her ear. "What is this about, Grant?"

"Good morning. I should be asking you that question."

"You saw the blog."

"Damn right I did. Raybelle, that's just not the way things are done in Washington."

"Things aren't done in Washington," she said. "That's the problem."

"You've been here as long as I have."

"Not hardly."

"All right." His tone softened a bit; they were friends, after all. "Why didn't you talk to me about it first? I could have helped you."

"You mean talked me out of it. I've raised my proposal with you many times, Grant, and for some peculiar reason could never get you to commit." She shifted under the bubbles. In spite of herself, she always enjoyed bantering with him. "Is it true after all what they say, that men are afraid of commitment?"

"If this is some ploy to make you look like a Washington outsider—"

"Are you saying my party has no place anymore for anybody, except a family values nutball? Any advice on marriage, Grant?" Raybelle let out a whoop of laughter.

"Fuck a duck," Grant said.

"Now, I don't think even I can seriously countenance that."

"Stop trying to change the subject. The Defense Department is totally against a new GI Bill."

"Grant Rivers, since when are you a shill for the Department of Defense?"

"I'm concerned about retention, Ray. The more volunteers we keep in career military service, the fewer reservists and national guard troops we have to call up for extra deployments in war zones. It's a win for everybody."

"Can you really sit there," (she knew Grant never stood when he could sit) "with a straight face and use the word *win* with regard to these conflicts? They've been disasters."

"There's only one thing we can do when we're already involved in something like this," he said, "and you and I both know what it is. Just minimize casualties."

"Yes, well. If you don't want a casualty on your hands right now, Grant, I suggest we wrap up this conversation. My bathwater's getting cold, and I'll get hypothermia."

There was a pause; she hoped he didn't have a dirty picture in his mind. "Did you ever consider it, for one minute?"

"What's that?"

"Marriage."

She laughed, a dick-shrinking cackle if ever there was one.

Now he was angry. "How far do you think you're going to get without my support?"

"I'll take my chances."

***

"She's playing with fire," Grant Rivers said, an unfamiliar trickle of sweat forming on his lip.

"So burn her," Perry said. "We've gone along with this too long. It's time to burn the bitch."

"Who the hell got that stuff to her anyway? I thought you said the people we hired for this were good."

"It doesn't matter. Don't you see? The end results are what matter. It doesn't matter what shape the final facility takes, as long as the correct people end up there drawn and quartered. It doesn't matter who pays our soldiers as long as they win the war. And it doesn't matter who falls in the course of this campaign, only that we win it in the end."

Grant rubbed his eyes. "Somehow I don't think you're talking about the election next year."

"I'm talking about the war. There's a war on, and no matter what she says, the war's not in a foreign country. It's in our country. You know the expression 'winning hearts and minds?' We're fighting for American hearts and minds. Americans have to stop thinking this is like World War II, when the enemy committed atrocities and we didn't. When everybody pitched in to defeat them, then came home and went to school on the GI Bill. It's not the twentieth century anymore. There's no such thing as an atrocity. We need to get the most defeat we can, at the best price."

"Don't you mean victory?"

"That's what I said."

Grant shook his head. There was no point arguing with Perry. For a moment, he almost felt sorry for the man he was cuckolding, and financially beholden to.

He needed to see Barbara. It had been awhile, and the elusiveness had started to wear thin. He thought with some amusement of Raybelle's mentioning marriage. Marriage seemed like the opposite of what it was supposed to be, a preserver of families. Nothing wrecked families faster. You signed up for unlimited sex with one person, and if you were lucky, you ended up with limited sex with someone else. Grant wondered where Perry was getting his, the tightass. Probably nowhere.

In an odd way, his affair with Barbara was discreet. They were keeping it in the circle of the powerful. What was with these crazy bastards who had to pay for it, or pick up guys? Then they'd trot their wife out in front of the camera for the public apology, which they didn't mean; they were only sorry that they got caught. The wife never mattered as much as she did the day she stood up for her humiliator. Grant would never treat Jean that way. He pictured Perry having to stand up with Barbara and say he was sorry—for what? Four thousand American deaths? Pissing off the Iranians?

"You haven't heard a word," Perry was saying. Sounded exactly like Grant's wife.

"Sorry. I was thinking about our families. How's Barbara doing?" Grant couldn't believe how disingenuously the words slipped out of his mouth.

"Fine."

"Been too long since I've seen her." Which, by his own standards, was true.

"Come on, I hate small talk."

Grant had to smile. "That's why you'll never get elected to anything. You don't sweet talk enough."

"I leave that to the experts," Perry said, and Grant had a sudden mental image of himself with Barbara, pouring her wine, receiving her favors although he wasn't much to look at. Not that her husband was. Power was all about saying the right things. Perry had the money, with a hand in the company running all these construction contracts, from the Middle East to Diego Garcia. But he really didn't know how to gain power.

Grant knew that history would judge men like him and Perry kindly. People said they were overreaching, taking away civil liberties, violating the Constitution. But they weren't doing anything Abraham Lincoln hadn't done, in the name of preserving the Union. Look at the threat to the Union they faced now. Lincoln hadn't faced terrorism on a global scale, and now he was considered the greatest president. Business was just the practical means to get things done.

CHAPTER TWENTY-SEVEN

Grant Rivers's wife was the last person Raybelle had expected to buzz in to her apartment that morning. "Jean! Come in," she said, her southern manners taking over.

But Jean just stood at the door, arms crossed, a tight smile on her face. Too tight.

"Where's Grant?" Raybelle said.

"I was hoping you could answer that." Jean still made no move to come inside.

"I haven't seen him. Jean, I wasn't expecting company, so it's a mess. But please, do come in." Raybelle had never had Jean in her home. Grant must have told her where she lived.

Jean clunked her purse down on the coffee table, with a

ladylike refusal to notice the Dorito bags and dip in the middle of it. Raybelle was careful not to belch.

"Can I get you something? Iced tea?"

"Sweet tea, if you have it. Please." Jean sat forward on the edge of the couch, back straight.

"Not that there's any other kind," Raybelle said. It was the kind of gratuitous thing you had to say when entertaining another southerner. She fixed two glasses of sweet tea and set them down in front of Jean. "Yankees, they think you can just serve cold tea and stir the sugar in afterward, but the stuff doesn't dissolve. It's so bass-ackwards, it's—"

"Raybelle."

Raybelle sat up, all attention now. After all, Jean Rivers was a constituent. "What can I do for you, Jean?"

"It's not business, Raybelle. Otherwise I'd have come to your office."

The formality unnerved her. "Is something the matter? Is Grant all right? I just talked to him."

This admission caused Jean's eyes to narrow. "I came here half expecting to find him with you."

For a moment Raybelle stared, utterly flummoxed. Then she laughed, a big, gut-busting laugh. "I'm sorry," she said, for how could you tell a woman it was absurd to imagine anyone having an affair with her husband?

"Part of me is relieved he's not here," Jean said. "But the rest of me is scared, Raybelle. If it's not you, then who is it? You don't know, do you?"

"I do not," Raybelle said. "Listen, Jean. This just doesn't make any sense. Are you sure Grant—" She couldn't bring herself to say it, just raised her eyebrows with the southern delicacy Jean would expect.

"I'm not sure about anything anymore. I don't know where my husband goes at night, I don't know half of what he does in the daytime. Help me." Her tone was imploring. "You're his best friend."

Not after the conversation they'd just had. But Raybelle thought it better not to mention that now. "Jean," she said, "I haven't been that close to Grant lately myself. It's been ages since we had breakfast together. I thought maybe he started watching his weight."

"Oh, why would he start now?" Jean clutched her glass; she'd made no move to drink the tea. "He's my husband, but I'm not a politician, Raybelle. I've never really understood what makes Grant tick. You must."

Raybelle resisted saying that she wasn't sure what made herself tick, these days.

"Something's wrong," Jean said. "I know he's not being honest with me, I just don't know who he's with. I was hoping you would know something."

"Jean, are you sure he's cheating on you? I mean, that just doesn't sound like Grant to me."

Jean sighed, picked up her purse. "Raybelle, I have been married to Grant Rivers for forty years, and I have no idea what he's like. He says things, you know, in the senate, on the campaign trail. Words come out of his mouth, but I don't know what they mean."

"I wish I could help you." Raybelle tried to sound more genuine than Jean's description made politicians sound. "But honestly, Jean, when I talked to him, he sounded fine. Has he called you?"

"Not for days." Jean's face relaxed, and Raybelle saw how tired she must be, holding the tension of a smile all the time. "Do me a favor. If you see Grant, if you hear from him again? Tell him to come home."

"I will."

Jean got up to leave, and Raybelle wondered whether Jean's lifetime habit of putting herself last would triumph over her doubts. The seed was planted in Raybelle's mind, though, and that was more fertile ground. If Jean couldn't trust her husband of forty years, then to what extent did Raybelle know Grant? Were they even friends?

She wasn't sure, as she shut the door behind Jean, that she even knew what friendship was.

***

Grant thought a moment before placing his next phone call.

He'd hoped to draw on their long friendship to put Raybelle off; it was what he'd invested for, long term. But for all her talk of Geneva Conventions, Raybelle had a cruel sense of humor. She wasn't there for him, and now his ego was smarting. She should pay.

"Connect me to Secretary Perry, please." When the secretary picked up, Grant said, "Henry? We have a problem."

"If this is about your friend," Perry started.

"Not my friend, Henry. You said you wanted her out, and I think now's the time."

"She will be out—of office—soon enough. And, as much as I hate to admit this, I'm not one hundred percent happy about it. She's been useful to us in the spotlight like this."

"How so?"

"Deflecting attention," Perry said. "We don't want it on us."

***

Tomas went through her workdays with her usual practiced smile and professional demeanor, but for the first time, she didn't feel at home in Chicago. She had gotten an e-mail from Ephraim, typed in a rush at some Internet café. It read like a telegram, shouting in all capital letters: TOMAS HELLO JUST TO SAY I AM BACK IN LONDON CASE GOING SLOWLY REGARDS TO MRS. MCKEEHAN. Why did he have to mention her? Like they were seeing each other. The thought made Tomas's heartbeat feel irregular, which took her briefly back to her days as a medical student, when every time she read about a disorder or complaint she felt symptoms herself. Sympathy pains.

She wasn't used to sympathy, only detached compassion. She wasn't used to the displaced feeling that Ephraim must have, that Dennis must have had, to wander halfway across the world for the dubious benefit of people he'd never met, or must have wished he'd never met. Nor had she ever considered the ramifications of a career choice like the military. She was a doctor, she always knew her work made people's lives better. To live with the consequences of a mission like Dennis's had moral implications, and Tomas wasn't very good with those. *Moral* connoted *moralize* to her.

She needed not to think about the gnawing, empty space inside her, only recently vacated by the long-absent Alicia. A space that couldn't be occupied by lust alone. She needed to go back to Washington, DC.

***

On the plane, it was getting harder and harder to concentrate. Every time she opened her laptop she wanted to check Raybelle's blog. Might as well set it as her damn home page.

She decided to look at it offline, whatever the page had stored before they lost Internet access in flight. The sky was the one place you could be safe from contact, and Tomas was sure it was only a matter of time before people got online there, too. Once Al Gore figured out a way to make it carbon neutral, he'd probably say he invented it.

She chuckled. Wasn't it just like the Democrats to eat their own? That's what Raybelle would say. Raybelle, Raybelle...what was she blogging about now? Tomas read the impassioned case for her new GI Bill; it referred to the "inhuman deployments" and "starvation wages" of the troops, and provided links to the healthcare scandal already being covered. There was Tomas in her glamour shot, scowling, a chunk of plaster in her hand.

"The Department of Defense treats our servicemen and women shoddily," the post concluded, "because it thinks they can be replaced with private contractors. Anyone who's ever had a job 'outsourced' should know better. Expect worse treatment, a longer war and needless deaths. Tomorrow, Part 2 of why Defense can't be trusted with the defense of America."

Tomas felt unreasonably proud. Unreasonably, because Raybelle didn't belong to her, and it certainly shouldn't concern her what some politician said. Proud, because it seemed that Raybelle had listened to her after all. Raybelle would never admit it. Couldn't show weakness. Tomas wondered how much of that was political instinct, being a tough woman in pursuit of a political career, and how much was resistance to her. She tried not to take it personally.

CHAPTER TWENTY-EIGHT

After she'd bathed, Raybelle dressed. A blouse and trouser suit, ironed sharply enough to cut flesh. No doubt about it, she was doing battle today. These blueprints didn't come out of nowhere, and she wasn't waiting to be invited on a Sunday press show to air her suspicions.

She and Melody were on their way to the senate chamber when Clyde Wheatley came running down the hall after them. "What's with this 'private contractor' shit on your blog this morning?" he said. "For chrissakes, you're pro-business. Next thing you're going to be outed as a closet protectionist."

"Don't take Christ's name in vain, Clyde, you're on camera." Raybelle flashed her smile to the right, where a bank of cameras waited, not unexpectedly.

"Senator McKeehan," someone shouted, "is it true you're launching your new GI Bill in defiance of the Defense Department?"

"Actually, the Defense Department is blocking me. I'm defending American veterans from people who supposedly have their best interests at heart."

"Doesn't offering free education to returning veterans encourage soldiers to leave Afghanistan?"

"Well, that's what they should be doing anyway," Raybelle said. "Our soldiers have already been there too long, and we've asked far too much of them. I'm just interested in making life better for them stateside, so they can contribute to our country instead of giving their lives for somebody else's country."

"Senator, what do you make of Secretary Perry's response yesterday to the news that sixty percent of Americans think his leadership of the war has led to unnecessary loss of life?"

"I haven't heard his response," Raybelle said. "Can you repeat it back to me?"

"'So?'"

She blinked. "Was that his exact word?"

"Yes." An uncomfortable calm. "What do you make of it?"

"I don't respond to rudeness." She brushed at her sleeves. "If Henry Perry wanted to go to war against the American people, he ought to be working for the enemy." She raised her file folder, ignoring Clyde and his posse, and invoked the demon spirit of her Senate predecessor, Joseph McCarthy. "I have here in my hand evidence that the Department of Defense is building a facility for the detention of prisoners, in non-US territory in the Indian Ocean. Territory leased from the British government. These plans were disposed of so carelessly that they ended up in somebody's trash room. Now either the contractors charged with making these plans are a bunch of incompetent boobs, or this was a malicious leak. But either way, somebody isn't doing their job."

There was an uproar, a cacophony, which was what Raybelle had counted on. Made her feel right at home. She chose this question to hear and answer: "What makes you think private contractors are involved?"

"Listen up, people. Private enterprise doesn't always mean better business." She waited for the earth to open up and swallow her for this unspeakable heresy. "Maybe they're getting paid more, like the soldiers of fortune over there substituting for our troops, and getting into all kinds of trouble 'cause they don't follow the same rules. But maybe they're getting paid less. There's no incentive. To be careful with your work, to do the best job."

"Senator, what's your hunch as to whether this was incompetence or malice?"

Raybelle stuck a Bic ballpoint between her teeth, like a thin cigar. "Given two possible explanations, stupid or evil, I go with stupid every time."

"Where is this facility going to be?"

"For all I know, James, it's been built. The island is called Diego Garcia. Ever hear of it?"

***

Sometimes what Grant most enjoyed was just to watch Barbara move about the hotel room. Sex was always the end of it, and the beginning. But he enjoyed the thought that as the power games of Washington swirled around outside, like flakes of snow, he was inside, playing the only game that mattered.

He'd come to feel things for Barbara, and that surprised him. He thought himself too far along for that sort of complication. The Perrys, and everyone else in Washington and indeed beyond, were pieces in his game. Grant had congratulated himself on how well this was working, because Perry, a pawn himself, believed that he was in charge of moving the pieces around. But when one of those pieces, Barbara, approached Grant, smiling over her always-full glass of wine, he felt something. Hesitation. Maybe that was all it was.

He'd intended to tell Henry today. He thought it would crush him, and Henry Perry needed crushing. Grant knew that Henry wouldn't publicly reveal his own role, as the cuckold; it would be too humiliating. He would either resign, or at the very least, become human again. His absorption in personal pain would allow Grant to move on freely, with everything he needed to do.

Yet, when Grant touched Barbara now, he felt he shouldn't sacrifice her, quite so thoughtlessly, or so soon.

CHAPTER TWENTY-NINE

Tomas couldn't relax around Raybelle McKeehan. She'd requested absolute privacy, which was why she sat in a stuffy and neglected corner of the senator's offices. She hadn't intended her first words to be, "I don't ever want to hear about marriage from you again until it's legal marriage for same-sex couples. At the federal level."

But Raybelle was like a queen; she could respond to the most unusual opening as if it made perfect sense. "Why, Doctor Jefferson, I didn't take you for the marrying kind."

"Senator McKeehan, I am a big enough person to advocate rights I have no interest in exercising personally," Tomas said. "And don't think of saying 'states' rights' to me."

"So I was right, you're not the marrying kind." Raybelle seemed intent on making this a flirtation, and that caused Tomas to clench her fists. "I'm flattered, really I am, but I can't risk my career having an affair."

"It wouldn't be an affair," Tomas said before she could stop herself.

They looked at each other. If Tomas relaxed her fingers, opened her hands, she would want to run them over Raybelle's face, her shoulders, the curves and planes of her body. What was worse, she'd allowed the senator to realize this about her. She dug red, manicured nails into her palms.

"What do you want to talk about?"

Raybelle's tone was quieter. If Tomas didn't know better, she would almost say gentle. Probably it was just her own hypersensitivity, because she felt caressed, and she didn't imagine many people felt that when they heard Raybelle's voice.

"Tomas?"

She knew she shouldn't think Raybelle was beautiful. There was nothing more frustrating than longing for someone who wouldn't have her, when there were women in the world who would. Did the timing of these things ever make sense? When did she, a doctor and a scientist, lose control of this situation?

"It's about Dennis," she said.

Raybelle dropped into a chair. "It always is. Sometimes I feel like you care more about my brother than about…"

Tomas looked at her, as if to rap Raybelle's knuckles. "Me," she finished.

Tomas crossed to the window, which looked as if it hadn't been cleaned in years. Despite this, the outdoors looked hopeful, bathed by a changing wind. There really was beauty in this city, buildings that looked like they were built for aesthetics rather than just to make money. Ironic, considering that it seemed to be the main objective of all the scoundrels around them.

"Dennis told me," she said, resting her hand on the grimy windowsill, "that when the marines came to Diego Garcia to evict the people who lived there, the island was like a paradise. The people and their dogs just ran free all over, and splashed in the lagoons. Sometimes that's just how people remember their own homes, looking back, but Dennis was a man with a hardened perspective, and difficult memories. He would not have made this up."

Tomas expected Raybelle to interrupt with some sarcastic remark, but she was quiet, so Tomas went on. "The marines started—they were ordered to start rounding up the people. Dogs too. Everybody had to leave the island. The dogs were like members of the family—you've seen those stories on the news, where there's a fire or a flood, and the people get out okay but are distraught, because the family pet is lost and they can't find it." She was surprised she had to clear her throat, more than once.

"They gassed the dogs," she said. "The marines just took them away from the families, and gassed them. Hundreds, thousands maybe."

There was a silence but Tomas felt it, like her hand had broken through the glass. Then she heard Raybelle's voice behind her. "Did Dennis—"

"He did."

"'All my pretty ones'?"

Tomas recognized the quote. "*Macbeth*."

"That's my favorite play."

"God, why am I not surprised?"

They shared an uneasy laugh. What else to do? Tomas found herself saying things, and feeling things, around Raybelle McKeehan that didn't make any sense. Whether there was "sense" in an absolute sense was no longer at all obvious to her. Now she was starting to remind herself of Bill Clinton. When were they going to elect a Democratic president again?

"I'd vote against you, you know."

Raybelle said, "What?"

"If you were running to represent me," she said, "I'd vote against you."

"Because you're a Democrat?"

"Thanks for not asking if it's because I'm black."

"You're not recording this, are you?" Raybelle attempted another laugh. "I don't want this to end up on TV."

"Why, Senator McKeehan, you've gotten paranoid. Must be a consequence of living in this surveillance society."

"You're thinking of Britain," Raybelle said. "Or Great Britain, as it used to be called. And none of this security apparatus is my idea. I'm against all of it."

"Yeah, but are you changing the system? Or is the system changing you?"

"Oh, please. You sound like some sixties radical."

"I wasn't even born in the sixties," Tomas said.

"Don't rub it in."

Raybelle made an impatient motion. Tomas recognized it as the itch of someone who used to smoke, and occasionally still wanted to. "How long ago did you quit?"

"What?" For Raybelle, it was probably unconscious.

"How long ago did you quit smoking?"

Raybelle looked sheepish. "Whenever they started banning it everywhere. But really, before that. It was getting politically incorrect."

"Never thought you'd care about being PC."

"No, I mean that literally. Can't be seen smoking and get elected. It certainly isn't because I don't advocate someone's right to smoke, to the death. And you know I mean that literally, too."

Tomas noticed she hadn't said anything about health, which was the first thing she'd thought of. Raybelle's smoking, or not smoking, suddenly mattered to her a great deal. "Do you miss it?"

"Every day." Raybelle pushed papers around like unwanted food on a plate.

"What's the big sigh for?"

"Oh," Raybelle said, "it's these service members. I know some of them have been asked to do terrible things...but the forty-three cents out of every dollar this country spends on the military—it's not going to them, is it? Somebody's getting rich."

Tomas looked at her. "Dennis wasn't."

Instead of avoiding her eyes or getting angry, Raybelle sighed again. "No. Dennis drew the short straw, that's for sure."

Tomas sat down beside the desk and extended her hand toward Raybelle's, without touching. "What do you mean?"

"I don't know about you, Doctor Jefferson," Raybelle said, "but my mama told me not to talk to strangers."

Tomas laughed. "You talk to strangers all the time! It's your job."

"I didn't say I did what Mama said."

"And I'm not a stranger." Tomas felt more open with this woman than she could ever remember feeling with a lover.

"Everybody's a stranger."

"That reminds me of a Nanci Griffith song." Tomas couldn't believe she was referencing a country singer. Good thing Dana Rignaldi had forced the odd tape on her, in college.

"I love her. She's from Texas." Raybelle was quiet for a moment. "Do you remember when Ann Richards was governor of Texas?"

"Vaguely," Tomas said.

"When George W. Bush was running to replace her, with Karl Rove working for him, there was a whisper campaign about Ann Richards. All the Texas ladies had to go on was a vicious rumor, nothing to it, but it probably destroyed her candidacy. Those guys don't fight fair."

"I don't understand."

Raybelle looked at Tomas, and her eyes were hard again, the political animal. "Lesbianism."

"Is that a vicious rumor?"

Raybelle made a dismissive sound with her lips. "Anything goes in Illinois, you indict governors all the time; but in other states it is."

"Why won't you tell me about Dennis?" Tomas said, turning back to the first painful subject.

"What's there to tell? You knew more about him than I did."

There were fine lines of tension around Raybelle's eyes. Tomas said, "Talk to a stranger, Senator."

She waited so long for a response that she questioned whether Raybelle had heard.

"When we were kids—" Raybelle cleared her throat, as if she were hoarse from just having made a campaign speech. "I was eight, so Dennis must have been thirteen. We got a dog from the animal shelter. Dennis wanted to name him Oliver. I thought that was the most stupid name ever for a dog, but Dennis was older so he got whatever he wanted."

He'd probably thought the same about his little sister, but Tomas kept quiet.

"Anyway, the dog was dumber than dirt—bless his heart." Tomas recognized the automatic southernism from the Rignaldis. "Probably brain-damaged, that's why he was at the shelter, but we didn't know any better. Barked all night, shit in the yard. You know. And Dennis was supposed to train him, but how would he know how to discipline some poor animal when he'd never learned any discipline himself? I mean self-discipline or any other kind."

"Your mother was easy on him?" Raybelle had never mentioned a father.

"Didn't matter. Nothing sank in. I got all the discipline for both of us. Anyway we had this dog for eight years, drove us all barking mad." Tomas groaned at the pun, and was rewarded by what sounded like a genuine laugh. "Dennis was home on leave, and I had just learned to drive. I wanted to get my license the day I turned sixteen, like Dennis had, but Mama wouldn't let me."

"Why not?"

"Dunno. Because I was a girl? So I needed to get to the driving test center to get my test done, but in order to get there, legally, I had to have a licensed driver in the driver's seat, and she wouldn't let me go. I was so mad I asked Dennis to go with me." Raybelle smiled. "This doesn't sound like much in the way of teenage rebellion, I know, but you have to understand how much it would take for me to consider doing anything a little bit against the law. I've been planning to run for the presidency since the time we got that dog. Everything I've ever done counts.

"So Dennis refused. More than that, he laughed. For once, he was ahead of me at something. He was sneering in the passenger side window, refusing to get in. I was so mad I turned the key and just shot back out of the driveway. That was when I heard the crunch of bones."

Tomas listened to hear if Raybelle's voice would catch or anything, but it was as hard as her eyes. Tomas felt that if she touched this woman now, she would feel stone. She waited for the stone to move and speak.

"It was that goddamn dog," Raybelle said. "At first I thought I'd run over Dennis's foot, he looked so pale and pained. Then I realized it was Oliver. I froze. I didn't know what to do. If I'd moved the car in either direction it would only have made a bigger mess. The dog was dead anyway."

Tomas didn't ask how or at what point Raybelle had known this.

"Dennis freaked out. The dog drove us totally nuts, but Dennis loved him. He was screaming and crying like I'd never seen my big brother do. When our dad died, Dennis stood up in his little clip-on tie, so brave and solemn; I never saw him break down sobbing. Now here he was, a man and a marine, gone to pieces over stupid Oliver. Why'd the dog have to be back behind my wheels in the first place?

"Dennis was screaming at me to get out of the car. I was afraid to let it roll back down the driveway, so I put the emergency brake on and got out. Just left the car running. I looked back and there was Dennis on the ground, covered in blood. That scared me so bad because it looked like his blood. I knew when Mama saw us, she'd think I'd killed Dennis, and then she would kill me."

Raybelle's delivery was flat, as if she were reading from a teleprompter. Tomas thought how much of her life Raybelle must have spent like this, at a remove. Had it started then, in that Tennessee driveway?

"That wasn't the worst part, though."

Tomas felt the need to clear her own throat. "What?"

"The worst part," Raybelle said to the desk, "is that Dennis thought I did it on purpose. He thought I knew the dog was there, and he knew I hated Oliver. He thought I deliberately ran over his dog, because I was mad at him."

"Did you?"

Raybelle looked as if her own foot had been run over. "Of course not. I wouldn't hurt a living thing on purpose. I don't even swat bugs. God, Tomas, what do you think I am?"

Tomas couldn't help it, she extended her thumb just enough to caress Raybelle's hand. She looked surprised but didn't pull her hand away.

"Didn't Dennis believe you?"

"I never told him," Raybelle said. "I mean I tried to, but he wouldn't speak to me. He acted like I didn't exist. A few weeks later off he went back to the marines, and that was it."

With all she'd seen in her career, Tomas still found this hard to believe. "You never saw each other again?"

"Nope." Raybelle met her gaze. "Oh, Mama tried to get us talking, but it just didn't happen. Dennis rarely came home, you know, he was overseas, and soon I was away at school and then working."

"What about Christmas?" Not that the holiday was a big deal to Tomas, but they seemed like a family who would get together.

"He wouldn't come home. I think, for years, he would just get drunk wherever he was, party like a sailor. Not that Mama ever put it like that. Then later, in his fanatic phase, he was too busy doing Jesus's work to celebrate his birth." Raybelle managed a feeble roll of her eyes. "Actually, he was probably more Christian than I gave him credit for."

"Did you love your brother?" This wasn't the sort of question Tomas usually asked, and she didn't know why it mattered now.

"With all my heart." Raybelle didn't hesitate, but her answer seemed to surprise both of them.

Tomas didn't spend a lot of time thinking about love, or what it meant. And Raybelle was a politician, a fighter. But how could you love someone and not do anything about it? Not speak to him, not come when he was dying? If this was Raybelle's whole heart, Tomas hated to think what her halfhearted efforts looked like.

"I guess that's why you're here," Raybelle said.

"What do you mean?"

"To find out what kind of monster doesn't care, when her only brother dies on the streets."

"I'm here," Tomas said, "because you asked me to be."

"Because I asked you to help me out."

"No." Tomas spoke with more conviction. "Because you asked me to be here."

There was a moment, a leaning in, and Tomas felt Raybelle looking deep into her and could feel the breath from her lips. Then Raybelle drew back. "I'm sorry."

"Don't be," Tomas said.

"I don't know what I'm doing."

"None of us does."

Raybelle stood up. "I need to get to the bottom of this scandal," she said.

"I'm planning to go to London. To see Ephraim."

"Then I don't know when I'll see you again."

Tomas didn't know why she should hesitate. She'd been ready to kiss Raybelle a moment before. "If you keep digging with this investigation," she said, "it could mean the end of your career."

"I know that." She could see Raybelle steeling herself. "But I wasn't elected by the people of Tennessee just to keep running for reelection. I was elected to serve in the United States Senate. And that's where I'm going now."

"You're very unusual, Senator."

A flash of that longed-for smile. "I could say the same about you, Doctor Jefferson."

***

Across the Potomac in Perry's office, Grant Rivers set down his headphones. "We got her," he said, with a triumphant pumping of his fist. "You hear that, Henry? Burn the bitch!"

CHAPTER THIRTY

As soon as Tomas had left her office, Raybelle collapsed in her swivel chair, face in her hands. She couldn't possibly head for the Senate chambers in this condition. All she could think about was how close she'd come to kissing Tomas Jefferson. Here. In her Senate office.

Kissing a girl was something else she'd always wanted to do, but unlike becoming president, she had, when she was ten. The girl's name was Laurie, and they were just clowning around, dancing in the school bathroom. Laurie lived with her grandmother, just up the road from the McKeehans, and rode the same school bus. Everything Laurie did, she did with enthusiasm. When it was her turn on the playground, Laurie kicked the ball so hard her shoe flew off into the outfield. Raybelle was smitten. So, in the bathroom, she'd kissed her.

But Laurie wasn't smitten, nor was Miz Rogers, whom Laurie told, and who made Raybelle stand in the hall outside their classroom. It was the only time in the whole history of her schooling—or since—that Raybelle had been publicly disciplined, and the shock was almost as great as Laurie's when their lips had touched. She hated Miz Rogers. Would not go back to her class. Was so insistent that Mama, who would certainly not have understood about Laurie, went to the school and worked something out so that Raybelle could go to the other fourth-grade class for the remainder of the year. The kiss had stayed in her memory for forty years, tucked in behind her ambitions and other lusts. For power, for knowledge, most of all for respect. Until today, when she would have undone everything, forgotten everything she'd worked those forty years to achieve.

She wasn't stupid. For a McKeehan, stupid was the worst thing you could ever be, worse than evil. Even Dennis hadn't been stupid, just not as smart as she was. Raybelle wondered, for the first time, why that had been so important to her, why she'd had to rub it in. She'd been too smart, too farsighted about her own future to get her hands dirty with the military, though she cheered it as loudly as she ever had at a ballgame. Dennis was the grunt who did the work. It was parallel to her career: too often wheeling and dealing, lunch on the taxpayers' dime while they, those men and women she met every day but never really knew, sweated through the days and woke up sweating at night too. Over their mortgages, their jobs, their kids facing guns at school and real predators beyond the playground fence. There hadn't been a fence when she and Laurie had played kickball, forty years ago.

It had always been her intention, and policy, to stand up for the innocent. Once Raybelle was convinced you were innocent, she'd fight for you, in the figurative trenches of Washington. Dennis's great flaw had been to fall on the wrong side of the innocence divide. He'd abandoned everything—Raybelle, Mama, reason, sanity—and in turn, she'd abandoned him. Tomas's call, when Dennis was still alive, had shaken her, but not enough to revise her perception of her brother.

He had stood at the gate of hell, and Raybelle pushed him in. Gently. Like a devil sent by God.

***

For the second time in as many days, someone had requested a private audience with Raybelle. She was beginning to feel like the Pope. The ex-marine in her office wore civilian clothes, but he still had the haircut and the precise motions. "What can I do for you, sir?"

He spoke with the directness she had come to associate with lying. "I'm here about the security contract you're investigating."

"The one where the pile of building plans ended up in my assistant's garbage?"

"Yes." He paused, as if for effect. "With respect, Senator, things don't 'end up' in places. People do things."

"That was government speak, Captain. I despise it as much as you do. But I don't know who put the plans there, or if it was deliberate. Coffee?"

"Thank you, no," he said. "I do everything deliberately, Senator."

She felt a new respect. "You must have had a reason."

"I always do. I didn't feel able to approach you directly, since you aren't my military superior. I did try talking to them." He still seemed comfortable—as comfortable as anyone sitting with that stiff posture could be.

"So Plan A was telling your superiors. And it didn't work out."

"No passives, remember, Senator?" he said with a touch of humor. "They fired me."

"And you believe this firing was in retaliation for your speaking out?"

"Yes. To you or to them. I'm sorry, I'm not sure."

Raybelle smiled. "You don't have to be sure of everything."

He leaned forward with his elbows on her desk, as if they were intimates. He didn't have many gray hairs in his crew cut. "I try to be. If I'm asked to lead men—and women—into the face of death, I need to be as sure as I can be of everything that's out there. Otherwise, their blood is on my hands." He looked at his hands then, as if for Lady Macbeth's spot.

"That's a very admirable attitude," she said. "I wish every commander, at every level, had such regard for the lives of his troops."

He straightened back up. "I didn't bring up those plans to be critical of any particular commander. I brought them up because I didn't believe my commanders knew what was going on. If they did—if the contract were my responsibility, and *I* knew, I could never have allowed it to go through. The company that got this contract didn't know what they were doing, and that's unforgivable when you're talking about people's lives."

"Can you elaborate a little on what was wrong with the plans?" Raybelle said. "Because the Pentagon wasting money, while deplorable, is hardly the kind of news that's worth your job to reveal."

"You've looked at the plans, Senator?"

"I have. And I'm not an architect. But I do get the impression that they're somewhat…incomplete."

"I could defend the unit better with a shot and sling," he said, and for the first time his lip seemed to curl.

"What did you come here to tell me today?"

His face relaxed somewhat. "They sent us these 'experts,'" he said. "Anthropology graduates. Most of them didn't have a clue about where they were being sent, or know the language. They were paid a lot more than active duty service members, though. To go through people's trash and tell us how we should 'relate' to them. Save face, appeal to pride. Asian stuff."

"And you resented these civilians," she said.

"On the contrary. I'm engaged to marry one of them."

This was an unexpectedly personal turn in the conversation. Raybelle wasn't sure what to make of it, but she knew how to respond to good news. "Congratulations."

"Thank you. My fiancée is more impressive than a lot of the other advisers. More mature."

"More like you?"

He made a laugh-like sound. "Closer in age, anyway. She got a degree in Islamic studies, although she's a Christian who knows Arabic."

"Is that important?"

He lifted one shoulder. "Depends whom you ask. The military is like America, Senator McKeehan; you're really supposed to be Christian. I'm a Jew myself, but we all get free evangelical books. They don't come from the government, but the message is clear. Cross good, crescent bad."

"That wouldn't be everybody's sentiment here in Washington."

"Nor in the military. And it's not my sentiment, either. Anyway, a few years ago we were all having a beer one night—not a very Muslim thing to do, as you know. One of the guys said something implying Arabs were the same as Muslims or Muslims meant Arabs—I forget which, but neither is true. Started talking about the war in Iraq and whether Iran was next. It was a relaxed atmosphere, you know, everybody knew my girlfriend, though we hadn't announced our engagement yet. So she made a statement that any sane person would agree with, that she didn't want any more war and, *inshallah*, we wouldn't go to war with Iran."

"Meaning 'God willing.'"

"Yes. In Arabic. I know you know what it means, because I read your blog." His face tensed again. "No one would bat an eye at that statement on a university campus. Maybe in an airport security line. But for the guy in our company, it was like shouting '*Allahu akbar*—'"

"'God is the greatest.'"

"—and running into the street with a suicide bomb. An investigation started, and next thing you know, she was fired."

"What did you say about this?"

"Not much I could say. As commander, I understood where the man was coming from, but I didn't supervise *her*. Besides…"

"You were dating."

"Yes."

"And you didn't want everyone to know."

"Some knew." He swiped at his brow, a quick motion, as if he didn't want her to see his discomfort. "We just didn't want to talk about it. In the field, everything is everybody's business. Sometimes you just crave a zone of privacy."

"Like the Green Zone," Raybelle said.

"Have you been to Iraq, Senator?"

"I have not. Believe me, sir, if I had ever been anywhere near a combat zone, I'd be bragging about it all over the television."

"Well, we don't get a chance to watch much TV out there," he said, but with no trace of rebuke.

They sat in silence for a moment. Had Melody been there, she would have been a much better hostess. "You sure you don't want coffee?" Raybelle asked, refilling her own.

"Do you have anything to put in it?"

"Cream and sugar?" She reached for the tray.

"Whiskey."

She looked at him, showing no surprise. Then she reached into her desk drawer for a fifth of Jack Daniels. No telling how long it had been there. "Product of Tennessee," she said. "Will it do?"

"Fine."

No one ever came to her office without wanting something, and Raybelle prided herself on never letting anyone leave without making an exchange. "So, you've given me the blueprints for a slipshod job in Diego Garcia, a job you think went to incompetent people. And you're mad because your fiancée was fired for saying God willing we won't have another war. I sympathize with you entirely. But what can I do for you?"

"Besides follow the money?" He sipped his whiskey-with-coffee. "Take another look at those plans. That's not just a detainment facility. They plan to torture."

"Who plans?" Raybelle said, as cold as she felt.

"Does it matter who, Senator?" For the first time, the captain stood and began to walk around the room. "See, people always want someone to blame. So they shoot the messenger, like me. Or they court-martial some private for taking degrading pictures. But it's never about those people. When the world hears, they hear about America. I was taught that everything I did was a reflection on the country I represent."

"So was I." She stood too, as he appeared to be edging toward the door. When he got there, he shook her hand, firmly. "I came to see you," he said, "because of the state you represent." He looked around, as if expecting the enemy. "Take a look at Herald Aviation."

"Understood." Though, of course, Raybelle didn't understand. "Thank you for coming to see me today. I appreciate your taking the time."

His smile was rueful. "Time's all I have now."

She saw him out, then sank back into her chair, twirled a pen in her fingers. She did wish he hadn't used the word *torture*. Her desire not to believe these things, about the country she loved, was so strong that it could have overpowered her desire to hear the truth. Almost.

***

That night, Raybelle was home alone with her security system when the call came from Grant Rivers. "Grant, am I glad to hear from you," she said. "Jean was just—"

"Are you at your computer?"

"Yes. Why?"

"I've sent you an e-mail."

"Well, that's not like you, Grant. Why don't you just—"

"Turn on your speakers," he said, "and listen up." He disconnected without saying goodbye.

It took Raybelle the better part of fifteen minutes, plus a phone call to Melody, to open the link Grant had sent her. A grainy video, the indistinct figure of herself speaking and voting on the senate floor; the sound was a rapping beat, with words repeated over it in a "dub" style. To her horror, Raybelle recognized them as private conversations she'd had with Tomas:

"Same-sex couples. S-same, s-same, same-sex couples…"

"Having an affair. An affair, an affair, an affair, an affair…"

"Lesbianism. L-l-lesbianism."

She slammed her laptop shut hard enough to crack the screen. This was blackmail, plain as day. If she didn't do what Grant said in his e-mail—withdraw from everything she was investigating, withdraw her bill—he would ruin her with this. The video was probably being uploaded to YouTube as she sat there.

But what was to stop him from releasing the video anyway, even if she did comply?

She opened the computer again and looked at the clock in the corner. Too late to call Tomas. Besides, she wouldn't mention this in any context that might also be recorded.

No, she wouldn't listen to Grant. Let the truth come out, if truth was what it was.

CHAPTER THIRTY-ONE

When Tomas arrived at the hotel in London, she immediately began unpacking. Since the new "security" measures, she'd taken to traveling with only one carry-on bag, though this meant she had to buy liquid toiletries and razor blades each time she arrived at a new destination. It also meant she was now one of those people who annoyed other passengers by wheeling a big bag onto the plane. She traveled business class when she could, but wasn't it every man for himself?

She unpacked her clothes, folded with a horizontal crease that would drop out when she put them on hangers. This was a trick Alicia had taught her. They had met when Tomas was in medical school and only dimly aware of clothing other than scrubs.

For the first time, thinking of Alicia didn't upset her. She waited to feel something, like testing an icy surface. She felt, almost saw, her relationship with Alicia recede into the past, where it was part of her.

Halfway through hanging up the clothes, the just-reconnected cell phone (or "mobile," as the British called it) rang. Tomas was tempted to hang it up too. But she could see from the display that it was Raybelle, and she was thrilled to hear from her. Even though she really, *really* got on her nerves. "Hey."

"Hey," Raybelle said. "How's London?"

"Well, I haven't seen any of it yet," Tomas said. "I just got in from the airport."

"Sorry."

"Don't apologize. How goes the bill?"

"Interestingly," Raybelle said. "I'm not getting a lot of support."

"Do you think you can beat the administration?"

Tomas could almost hear Raybelle's shrug. "My issues are too important to be drowned in the party in power," she said. "Everybody else is about the 'war on terror.' Nobody will say anything about it—the Democrats are turning Republican."

"What issues are making you unpopular?"

"Civil liberties," Raybelle said. "Limiting executive power. Not going in to places that haven't attacked us, just to fight wars."

"I thought you were pro-military."

"I am," Raybelle said. "Too much to waste soldiers' lives like this administration has done. All the administrations before them, too."

"Carter?"

"Oh, don't make me laugh." But Raybelle was laughing.

"Why?" Tomas said. "Don't you like it when I make you laugh?"

There was so much to a silence, even an expensive transatlantic one.

"I believe the government has let down the people who serve this country," Raybelle said. "What are they doing in all these overseas places?"

"Like Diego Garcia?"

"Yeah. It should be sovereign territory. It's not American, or British. We talk about 'nation building,' but we destroyed a nation.

We're supposed to be about fighting terrorism. What we did to the Chagossians was a terrorist act."

"You realize that by that reasoning, we should give our country back to the American Indians, and send Africans home free."

"All the slaves are dead," Raybelle said. "But Ephraim is a living man. I can do things for people I can see."

"I wish I could see you." Again, Tomas didn't know where the words were coming from, only that she had to say them.

"Tell you what," Raybelle said. "You take care of your business in England, and I'll do whatever I can for you when you get back."

"To DC?"

"To the States. I'll meet you somewhere, if you'd rather. Buy you a nice dinner, whatever you want."

Tomas smiled into the phone. "Are you asking me on a date, Senator McKeehan?"

She expected denial, but got defiance. "I can do whatever I want in my private life. But I have less time than ever to pursue it now. I'll see you, Tomas."

"'Bye."

She wasn't entirely clear on what business she did have in England. Ephraim wanted her to testify in the Chagossians' court case, as to his injuries and intimidation by forces unseen. They'd agreed that Britain would be slightly more receptive than America to the notion of US brutes running roughshod over human rights in the pursuit of "terror." To be sure, anything that had been done on that score in the US had probably been done in Britain first, and for longer, but it was public perception that mattered, and the public was far more antiwar over here. How much of that public perception would be reflected in the magistrate, or whatever the appeals person was called, was anybody's guess.

Tomas was tired. She hadn't slept on the plane, and knew she couldn't sleep now. If she tried it, it would screw up her schedule for the rest of the trip.

A run, she decided. A run would get her blood pumping, distract her from her feelings about Raybelle. When she got back she could have a long soak in the oversized tub she'd been eyeing in her hotel room. She took her sensual pleasures where she could find them.

She changed into running clothes, and stuck her ID and room key in the Velcro back pocket of her shorts. She wore men's tennis shorts. They were so much more practical, with pockets that would actually hold something while you were running around. Sometimes she wondered how women put up with it all.

She jogged the length of the carpeted hotel corridor, bouncing on her toes in front of the "lift." Smiled at a fellow guest, some worried-looking City investment type. Not the sort of thing Tomas ordinarily bothered to do, but he looked less comfortable than she was; his suit didn't seem to hang right from his shoulders. They rode down together to the ground floor. He hesitated as to which direction to go, so Tomas ran off. There were advantages to being on her own. She could decide, on the spur of the moment if desired, what to do and where to go (jogging, London). Nobody to answer to. Free.

The thought, in itself, didn't lighten her heart so she bounded away, toward Grosvenor Square. It was an easy way to orient herself to London, which was a bit of a challenge to an American accustomed to cities laid out on a grid system.

As she approached the US embassy, she slowed for a better look. She first noticed a statue, set high on a kind of planter pedestal to discourage vandals, or recognition. She had to look at the sign to verify that it was Ronald Reagan, of all presidents.

State flags lined the front of the embassy building. She wasn't sure which flag was which, but the Stars and Bars of the Confederacy leaped out at her from the flag of one of the southern states. Then she came to the security entrance where American citizens had access. There was a sign with helpful illustrations indicating items that were banned. Cameras, okay. Mobile phones. But really, a cartoon of a cherry bomb, like something that would blow up Wile E. Coyote? Who had to be told that oh, darn, I left a bomb in my backpack, along with my camera? Tomas almost laughed. She'd left her phone in the hotel, could walk right into the embassy.

An arc of bollards lined the sidewalk in front. Tomas set off on her run again, dashing between pairs of bollards, like a kind of obstacle course. She was starting to enjoy this when she was grabbed from behind. Instinctively, she slammed her elbows into the body behind her, but another figure emerged and Tomas felt herself pinned between dark coats, her arm twisted painfully. Within seconds she was being hauled away—not into a car; where would they park one? She shouted "Help! Get off me!" but no one paid attention as she was dragged inside. Tomas recalled the great British politeness. You could take off all your clothes and sit down in the middle of the high street, and your average English person would just avert his or her eyes, get on with the business of the day. Tomas almost wished she'd had the luck to be abducted in Chicago. Americans might not care, but they would notice, and they were loud.

Beyond the blank American zone of the embassy, she supposed, traffic continued to go by, oblivious people. How stupidly tourist of her, to spend her whole adult life in Chicago, and only in a European capital become the victim of a crime.

Her captors were British, that's all she knew. English, probably. Tomas wasn't familiar with the accents, but she didn't hear a particular lilt, or brogue. They didn't talk much, but when they did, it was only to each other. They said no more to her than if she were something bought off the butcher's block, in one of those ghastly English markets.

Nor did they bother to gag or blindfold her. She was slammed upright into a kind of armchair, and for the first time could see her captors clearly. Two white guys, not very tall, bad haircuts, dull suits. She recognized one of them as the "guest" she'd shared the hotel elevator with. He looked no less worried now. Perhaps he wasn't trained in thuggery.

"ID," the other man said.

"I should ask you for that. Who the hell are you, snatching an innocent jogger off the sidewalk?"

"You were running past the American embassy," he said, as if here were an obvious indicator of guilt.

"You don't sound American," Tomas said. "What are you doing protecting our embassy? Besides, I'm not aware that it's a crime to go running in America. Though you might think so from our obesity rate, I'll grant you that."

"It is through a secure zone." He sounded smug, and Tomas hated him already. "Now you're on British soil, and you're going to answer our questions."

"I'm in the US embassy!"

He made a clucking sound and held up two fingers, entwined. "You think you're going to get some sympathy from the American embassy in Britain? We're like this."

"Who are you?" she asked again.

At last, Hotel Man spoke. "Homeland Security." In his English accent it sounded more ridiculous than usual. Tomas had always thought the name of that particular invented department had the ring of *Volk* and Fatherland about it.

"You have got to be kidding me," she said. "Homeland Security nabs people who go running past embassies overseas?"

"Or through airport security checkpoints, or other areas of high security significance."

"Like my hotel?" Tomas knew from cop shows that she ought to request legal representation if she was under arrest, but no one had read her her rights. Perhaps in Britain, a country without a written constitution, she didn't have any. "You followed me."

"You're a person of interest," the first man said.

"Oh, that's very flattering. To whom? Someone attractive?"

"Of interest," he said, his teeth on edge, "in the war on terror." She was getting on his nerves now. Good. He was getting on hers.

Hotel Man spoke next; it was like watching a tennis match between two Serbs she'd never heard of. "You entered Britain on the pretense of visiting a friend—"

"I am."

"—when, in clear contradiction of what you told passport control, you are actually here to interfere in sovereign British affairs. By lying about your passport, which is the property of the US State Department, you are in violation of the laws of the US."

"This is not true," Tomas said, "and I fail to see how you could possibly consider me a security risk. I'm not carrying so much as a nail clipper, and we all know how dangerous those are."

The first man drew a pen from his pocket and rolled it around in his hand. It was meant as an intimidating gesture, and she took his point, that anything could be a weapon. Watch for pens to be banned from flights. How, then, would passengers fill out increasingly invasive customs forms on board? "You must surrender your passport," he said.

She was incredulous, but it didn't matter anyway. "I haven't got it with me."

Hotel Man said, "If it is with your personal effects, it will be seized."

"By whom? It certainly doesn't belong to you!"

"Customs." He sounded bored now. Must be relaxing into his role.

"I cleared customs this morning." She sat up straighter.

"In violation of passport control," he said. "And you will not leave this room, nor will you have access to your belongings, until our investigation is finished."

"You're holding me *prisoner*?"

"Relax, Miss Jefferson." Motherfucker actually smiled at her. "You'll be no more inconvenienced than you might be by a routine airline delay."

"For the record—because I know you're keeping them—it's Doctor."

"Just sit here," the first man said. "There's no use doing anything else. No one knows where you are."

He trained his pen on her. She shivered, remembering that she was still in her running gear. Hotel Man departed, presumably to ransack her room. She couldn't believe she'd been stupid enough to come out without her phone. Not that she could have had it in the embassy.

"US embassies don't detain people," she said. "That's a scam."

"You've not been detained," he said. "You're being intimidated." Tomas trained her eyes on him. "Am I?"

***

Raybelle took the stage at the Beef Cattlemen Association's dinner as naturally as she had every podium since the fifth grade. She wanted to stand her ground, a middle ground of positions that would truly keep the country secure. Anyone, Democrat or Republican, who wanted to join her would be welcome.

"Guantánamo Bay," she began, "is an illegal prison in Cuba.

Anything strike you as strange about that? Why are we in Cuba? A country so wicked that American *citizens* are not allowed the freedom to travel there. By our own government. Isn't limiting travel, by their own citizens, something that, oh, I don't know, *communist* governments do?"

She was riffing now, and she knew it, but she also felt the crowd, and the whole thing was being filmed. "Almost fifty years—ladies and gentlemen, my entire lifetime—the United States has been unable to get rid of a dictator living a few miles away. He's now the longest ruling leader on Earth, if you don't count really undemocratic rulers, like queens! And what is it dictators do that's so terrible? Lock up people without charge, right? Build secret prisons. Torture. Ladies and gentlemen, it is time we stopped becoming the monster."

A cell phone rang behind her. The tune was someone rapping over "Cantaloupe Island." Melody approached from the rear of the stage and whispered, "It's Doctor Jefferson. She needs you. It's urgent."

Tomas was the one person who could make her forget everything else. "Tell her to stay on the line," Raybelle whispered back. Then she turned back to the cattlemen, her stage smile locked. A rictus.

When they finally connected, Tomas said in a ragged voice, "I've just been released from the embassy in London. Do you know anything about this?"

"What do you mean, released?"

"Homeland Fucking Security, or rather their British stooges, nabbed me in front of the embassy and held me incognito for *twelve hours*," Tomas said. "I figured you tipped them off."

"What are you talking about? I was in the middle of making a speech against the unlawful imprisonment of Afghan teenagers and Iraqi taxi drivers," Raybelle said. Then, more quietly, "Did someone hurt you?"

"I'm fine. Just outraged. Someone's got Ephraim, though."

"'Got' him?"

"He's gone. Disappeared."

Raybelle ran through the possible scenarios. She was a politician; she ought to be good at this by now. A foreign national, already intimidated in the United States, is whisked away from Britain by forces unknown. The odds were not good that Ephraim's "rendition" was anything less than "extraordinary."

"He could be anywhere."

"Saudi Arabia would be my guess," Tomas said. "We'll let the Saudis get away with anything. They come blow up our buildings, and we bomb everybody else."

"Well, at least we're on the same page there," Raybelle said. "But Ephraim has nothing to do with the Middle East. The interest in him must be because he's calling attention to something beyond the present war. Guantánamo—even the military court personnel are quitting, the process is such a travesty. But Diego Garcia will be used as long as this country fights wars."

Tomas didn't hesitate. "Then we have to stop them."

"We?"

"You. Me. Us."

***

Without Tomas having time to recognize the change, let alone stop it, Raybelle had altered the way she thought and acted. Tomas used to obsessively count words, not wanting to waste one, hadn't had a spare moment since college, and now she spent them with abandon, like dollars on a vacation. She wanted to cover this woman with words, with her hands and her body. She remembered this feeling, albeit distantly, and thought it might be what was meant by falling in love. The thought terrified Tomas more than being held, incommunicado, within shitting distance of the pigeons in Trafalgar Square.

CHAPTER THIRTY-TWO

"I don't understand what you're telling me, Melody."

Melody tapped at keys, looking ineffectual. "It's not letting me in."

A call to the IT department had proven fruitless. That in itself wasn't unusual, but never before had the simple matter of booking a transatlantic flight turned into such a production. For the first time, Melody seemed unable to hack her way through the unexpected red tape.

After a day and a half, the best the airlines could come up with was that, no doubt through some embarrassing mistake, Senator McKeehan's name had come up on a "no fly" list. The senator herself asked why they, the airlines, couldn't do anything about it, since they were private companies and had been deregulated by Reagan.

"I'm telling you, Melody," she said, "the airlines are the worst. The minute their stock falls or any other normal business event, off they run crying to the government. Who in tarnation has mixed my name up with Cat Stevens or whoever else is on this 'no fly' list?"

"That's what I've been trying to figure out," Melody said. "I can't get anybody to tell me why, but apparently, it wasn't a mistake. Your name, and title, were put forth quite specifically. By order of the president."

"President, my ass," Raybelle said, and liked the sound of it. "That move's got Henry Perry all over it."

"There's no way he'd dare," Melody said. "This is just more of his malicious messing you around. He's trying to get you to explode in public, say something intemperate like you're against everything security related. Then he can make it sound like you're in favor of planting bombs on planes."

"You think I don't know that?" It was a question of who, Raybelle or Perry, could make the other look like a bigger fool. "No. Let's play along for a little bit. He won't be expecting that."

"You mean, actually take the flight ban seriously?"

"Just till I can get down to Tennessee. This ban, it's for scheduled commercial flights only, right?"

"That's what they're telling me."

"So we hop down to Tennessee and take a look at Herald Aviation. I've been meaning to do that anyway." As she spoke, Raybelle was grabbing her bag. "I'll call my flight attendant friend. He knows everybody in the state who knows how to fly."

Moments later, she was on the phone. "Yeah, Geoffrey? I need a favor."

***

The last thing Henry Perry needed right now was his wife in his office. She had rarely visited him there, not that he blamed her. It was his withdrawal into this office, not only its physical space but the office of Secretary, that had broken whatever link remained between him and Barbara after the death of their daughter. The oak desk, not their bed, was the locus of his most intimate moments. Perry would stay in this office for hours, whether or not there was real compulsion for him to be there, with all the BlackBerrying and other ways that he could do his work from bed if he wanted. And it was all because this, not the house he'd bought with Barbara in the seventies, was where he felt at home. Here, he was competent, adequate, alone. It was what he liked best, solitude, a pinnacle of power where he didn't have to consider anyone else's viewpoint, least of all hers.

Barbara looked dignified in the context of his office. He wasn't used to seeing her like this, standing before him, conveying the power that for his wife went with his position. He rarely thought of Barbara in terms of power at all; he'd long since turned off any influence she had over him, the way he'd ignore a dripping faucet when she'd asked him to fix it.

He decided to try diplomacy, a language at which he was rusty at best. "Barbara," he said, "can't this wait? I've got something important that I should wrap up before I leave."

"Then stay late. Like you always do."

"I don't expect you to understand the complexities," he began, feeling the condescension rise like bile.

"Let me guess," she said. "One of your little deals has fallen through. Aircraft? That front at the Tennessee Bible college?"

Perry felt a rare sense of being one step behind. "You know about that?"

"I do listen."

Now he was truly alarmed. He was certain he'd never mentioned Herald Aviation at home, or anywhere where Barbara could have heard. "Are you spying on me?"

She laughed, but there was no mirth in her laugh. "That's your remit. Bugging innocent people, flying suspects to torture states. You know what makes you almost beneath contempt, Henry? You aren't even a true believer. You can pose on television, but I know you're only in this to make a quick buck."

For once, he felt powerless to deny the truth. Normally it was as easy for him as drawing breath. "Won't you sit down, Barbara?"

"I prefer to say this to your face," she said. "You've been cashing in with Senator Rivers for the past seven years, but you don't know him." He detected a smile. "Not like I do."

"What are you saying?"

"I'm saying, I respect a believer. He may be crazy, but at least he isn't venal." She crossed her arms, and Perry was aware of surprisingly pert breasts underneath her royal blue jacket. He hadn't noticed them in years.

"Grant Rivers?" he said.

"Yes. I'm leaving you, Henry."

He sat there, stunned. He hadn't felt so paralyzed, so incapable of making a move or any decision, since the day they heard about Kelly.

"For him?" he finally said. "For Grant Rivers? Grant doesn't love you."

Barbara sniffed as though love were the furthest thing from anyone's mind. "Not for Grant." She lifted the glass paperweight from his desk, hefted it, as though debating whether to stone him.

"I'm not the adulterer," he said aloud.

"Not for Grant," she repeated, his accusation flicked away. "For me. Me, Henry. I'm a person too. The person you've been looking over, past, and through for twenty-three years."

Perry couldn't lift his eyes from the paperweight. In his mind, he saw stones, raised in the hands of men he'd never seen. His accusers were those who had lost their lives through his security policies. For his profit.

"Look at me, Henry."

They all had Barbara's eyes. He remembered, as he had tried to forget since 1984, that her eyes were also Kelly's eyes. And that there was still one human being, living on earth, whom he loved.

What he said was, "I want you to stay, Barbara."

"You're not listening," she said. "You can't just have something, because you want it." She set the paperweight down. Then, at the door, she added, "I've stopped drinking."

Stopped? He'd long since given up on the one thing he needed from his wife. The more she lost control, the more he had craved it, clung to it, until there was hardly anything between them at all. If she had stopped drinking, then he truly didn't know her.

Barbara had lost a daughter too. Somehow, he'd forgotten that.

He just needed to shut down Rivers and Herald Aviation before McKeehan got hold of the story. No reason anybody had to find out what had gone on there. It was over now, no permanent harm done. Nothing was permanent but death.

Perry wasn't accustomed to second thoughts. "Burn the bitch" had just been rhetoric. So had his instruction to Rivers, in a similar vein, to get rid of that troublemaking island person. Perry was a civilian leader, and careful.

But there were important differences between the islanders and Raybelle McKeehan. She was a senator, a US citizen, and a white woman, in a world where such things mattered. The Chagossian was stateless, and potentially an illegal immigrant; after all, he wanted to stay with his homosexual lover. Anyone less sympathetic to the average American would be hard to envisage. Given the extent to which Rivers was involved in the rendition business, it would be tempting to him to take Perry's order literally.

It had, Perry admitted to himself, been careless of him to give vent to emotion. Rivers was an excitable creature. It was time to rein him in, and close down the operation with the planes. An unnecessary distraction. It wasn't making money anyway. Better to prepare for leaving office, and throw people like Senator McKeehan off his track, preserving opportunities for later.

CHAPTER THIRTY-THREE

Raybelle wondered who else could betray her and what else she could lose. Her brother was dead, with no chance for reconciliation. More disturbingly, someone who had become important to her was in trouble. Tomas was risking her career, and now it seemed her freedom, for a man Raybelle had never met. But Tomas cared about him, and she cared about Tomas. And that was enough reason. All along, she realized, the political really was the personal.

Running for office meant crisscrossing the country, bowling or looking at butter sculptures, throwing back shots and beers. Raybelle could use one now. She'd grown up on the land, a country girl, but what kind of country—"homeland"—was she working, fighting, to preserve? How could love of the land not be respected, if not for "enemies," like in Iraq, at least for innocent third parties like the Chagossians?

What could they be doing on those islands that they had to keep secret? That it was worth firing a marine and attacking Ephraim? In the past, she might have trusted Grant enough to ask him. Now Grant was the last person she could rely on.

Raybelle made sure she and Melody were on their way to the airport before she called Henry Perry. "Hey there, Dick," she said to the Secretary's secretary. "Senator McKeehan. Please connect me to the man who hates me most."

When Perry came on the line, he sounded more than usually conciliatory. "Senator McKeehan," he said. "I'm so glad you called."

Raybelle was reduced to the southern expression of incredulity: "Do what?"

"Yes," he said. "There's been a slight—complication in your travel plans recently, and that—well, I've taken care of it..." He seemed to run out of words, like a car stalling.

"Don't waste time trying to apologize. I know you won't be able to get it out."

"We're in the process of closing down a facility in your hometown—"

"Herald Aviation? I'm on my way there now."

"But how did you—"

"A little woman told me. Listen, Henry. Much as I'd love to chat, the person I really need to talk to about this is Senator Rivers. He needs to explain to me why the aviation school is closing."

She could tell Perry was sitting up straighter. "That's far too sensitive. Senator, I'm terribly sorry about the travel matter, I don't know how that could have happened. But I'm going to have to ask you not to go to Herald right now. It will attract all kinds of attention and due to national security—"

"Relax, Henry, I'm not traveling in a motorcade. I'm just going to see for myself what you carpetbaggers have been up to, in my backyard. Did you expect I wouldn't find out about Grant's involvement in this?"

She could tell he didn't know how much she knew.

"Senator Rivers and I will be coordinating the announcement of the planned closure."

"Oh, I don't think you will."

"I beg your pardon?"

"I'm going now," Raybelle said, "and you'd better pray I like what I find."

She tossed the phone to Melody. "Take pictures."

***

The propeller plane landed at Herald Aviation's airfield, and Raybelle was curious to see the place from the air. It didn't look menacing, as if evil were going on there. It was the same beautiful country she was used to seeing when she flew home. Hills still green from the recent summer, rolling away toward the flatlands of the Mississippi to the west, and the Atlantic coast to the east. It was her home, the most beautiful place on earth to her.

This must be how Ephraim felt about his island. It was wrong, just flat-out wrong, that a place of peaceful beauty, her Appalachians and rhododendrons, should be a place of pain and unreason.

She and Melody were met at the plane by an obviously armed guard. "Senator McKeehan," he said, "I've been asked to look after you here."

"That won't be necessary, Mr. Shepherd," she said, reading the name badge. "Nice biblical name, though. Is that a requirement for working here?"

They were halfway to the terminal when something moved in the corner of Raybelle's vision, like when there'd been a mouse in her apartment. Someone shouted "Get down!" and a crouching figure outside the building pointed a gun. Raybelle registered abstractly that it was aimed at Shepherd, not her.

"Federal agent," the figure identified herself. "Disarm, Shepherd, for God's sake."

The word "God" must have turned the trick. Shepherd was soon out of his unseasonal jacket and the federal agent was at Raybelle's side. "Sorry about that, Senator," she said, "but under no circumstances should your visit be hampered in any way. I want you to see what you came here to see."

Raybelle dusted herself off and shook her hand. "Not the way I usually start a visit, but thank you, Agent—"

"Rignaldi. Dana Rignaldi."

Raybelle drew back, startled. "Edith's daughter?"

"You know my mom?"

Melody interrupted. "I'm Melody Park. We can get to know each other later. Right now, let's gather the surveillance and the documents." To Raybelle's look of rising disbelief, she said, "I'm your right-hand woman, remember? You don't think we'd come here without my having thrown your weight around in advance?"

Dana Rignaldi guided them to where the records were kept—an inauspicious little room at the back of the control tower. It smelled of stale coffee. The security surveillance and documentation showed everything: the use of the aviation school as an "intelligence" front, the missions of the pilots turned from Christian ministry to extraordinary rendition. There were recordings of Senator Rivers swinging the deal for his home state, and of Secretary Perry on site, giving orders for the whole bloody business. Everything was there, behind the control tower in Poudre Valley, Raybelle's own backyard. She felt ill.

"Take everything," she said to Melody. "Agent, will you ride with me? I want you to shoot anyone who tries to stop us."

"No shooting necessary," Dana Rignaldi said. "Shepherd was the only one allowed on Herald property with a gun. They like to keep their hands clean here."

"How did you get in?"

"I infiltrated as a student, but it's very male-oriented, so for the first year no one would let me near the planes. Couldn't argue with my knowledge of the Bible, though. I was raised with that."

"So the aviation school was a CIA front," Raybelle said. "I can't get over how it was right here in my state. The bastards."

"You know our different agencies don't trust each other; our job as FBI is to police the country, not spy. And I know it hasn't always been that way, but that's my job now. This whole operation was set up after September eleventh. It was supposed to be part of a program to keep crazy foreigners from learning to fly at US aviation schools. Which sounds like a great idea, till you factor in domestic crazies. Someone like Timothy McVeigh, born in the

USA and with the zeal of the Lord, training as part of a 'night flying' program to nab suspects and ship them off to overseas torture centers."

"If I may play devil's advocate for a moment," Raybelle said, "presumably what was going on here was legal, or said to be. Executive orders and so on. What made the FBI go after that?"

"We're law enforcement. Our loyalty is to the Constitution, and we can't be letting some citizens commit what amount to crimes, potentially against other Americans. And you know, Senator, just because the president signs something does not make it law."

Raybelle had never held unelected federals in higher regard. "Thank you, Agent," she said. "Clearly you're someone who's actually read the Constitution, rather than just talking about it."

"Sort of like the Bible," Dana Rignaldi said.

***

When she and Melody got back to Washington, Raybelle said, "You mind going back to the office and fielding phone calls? I've got a plane to catch."

"Going to see the other person whose opinion matters to you?"

"Don't push it, Melody." Raybelle stopped at the corner of Twenty-third Street, searching for a taxi. "I'm going to see what kind of country I can leave to other people's children."

CHAPTER THIRTY-FOUR

"Tomas, it's me."

Raybelle's voice on the phone. Tomas said, "Where are you?"

"Heathrow. Where are you?"

Not for the first time, Raybelle's words caused Tomas's knees to weaken. Quickly, she stepped off the treadmill in her hotel gym. The last thing she needed was to fall off and hit her head. She might be a doctor, but she was a terrible patient.

"Tomas, I just cleared passport control. Help me out here."

Tomas gave her the hotel address. She wanted to see her. "I'll be right there," Raybelle said, and disconnected without saying goodbye. Fuck, she drove Tomas nuts.

Forty-five minutes later one of those famous London black cabs pulled up in front of the lobby window. Tomas wasn't sitting there, but well back; she'd gotten a bit paranoid since being kidnapped. After the first shot she ordered, the barman served her Jameson's every time she sat down at the hotel bar. She usually didn't drink whiskey, but he made her feel too welcome to change her order now.

She stopped breathing momentarily when Raybelle strode in. The woman always looked magnificent, and walked in as if she owned the place. No matter how many times Tomas had seen her this way, whether at the Poudre Valley bike-a-thon or on Capitol Hill, she was impressed. "Hi," she said, her own voice sounding small in this field of human energy.

"Pint of bitter, please," Raybelle said to the barman. Then, to Tomas, "I've always wanted to order that in England. Is that what you're drinking?"

"Chaser."

Raybelle eyed her with something like concern. "You getting drunk, Tomas? It's nine o'clock in the morning."

"No, it's two in the afternoon. Get with the time zone. And I'm not drunk." She drained her latest shot, as if to prove it. The barman served up Raybelle's pint and they clinked glasses.

"So," Tomas tried. "How's it going?"

"Oh, honey. I need to fill you in on a few things."

As Raybelle summarized the events of the previous day, she rapped the bar, and Tomas again glimpsed the ex-smoker. When Raybelle put her hand on Tomas's arm, Tomas felt lacquered nails and imagined them scraping down her back.

Raybelle was saying, "What I want is to find out where Ephraim went. I'm worried about him."

"I have an idea of where he might be," Tomas said. "When he was attacked in Chicago, the threat was to send him back to Diego Garcia."

"You think he's been 'extraordinarily rendered' too?" Raybelle sneered over the rim of her pint glass.

"You have the plans for that detention facility, don't you?"

"Right here in my carry-on. There was lots of room after I took out all the banned liquids."

"Doesn't that prison seem like a logical place to look?" The whiskey was kicking in; Tomas could feel it. "Don't you think that's why the plans were passed to you?"

"Then let's go." Raybelle drained her glass and stood.

"What, now?" Tomas wasn't at all sure she could stay on her feet. She was certain no one would let her board a plane.

"I'm packed. How much stuff do you have?"

"Not much." Tomas rose. "It's all upstairs."

Raybelle seemed to be standing very close; the lights of the bar blurred around her profile. Tomas imagined there was more to her tone and expression than merely the suggestion to pack luggage. Then she wasn't aware of anything.

***

Tomas came to some time later, still in her clothes and shoes, flat on her back on the hotel bed. Raybelle sat beside her, holding a wet cloth against her forehead. "I set the wastebasket here by the bed," she said. "Just in case you start throwing up."

"Ugh. I didn't, did I?"

"Not yet," Raybelle said, in an obscenely bright tone. "How's your head? I tried to keep you from banging it when you fell."

"Oh, fuck." Tomas didn't feel sore in one particular place, just that all-over ache that she associated with being sick. Which she hadn't been in a very long time. She groaned, more with embarrassment than from pain.

"You going to be sick now?" Raybelle said. "I haven't nursed somebody through a drunk like this since college."

"I never did this in college," Tomas said. "Maybe once, when I graduated from medical school. Dana did."

"Dana did what, honey?"

There it was, "honey" again. Tomas was in bad shape, but not bad enough to forget what Raybelle had called her. She groaned again at the disgraceful circumstances that had brought the senator to her hotel room. "Dana. You met her?"

"She's an FBI agent. Remember?" Raybelle stroked her hand softly, with a calloused thumb.

Everything in Tomas's head was fog; she could not concentrate on what Raybelle had said about the present, only the past. "Dana was the wild partier when we first met. Not me. I was always nose to the grindstone."

"You lived together how long?"

"Three years." Now that she thought about it, sharing that dorm room with Dana was her most stable adult relationship, if not the longest.

"Was she in love with you?"

What the hell was Raybelle doing, asking these questions when Tomas was so vulnerable? "I thought she was, at one time. I never asked and she never told."

Raybelle chuckled. "I know how that is."

Tomas was relieved that the question wasn't, "Were you in love with Dana?" She wouldn't know how to answer that. For most of her life, including most of her time with Alicia, she'd only been in love with her work. Work was satisfying, and she didn't have to explain its value to anybody. There was an objective reason for going to all the trouble for an important career. Who could say that about loving relationships?

"Stop thinking." Raybelle put a hand on Tomas's forehead. "You're going to make yourself sick."

"Is it that bad for me?"

"Well, I wouldn't know," Raybelle said. "You're the doctor."

"And you're a politician."

"So I don't have much experience with thinking!"

Tomas reached up and held Raybelle's hand, where it rested on her hair. "You're smart enough not to get hammered," she said. "I feel awful."

"It'll pass."

"No. I mean I feel awful, passing out in a bar while Ephraim is fuck knows where having fuck knows what done to him."

Raybelle moved away and brushed her hands together, as if to say, *That's one thing sorted.* "Well, we're just going to have to go and find out for ourselves. The kinds of diplomatic junkets senators swing, I'm sure I can take you on my trip to Diego Garcia. Now that the flight ban's sorted out."

"What flight ban?"

"Lord, we do have a lot to catch up on." Raybelle patted Tomas's hand. "Rest, now."

***

Tomas woke in the disorienting hotel time that could be any hour of the day or night. She felt much better, but very dehydrated.

She stumbled out of bed and stopped partway to the bathroom. Raybelle half-sat, half-sprawled in a grim brown armchair, eyes closed, looking more alone and vulnerable than Tomas had ever imagined her.

Her guard must be staying in the next room. But Raybelle had stayed here, with her.

She took her time in the bathroom, drinking a full glass of water before refilling her glass to take back to bed. She paused again in front of Raybelle's chair. Couldn't stand to see her so uncomfortable.

"Raybelle."

The senator stirred. Tomas set the glass down and set both hands on the arms of the chair. "Why don't you go to bed? I'm fine."

Raybelle's arms came around her and there was no stopping it, Tomas leaned in for the kiss. Raybelle's lips were warm and soft. There was no comparison to the way Tomas had imagined them. There was no comparison, because, for once in her goddamned life, she wasn't thinking, wasn't, some part of herself, perched above, analyzing the whole situation. She felt no resistance from Raybelle and so kissed her harder, opening to the surprise of her openness, tasting her. Tomas felt her everywhere, although it was only a kiss.

When they broke apart both were breathing hard, and Raybelle's blue eyes were open. "I thought I was dreaming," she said.

Tomas fought not to dive on top of her again. "Just as well your security detail wasn't in the dream, then."

Raybelle looked around awkwardly, as if trapped in the chair. "Here," Tomas said. "You can't stay there. Come on."

"I should—"

"You can go back to your room if you want to," Tomas said. "Or you can stretch out here, with me. If you want to dream some more."

Raybelle was on her feet, crushing Tomas in her embrace. Tomas had the sense of being swept into a powerful whirlpool, and she kissed Raybelle for all she was worth. She couldn't remember ever just kissing, just reveling in fully clothed pleasure, without the promise of dragging each other off to bed. Whereas no one was dragging Raybelle McKeehan anywhere.

At last, Raybelle released her to arm's length. She looked, for the first time since Tomas had known her, as if she had no idea what to say.

Tomas didn't either. She'd already suggested bed, but with Raybelle it wasn't the way it was with other women. It might still be a dream with Raybelle, and if it was, Tomas didn't want to wake her up.

"We've got a plane to catch in the morning," Raybelle finally said, still holding on to her.

"Do we?"

"Yes." Raybelle's facial muscles moved, as if still rearranging after the kiss. "So we should both get some sleep."

"Okay."

"Goodnight."

Tomas picked up her glass and put it on the bedside table. Her hand shook a little and the water sloshed. From the doorway, Raybelle said, "Sweet dreams."

"You too."

The door closed on Raybelle and her safe world. Tomas stretched out on top of the covers and shut her eyes. Her body hummed with frustration and desire. Even so, she felt much better.

CHAPTER THIRTY-FIVE

Flights to the Chagos Islands took a long time. This was the longest trip Tomas had been on since Tanzania, back in college. She supposed Dana had been in love with her then, but she had been too busy diving to pay attention to the woman right next to her. She wouldn't make that mistake again.

"So," she said to Raybelle. "You must be in shock, over the whole Grant Rivers thing."

"Yes. It's personal now. Grant betrayed a friend."

"Yeah." Tomas put a tentative hand on Raybelle's knee. "That must have hurt you, to have him turn on you like that."

Raybelle removed Tomas's hand, but gave it an affectionate squeeze.

Tomas had flown all over the world to go diving. She marveled now that she could cross oceans and go to the bottom of one, but she could not escape women. The memory of them, of the most casual affairs, of her failures at love. She wondered why it was no longer enough to pursue the body of any attractive woman, why she had to have this one, and she couldn't. How could she reach through? What sounds could she make to convey to Raybelle McKeehan that this was what she needed? Was it preposterous of her to imagine that Raybelle needed it as well?

When they reached Diego Garcia, Tomas felt that they'd left the world she knew behind, almost as soon as the senator's party deplaned. This was a US base, but it could not have been further from the country that possessed it. The atoll looked like it had been a paradise of lagoons, just as Ephraim had described. A paradise that had been taken from him.

"We don't belong here," she said. She didn't just mean Americans. She wanted to climb right back on that plane.

But Raybelle didn't answer. She had seemed more preoccupied the closer they got to the base, and by the time they were met by two young Americans in army fatigues and boots, Tomas felt that Raybelle had forgotten she was there.

"Hello, soldiers," Raybelle said. "What have you got for us?"

"Sergeant Baker, ma'am." The young woman nodded. "This is Corporal Wilson." The soldiers looked from Raybelle to Tomas, to her security detail.

"Senator," Baker said, "we know you're here to inspect the facilities. We thought you should know—you're right about the flights."

"We dumped a body," Wilson said. "In the water. We marked the location for you."

Maybe it wasn't Ephraim. Tomas just needed to verify that what they were saying was true. "Where is the body?"

"Doctor Jefferson is a diver," Raybelle said.

The soldiers looked at each other. "Never know what kind of ordnance might be down there," Baker said.

"You know where the term *ordnance* comes from?"

"No, ma'am."

"Why, it's the same word as *ordinance*, meaning law. Started using the word for weapons because, let's face it—weapons are the law. Are they not?"

He seemed uncertain. Baker answered for both. "We follow the laws of the United States here, Senator McKeehan."

Raybelle nodded. "That's good, see. Because I'm a United States lawmaker, and that means I make the laws of the United States. I bring the law to these islands. And the law says, Doctor Jefferson is here on vacation, and you take her wherever she wants to go. She asks to dive to the bottom of the lagoon or run up the flagpole, you take her. She's here under my protection. Understand?"

Baker turned to Tomas. "Come and see, ma'am."

While Raybelle and her security detail went one way, the soldiers took Tomas to an equipment hut.

She grimaced at the unsanitary conditions. If this was how the soldiers lived, how well could she expect their prisoners to be treated?

The wetsuit they found didn't really fit her; she was about the same size as Baker, but the suit squeezed her in the carotid artery. Tomas knew this was not as dangerous as it sounded, and the alternative, one of the men's wetsuits, would just fill with water. No insulation at all against the thermoclines.

She took hold of the tanks being passed to her and grunted under the weight. It was easier to carry two than one, but clearly, Tomas needed to work out more once she got back to the States. She checked her pressure gauge and regulator carefully. This was a lot further from the US than Cuba, and she'd heard nightmare stories about the quality of diving equipment there.

They boarded a boat, and she checked the tank valve again, made sure the buoyancy control device and regulator were both receiving air. It took her most of the ride to finish the tedious task of threading weights on her belt so that they'd weight her properly without tilting her to one side. They still dug into her hip bones, and she missed her own BCD.

When the boat stopped, Tomas spat into her mask to defog it and rinsed it over the side.

The dive itself was like a dream. Tomas felt the water flowing by her, like tears she hadn't shed. The sounds beneath the water were muffled, unearthly. She felt them, inside, like the communication she wanted, longed for with a woman. She pushed through the water, past fish of brilliant yellows and purples, and was shocked by a sudden layer of much cooler water. All the world looked blue, and Tomas relied on the precise instructions from the soldiers to show her what she didn't want to find.

The body was only partly tangled in seaweeds that fastened it to the shallow floor of the lagoon. Tomas had seen bodies in many states of mutilation and decay, but she was not prepared to see one this badly damaged and still recognize it as someone she knew. For it was Ephraim. If her gag reflex had permitted it, she would have thrown up, a dangerous thing in scuba gear. The swelling and grotesque distortions of his features could not solely be due to his being in the water.

At the surface, Tomas said, "You going to bring him up now?" She knew better than to be angry at the soldiers—they were trying to do the right thing, if belatedly—but she could not contain herself. "What are you waiting for?"

It took a long time to recover the body. Ephraim hadn't been a heavy man, but his body cavities would all have filled with water, making him almost impossible to lift. "Him," she uttered aloud. Was this body, grotesquely distorted, really Ephraim at all? The body, without its life, was missing something sacred, even to Tomas.

When they returned to shore, Raybelle was waiting for them. She spoke as if the hideous smell could not reach her, or soil her business clothes or disturb her perfume cloud of diplomacy.

"Ugly as hell, isn't it?" Raybelle looked at Ephraim's scarcely recognizable face and, to her credit, didn't flinch.

The nausea overwhelmed Tomas and she threw up into her mask, holding it before her with incongruous delicacy. The contrast was so great she felt dizzy, as though she might tip backward off this island, like she'd tipped backward out of the dive boat, and into a world that made more sense. She felt Raybelle's cool hand on the back of her neck. This was the second time she'd been sick in front of Raybelle, and she was a doctor. Christ, how humiliating. She sank to the ground, cradling her head in her hands.

"Sorry about your friend," Raybelle said softly.

"They dumped him for the goddamn fish?" Tomas's head hurt more when she shouted.

"Ma'am, we're angry too," Wilson said. "I went into the army six years ago this month, September. I thought, my country's being attacked, I want to protect it."

"And that's what we're doing. We don't want any more of this," Baker said. "Not on our base. Or under our flag."

Raybelle turned to Baker and Wilson. "Can you get this body somewhere it can be preserved for autopsy?"

"Yes, ma'am."

Tomas said, "You don't expect me—"

"No," Raybelle said. "I'm afraid Ephraim's body now becomes evidence. He has to be preserved."

Yes, Tomas thought, evidence. The gold standard in medicine, and in crime. "It'll make a change to have evidence, won't it?" she said. The rage erupted in her now, like pain returning after numbness wore off. "Evidence, instead of banging people up without charge or trial. Evidence, instead of rumors and innuendo."

"Well, rumor and innuendo you don't have to worry about," Raybelle said, "'cause this is real." She reached out her arms and gathered Tomas in, seeming not to notice the vomit, or the pissed-in wetsuit. You'd think she'd trained as a medical professional, not a lawyer.

Sgt. Baker spoke very quietly. "Me and Wilson," she said. "That's not why we joined up."

CHAPTER THIRTY-SIX

When they arrived back in Washington, Raybelle had no idea what time it was. She felt she wanted breakfast, since that was the last rubber meal she'd been served on the plane, and she had rejected it.

She wanted a meal with Tomas, and she didn't want to have to share it with anyone: the public, even a waiter. There would be no food in her apartment, of course. But she needed to be home, away from her overseas detail. "Come to breakfast with me," she said before Tomas could get a taxi.

Tomas's look was more of annoyance at the peremptory tone than anything else. "We're not on a base anymore. No orders."

"Would you like to have breakfast with me?"

"I don't know," she said. "The last coffee you bought me was so bad, even I couldn't drink it."

"We're not going to the senate cafeteria." Exhaust mingled with the clear fall air outside the terminal. "We're going home."

Tomas coming with her was assent enough.

When she unlocked the door of her empty apartment Raybelle had the unfamiliar sense of being free. No security detail, and certainly no surveillance. Maybe it had to do with the end of her senate career. How ironic that she should have been working for personal liberty all her life, and only now felt it herself.

She wanted to talk to Tomas about matters this important, what freedom really meant, but she'd promised her breakfast. Well, coffee. Coffee she could make.

Tomas stood inside the door, her back against it and arms crossed. "Aren't you worried about people knowing I'm here with you?"

Raybelle crossed to the kitchen area, which included a rather charming breakfast bar she rarely used. "I've been halfway around the world with you, and I'm about to resign," she said. "Honestly, I couldn't care less. Instant okay?"

Tomas's shocked expression made her pause with the teaspoon halfway out of the jar of coffee. But she did not address Raybelle's casually delivered announcement. "Are we still in England, where they don't understand that coffee is brewed?" Tomas said. "How many bad cups of coffee am I destined to have with you?"

"How many would you like?"

Raybelle had no precedent for this experience. The seconds and failed attempts ticked silently in her head before Tomas, seeming even more fed up than usual, strode over and started filling the teakettle with water. She banged it on the stove and turned the burner on as if she'd been in Raybelle's kitchen many times before.

"I'd like two sugars, please," Tomas said. "Do you have any sugar, Raybelle? Or any food? You really take care of yourself, don't you?"

Raybelle's arms wrapped around Tomas, and she tried to remember a time when she'd been drawn to another like this. She felt herself lean, her body's center of gravity shift. The fabric of Tomas's shirt, grasped in her fingers, the sense that if Tomas stepped out of her arms without warning, Raybelle would fall. All that young leanness against her, so strong. She could feel Tomas's lips at her neck. She didn't want to stand here kissing her, but if she tried to step back her knees would buckle and—

"Shall we adjourn?" she said.

Tomas said, "Are you propositioning me?"

Raybelle grabbed her hand and from it drew the strength to lead her out of the breakfast nook. "No propositions." Not looking at Tomas gave her the nerve to walk back to the bedroom, which, to her immense relief, was clean. She sat on the bed and motioned for Tomas to sit next to her.

"I've never," she began, but Tomas was having none of this. Her kiss broke over Raybelle with the force of a wave. She put up her hands as if to keep herself from falling, but she wanted to fall.

Her fingers were in Tomas's hair and a hand was sliding up her thigh when Raybelle heard a growing, persistent whistle from the kitchen. She moaned. "The teakettle."

Tomas's palm pressed firm on her chest. "Don't move. I'll get it."

It could only have taken less than a minute for Tomas to turn off the stove, but it was long enough for Raybelle to re-engage her mind. She was about to get naked with a body younger and more attractive than her own. There had never been anyone else here with her, not in this bed. She hadn't slept since they'd left Diego Garcia, but this, her home for eleven years, was at this moment the most foreign place she'd ever been.

Tomas came back and stood by the bed. Her gaze was fierce, as it had always been, but Raybelle perceived something else there too. Tenderness.

Not taking her eyes from Raybelle's, Tomas stripped off her shirt, and then her bra, so swiftly it was as if a vision had appeared. Raybelle reached up but Tomas stopped her. "I said don't move."

Tomas was breathing steadily, but hard. Raybelle's admiration was having a visible effect on her; her skin was tight and glistening. She reached to unbutton Raybelle's blouse. "No," Raybelle said. "I'll do it."

She couldn't face Tomas while she undressed, not in the light of the bedroom window that the shades did such an ineffectual job of blocking out. This wasn't fantasy. This was a first time, with all its clumsiness, and she didn't want to see disappointment if that was what was there.

But she hadn't said Tomas couldn't touch her, and before she could turn around Tomas was pressed against her bare back, arms circling her from behind. She felt warm lips against her ear, and practiced fingers resumed their dance on her thigh. Raybelle surrendered to the moment and stretched out, turning to Tomas and pressing close enough so that the beating in her heart felt less like panic. There was moisture on her thigh. It didn't feel like disappointment.

"I'd rather—" Raybelle began.

Tomas shut her up with another searing kiss. For once in her life Raybelle stopped worrying about what she was going to say, or do in the moment after this one. She let Tomas on top, which was where she'd wanted her in the first place, and felt lips trailing down her neck and along her collarbone. She sensed hesitation so she dragged her nails down Tomas's back and heard the groan of appreciation. Sometimes she opened her eyes to watch Tomas kiss her, first her breasts, then lower. It was so new and strange, not to think about what she was doing or break it down into steps. Just to feel.

She couldn't have done any more anyway as she was totally laid waste. She sat on the edge of the bed; Tomas knelt on the pile of clothes and took her in her mouth, with exquisite skill.

Raybelle shook with wonder. *I'm giving you everything*, she thought.

***

She could barely move, and didn't want to. She couldn't feel hunger, or lust or the need to control anything. What she felt was something as unfamiliar as anything else she'd felt in the past twenty-four hours. Satisfied.

Tomas stirred beside her and, with lazy effort, Raybelle turned to drink in the sight again. "Do you do a lot of crunches, or what?"

Tomas looked pleased and, Raybelle imagined, a bit shy. "I do work on my abs," she said.

"And everything else. I guess this isn't the first time they've gratified someone."

"Not like you."

Raybelle snuggled in. "I'd love to go back to sleep with you for the rest of the day—"

"But you need to check your messages."

"How did you know?"

"You haven't turned on your phone since the plane landed. I'd be going crazy."

Raybelle grinned, and saw a return spark in Tomas's eye. "You're beautiful, you know that?"

"Stop making me self-conscious." The admission was as sexy as everything else Tomas had done. "Coffee?"

Raybelle started to sit up, but Tomas motioned for her to stay where she was. "I'll get it."

She finished getting dressed and Raybelle was awed. At her beauty, but also at a woman making herself at home in her bed, in her kitchen. How was this going to work?

CHAPTER THIRTY-SEVEN

Raybelle turned on her cell phone for the first time since they'd left the island. How had she ever lived without that phone? There was a series of urgent text messages from Melody, but no news in any of them.

"What's up?" she said as soon as they were connected. "I just landed."

"Senator." Melody's voice lacked its usual perky edge. "I didn't want to talk on the phone. You've got to come into the office and see this."

"All right."

When she got back to the bedroom, Tomas was dressing. "Whoa, hey, where're you going?" Raybelle sat and, still tentative, stroked the tight curls on the back of Tomas's neck.

"I have a flight back to Chicago in three hours." Tomas looked regretful, but not regretful enough.

Raybelle didn't know what to say. *But we just made love? Stay with me, I need you?*

"I have patients, appointments." Tomas still sounded as if she were trying to justify herself. "And you have a resignation to take care of. But I don't want to be the reason."

"The reason for what?" Raybelle found her voice as Tomas stood and finished buttoning her shirt. "For resigning? Or for making it seem worthwhile?"

She followed Tomas to the living room, already regretting this degree of vulnerability. Tomas reached for her trench coat. Her embrace was tender and warm.

"Raybelle," she said. "You can have me here once, but more than that and people are going to know. I don't think you're ready for that."

She kissed her, slowly, a tongue so sharp that could caress so sweetly too.

"I'll call you." Something Tomas had probably said to a hundred other people.

"Is that how you talk to a senator?" Raybelle said.

Tomas's tone was gentle, but not intimidated. "You need to figure out who you are when you're not a senator," she said. "When you're just Raybelle."

She left Raybelle with the sound of her own name, in Tomas's voice, and the question she'd asked. Who was Raybelle McKeehan when she wasn't in office? If the next campaign, the presidency, was no longer there, what would drive her? Where—and whom—did she care about enough to get up every day, even when nobody was filming, recording or voting?

***

Raybelle brushed her hair back. She looked as if she'd been up all night, but nobody in the office would know what she'd been up to. Would they?

When she got there, Melody was waiting. "Honestly, Melody, what is so important that we had to talk about it here and now? I haven't even had a shower!"

"This story was on the Internet yesterday." Melody tossed a copy of the September 9 *New York Post* on her desk. "Now that you're back, you can read about it in your preferred medium."

Raybelle picked up the paper. The story described how a website called Wikileaks.org had revealed loads of secret US Army documents, for everyone to see. All the equipment being bought in Afghanistan, and the money spent on it. There was nothing outrageous reported in the article, but that could change.

"I think we should use this," Melody said. "Put all the Herald Aviation evidence, and the stuff from Diego Garcia, and publish. Here." She lifted a large Jiffy bag. "It's all here."

This brave new model was tempting. Raybelle could leak what was happening with Perry, Grant Rivers, Ephraim, all of it, anonymously if she wanted to. Then watch the fireworks. Rivers's blackmail would be moot.

Or, she could leave the party, with an ultimatum for the president that the buck must stop with him. She might not hold his or any other office in the future. But she'd keep on fighting on other fronts.

"Hold off on that for another twenty-four hours, Melody." She stood and tucked the Jiffy bag under her arm. "You have copies of all this?"

"Goes without saying, Senator."

"I'm going to see the president," Raybelle said. "If I'm not back by the end of the day, I've been rendered somewhere."

"They wouldn't dream of it," Melody said.

"Oh, they already have."

***

At home in Chicago, Tomas sifted through the images. Unlike at the White House, she had full documentation this time. She wished that was all she had, that it wasn't also imprinted on the camera of her mind. Photos from which Tomas would document the injuries inflicted on Ephraim before his death, and the probable cause of those injuries. Clinically and objectively. It was difficult for her to present that way, because the body was not a data set to her; it was a man. Her friend. Tomas wondered what a friend was, how you had and kept one. She didn't have much practice at that.

The images stayed with her as she looked at other images that day. Mrs. Hope's chest X-ray. Tomas had called Tim as soon as she got back to the US, but she hadn't seen him yet; she'd need to wait until after work. Mrs. Hope's X-ray wasn't good news either, but Tomas didn't need a dress rehearsal. She'd broken the hearts of so many Hopes in her career.

"Mrs. Hope." She was careful to address the patient, although her daughter was there too and seemed used to being in charge. "Your X-ray shows it's very serious."

"I don't understand." Her daughter spoke as the blank walls of the examining room closed in. "It's a virus, right? Can't you treat a viral infection? It's like a cold!"

This wasn't the time to remind the younger Hope that no one could treat a cold either, that you just rested and let nature take its course. A virus could come from somewhere distant and exotic or deep within our bodies, and sweep away life and health and everything else in its path.

"I'm afraid your health, and age, don't permit surgery at this time," Tomas said. "We'll do everything we can to keep you comfortable now." There was never any other time.

***

That night, Tomas knocked on Tim's apartment door reluctantly. She'd let him know the worst right away, on the phone. And he'd deserved to know. But she regretted not being able to give him the news in person, and regret wasn't a feeling Tomas was used to. Seeing Tim face to face, now, was going to be harder.

When he answered, there was a desolation on his face like nothing she had ever seen in him before. And she'd broken so much bad news, to so many patients and relatives. No, you can't have children, I'm sorry; no, your dad isn't going to get better, I'm sorry; there's nothing more that medicine can do. I'm sorry, I'm sorry, the empty apology echoing through hospital corridors and memory like a goddamn mantra. Show empathy without getting emotional. Help the patient but don't offer false hope.

This was worse than any of them.

Tim let her in, or rather she walked in, as he didn't seem capable of gesture or speech. His expression made her think of a First World War battlefield after the guns had gone quiet. In a way, he seemed composed. He had shaved; his eyes weren't bloodshot, or swollen from tears. Did men like Tim cry? Her examination was reflexive but it told her nothing about him, really.

"I'm glad you could come," Tim said, as if to a guest he'd never met before.

She sat on the couch. He offered her a glass of wine, and she offered him a smile. Tomas couldn't hug him, not in this moment. She felt brittle, as if his arms would break her. As if she would break if she tried to embrace someone else.

They were both into their second glasses of wine before Tim said, "You found him."

"I was shown the place."

"Raybelle."

She couldn't recall him saying Raybelle's name before. His own southern pronunciation made it sound homey and familiar. She feared she'd burst into tears, but that was absurd. Tim was the one who had lost his lover, and she wasn't sure what Raybelle was to her.

He drained his glass, reached for the bottle on the floor between them, without looking. "I don't want to talk about it," he said, "if it's all the same to you."

Neither asked why she was there, then. Neither reached out to touch the other, or said a word. It was enough to sit together, share a bottle of wine, and commune with the memories.

This, Tomas realized, was the rare thing. Not lovemaking, nor somebody to live with, who would sit with her at the end of the day. The truly rare thing was the presence of someone who would intuit what was needed, and provide it. Not ask, or tell, not be afraid to receive in return.

CHAPTER THIRTY-EIGHT

Raybelle was irritated by her limited capacity to dislike the president. She couldn't stand what his administration was up to, or some members of it, but the same was true of Democrats like Grant. She got along with the president personally, and she understood his folksy appeal to some voters. Today, she would operate on the hypothesis that he was just a poor judge of character.

"Mr. President," she said. "Thank you for agreeing to meet with me at such short notice."

He looked at her without intelligence. Maybe he really didn't know.

She started pulling photos and documents out of the unprepossessing Jiffy bag. "Sir, what I have here is evidence of some pretty serious misdoing by the Department of Defense. And, you'll be relieved to know, my senior Democratic colleague. Among others."

"What kind of misdoing?"

He was a busy man, and there wasn't time enough to reconvert him to his oath to defend the Constitution, or explain why torture was wrong. "Our wounded troops were left to rot, while contract workers were being paid to…interrogate prisoners overseas. Contracts given to Secretary Perry's old buddies, who couldn't build their way out of a paper bag. Might have something to do with their illegal immigrant workers, who can't read a word of English on the labels of that cheap cement they ship in from China. Believe me, Mr. President, you don't want this in the public domain. You may think this type of treatment—" She'd found the pictures from Diego Garcia—"is a price worth paying in the 'war on terror,' but you don't really want people seeing it, do you?"

He fingered the photographs without evident interest. "Americans don't care what we have to do to stop these guys."

Raybelle took a deep breath. He didn't care that Ephraim wasn't a "bad guy," or that people would confess to anything under torture so what was the use? *Focus on what he does care about.* "Sir," she said, "I don't know who'll be running to succeed you next year. But you have Senator McCain, a former prisoner of war, speaking out against aggressive interrogation techniques, and Senator Obama saying that *he* believes you're motivated by what is best for the country. It's hard to know who your friends are."

"And I suppose you'll be running, Senator McKeehan. What are you getting at, my friend?"

"Fire Henry Perry." She slapped her hand on the pile of evidence like it was the oath of office Bible. "Get rid of extraordinary rendition, this aviation scam, all the dirty contracts. Everything he's implicated in. Make it like it never happened. Purge your administration of these tactics," she said, "and I'll purge the Republican Party of myself. Matter of fact, I'll resign from the Senate. After all," she jabbed one finger at the Herald Aviation file, "this was going on under my nose."

"And why," he said, his blue eyes cool and distant, "should I throw my buddy Henry under the bus, just for you?"

"Because if you don't, Mr. President, I will send a torpedo up the hind end of your party and mine. Everything goes on the Internet—everything, even the snuff film that makes what happened to John McCain in Vietnam look like *Teletubbies*. It all goes out tomorrow. The eleventh. Just in time to upstage whatever patriotic whoop-de-doo you've planned to mark the occasion." She leaned forward. "Now wouldn't that be a shame?"

Now he looked interested and engaged. "Lemme take a look at that file," he said. "Sit down, Senator."

CHAPTER THIRTY-NINE

Grant was not too surprised when Perry resigned on the eleventh of September. With all the anniversary aspects of that date, someone as cynical as Perry knew it was a great day to bury news. Grant heard the clichéd announcement: "I'm going to spend more time with my family." What was left of it.

What was he, Grant, going to say? That he was resigning from the Senate to spend more time with Perry's family?

He could stay, and just not run for reelection. The president might be able to get rid of his own defense secretary, but a member of the majority opposition was another matter.

No, Grant would ride this out. As long as he had the dirt on Raybelle, and didn't release it, she wouldn't betray him either.

***

Raybelle wasn't used to feeling this absence, this aching need for another person, as soon as she went through a gate or a time zone. Other people were always around, but since she'd left home thirty-three years ago, Raybelle could not remember needing one person in particular. It wasn't at all clear to her what having Tomas would mean, either—what she would do with her if she had her. She could hardly expect Tomas to come back to Washington. She had a career of her own and, apparently, a life. Raybelle wondered if she herself any longer had either.

The constant caring about someone else, worrying about Tomas because she wasn't around, gave Raybelle an inkling as to why men like Henry Perry were so implacable. If it were Tomas in trouble, if it were the plane she was coming in on, would Raybelle care that much how her fellow passengers were screened? Or where the information had come from, to keep one person safe?

But did that really mean torturing people? Kidnapping them in allied countries? Exercising the right of life-destroying, dog-gassing "eminent domain" over every acre of the world?

In the open letter explaining her resignation, Raybelle didn't mention the present events on Diego Garcia, or Herald Aviation. As she'd told the president, she wouldn't be unveiling military secrets. Leave that to Wikileaks.

September 12, 2007

For the past eleven years it has been my honor and privilege to serve the people of Tennessee as a United States senator. I didn't come into public service to fill a particular office, but tell you the truth.

And the truth is, for more than a generation now, we Americans have asked our armed forces to do dishonorable and dirty work on our behalf. We've asked them to steal land from people who never did anything to hurt us. We've asked them to lie to those people about what was being done to them. We've asked them to kill the innocent.

Whenever you see or hear news reports on the endless "wars" in the Middle East—wars not declared by Congress, or sanctioned by our Constitution—you often hear mention of the air base on Diego Garcia,

*an island in the Pacific Ocean. Is it an island that just happened to
fall into our laps, unoccupied? No. A gift from Great Britain? Wrong
again. We took this land, this tropical paradise, from its inhabitants by
force, lied to them and said they would be coming back. Men wearing
the uniform of the United States did this...including my own brother,
Dennis McKeehan. They even gassed the islanders' dogs.*

She knew that the mention of animal cruelty would move her
listeners in a way that speaking about people might not. People
from a funny island, moving around and asking Americans to
leave their base, wouldn't be particularly sympathetic characters;
too close to the presumption of terrorism, these days. But this
was Raybelle's farewell to political office, and what she talked
about was people.

*Before we send young people overseas, before we send a single American
to risk life and limb, we need to know one thing. We first need to know
what kind of country they're defending. How do we behave that makes
us know our way of life is just?*

*In the Second World War, the Allies knew we were the better side,
because of the way we treated the other side. When we captured Nazi
war criminals, we didn't hide them on an island, or torture them in the
dark. Not because of the kind of people they were, but because of the kind
of people we were.*

*The people of Diego Garcia aren't terrorists. In fact, they didn't
do a thing to us. But even when somebody does, let us remember the
Nuremberg war trials, and ask ourselves: What kind of people are we?
If our process of law and justice could be trusted to handle Nazis—and
it could—then it's good enough for any barbarian, in any cave.*

Raybelle knew that this, not sleeping with Tomas, was what
had ended her career in politics. She could have averted her eyes,
or made campaign ads that would continue to make her popular,
with puppies gamboling over a hillside. She could have stopped
with the dogs.

But justice was easy when it protected fluffy dogs, or
kidnapped kids. Everybody loved justice for the innocent. It got
harder when the lines were blurred, the minorities unpopular,

the victims guilty. To love justice then was no longer a matter of simple feeling, the first blush of love. To serve justice when the work was hard, when editorials decried her, when an office could be lost—that was love for the long haul. Raybelle loved justice because she needed to sleep at night. And she couldn't sleep unless she believed that her country was better than that. Better than an Islamist tyranny, or a military dictatorship. She wouldn't fudge that with cultural relativism or "the enemy of my enemy is my friend." She loved justice.

CHAPTER FORTY

Months later, and thanks, in part, to Ephraim's story and the publicity it had received, the Chagossians won a victory in the British courts. The courts had taken the extraordinary step of promising to return the Chagos Islands to their inhabitants, although this was contrary to the wishes of the United States. Maybe the Iraq invasion would turn out like this: something deeply unpopular with the British public couldn't be sustained forever, with or without the support of the American government.

Tomas now found Chicago changed. She looked at buildings she'd passed all her life, and they no longer looked the same. She found herself biting her tongue in the presence of patients, wanting to tell them for fuck's sake to stop smoking, or lose the extra pounds, or whatever was in their power to improve their own health. How else could she help them?

She'd phoned Raybelle when she got home, and likewise had heard from her. But Raybelle's career was in transition right now, and Tomas felt the need for a change as well. She wanted Raybelle but she wanted all of her, and that meant Raybelle had to figure out herself first.

Tomas had started looking at the job sections of various journals. One day she saw an advertisement for a position with the International Center for Victims of Torture. *Torture* was a word that drew Tomas's eye. It was a word that, for most of her life, hadn't appeared in mainstream news reports; even activist organizations were careful not to direct the word at governments they were criticizing; they called it "ill treatment." Now, though, torture had come out of the dark, skeleton-filled closet of the popular psyche. Mainstream news media had lost their fear of the word, and otherwise sane government officials debated the acceptability of the practice under American law. As for international law, that seemed to be something best left to other nations.

This ad was written in a style Tomas had not grown to love, an aggressive second person: "You are keen to support... You will actively participate." It always came back to those unnecessary words: *actively* participate. Was the alternative to passively participate, to let someone else carry the can, take no responsibility at all? Tomas thought it ironic that such terms should be used by a center for victims of torture. Things didn't just happen: people were doing them all the time—treating, dying, torturing.

As Tomas's eyes wandered down the ad, she was amazed to find that it called for medical qualifications. This sort of thing wasn't advertised in regular media; it should be in a medical journal's back pages. Then she wondered where governments advertised for their medical and psychological "experts" to assist in the administration of torture. In her own city, possibly in her own hospital, were people who had sold their souls to the devil, monitoring the damage done by waterboarding and so on. Mengele had done this. Many doctors had. They had given their names to syndromes, and still cropped up in the literature. Where would Dr. Jefferson prefer her name to be?

First, do no harm. She looked up the center's address.

***

Raybelle moved out of her Washington apartment with little fanfare. Melody's boyfriend, Brian, came with his friends, collected her things in taped boxes, and stuffed them in a truck. They offered to drive it, too, but Raybelle preferred to drive herself. It seemed fitting, somehow. She'd arrived from Tennessee decades earlier with what she'd lived with in her college room, and now she was headed back home.

She left a farewell message for her Senate colleagues, on a Post-It note. She never had understood how someone busy running for office could still claim to be doing another full-time job. No one else could do this, in other walks of life. It made her realize how little she'd done as a senator, and the fact that she had so few tangible things to show for her years in Washington only emphasized this. Traveling light. Letting go of someday being president and now, of what she'd enjoyed most: sticking it to the men who would be.

Her new GI Bill would be okay. Senator Snowe would handle it. One day with her as sponsor and it was a bipartisan effort already. Further than Raybelle had gotten it all year.

The day before she was to drive back to Tennessee, she took Melody out for lunch, just the two of them. Raybelle offered to spring for something nice, but Melody insisted she wanted a turkey and provolone sub. "For old times' sake," she said.

"Are you sure? I'd even buy you kimchi, if I knew where to get it."

"That's all right, Senator. I'll take you to Korea Town when you come to Chicago." Melody looked mischievous, as if she thought Raybelle might be headed there right away.

"That's what I wanted to talk to you about," Raybelle said. "Is that what you want to do, move back to Illinois?"

"I'm not sure. Brian and I are still in discussions." She spoke in negotiation terms, and Raybelle thought they'd all been in Washington too long.

"Well, I don't know if this holds any appeal," she said, "but I know a federal judge back in Poudre Valley who's looking for a clerk, and I couldn't recommend anyone more highly than you."

"Thanks, Senator. That means a lot."

"And if it didn't work out with David, you could always come back and work for me."

Melody looked curious. "David…"

"Payne. The judge. He's the man who beat me in the race for district attorney, many years ago now. So how bad can he be?"

***

In her car, on her second day back in Poudre Valley, Raybelle released the clutch gradually. She was still not quite accustomed to being on her own, driving a car without company.

This morning she'd received an engagement announcement from Melody and Brian. She should pick up a card for them.

On Avenue E she slowed in the right lane. There was a little dog running along the side of the road, darting in and out of the traffic. Stupid thing, liable to get run over.

Although it wasn't a good idea, she eased onto the shoulder of the road, and reached over to open the passenger door. There was a veterinarian's just up the road, she'd try and see if she could take the dog in.

When she opened the car door the little dog ran up, jumped in, and sat in the passenger seat, for all the world as if it belonged there. Raybelle was affronted, not least because she was nervous to drive with something that might jump into her lap. Fortunately she was back in Poudre Valley; no matter how she drove, other drivers were more likely to wave than to honk their horns.

On examination, the dog was white, with a panting mouth that seemed too big for its (female) body. Some kind of terrier, maybe part Scottie. No tags or collar, but somebody had taught her to behave properly because she wasn't barking at all. The little tail just wagged and wagged.

Raybelle grunted. Dumb dog, chasing cars. Get herself killed.

A few minutes later, she pulled into the parking lot of Dr. Stansberry's vet clinic. He didn't look at all surprised to see her with a wriggling small dog in her arms.

"Senator McKeehan," he said. "Good to see you back home."

She set the dog down on the floor, where she started scampering around again. "Can you tell me what to do with this thing?"

Dr. Stansberry said, "She's a dog. Is she yours?" His look suggested doubt, as if he thought Raybelle incapable of caring for anything.

She explained how she'd found the dog, couldn't identify if she belonged to anyone. "Maybe it's got one of those microchips," she said. "You know, Big Brother monitoring devices, like some nutsy-cuckoo parents want to implant in their kids."

Dr. Stansberry hmphed as he put the dog on the table. "Government would put 'em in all of us, if we let them. No offense."

"None taken, Doctor Stansberry. I've spent my life fighting that type of government."

After a few moments' work, he said, "Well, she's spayed already. No microchip. What I suggest is, get her her shots today, make sure she's up to date, then take her home."

"Home?" Raybelle felt that momentary surge of fear that always came when she was expected to nurture. "But she's not mine, Doctor. I was just hoping you could help."

"I can," he said. "What should we do first? Rabies?"

An hour later Raybelle, still stunned, turned the key in Mama's door. The dog trotted in behind her. The expression on the dog's face implied that she'd just landed on her feet, in just the place she was meant to be, and it was Raybelle's honor to take care of her. More like a cat than a dog.

Raybelle called her Angel, precisely because the name was sentimental, and she didn't mind what anybody thought about her anymore.

CHAPTER FORTY-ONE

She sat down by the wall phone in Mama's kitchen. She had already resolved that this was one call she could not make from her cell phone. This was not business, not casual enough to be accomplished on the run, dislocated from time and place. She didn't want to remember this conversation—whether or not it turned out to be an unmitigated disaster—as one she had while staring out a car window, or walking around her own property, her feet constantly in motion. She needed to be sitting down, trembling with the anticipation of a high school girl, making up for all those years when she'd been called and escorted by young men, and later not so young men, to whom she was physically indifferent. She'd been married to her career, that was certainly true, but now that the career was over, she no longer had to make what still seemed, after all this time, the universal woman's choice between them.

"Hey, Tomas."

"Hey, Senator."

"I think Raybelle is more appropriate," she said. "How'd the interview go?"

"It went well, thanks," Tomas said. "I think I've got the job."

"Great, congratulations." Raybelle wiped a damp palm on her jeans. "So you'll be staying in the midwest."

"What about you?" Tomas said. "Are you planning on staying in Tennessee?"

"I guess so. It's my natural environment. Listen," Raybelle said, "I called to invite you here. I need to see you. Before you start your new job, before you're too busy."

"Okay."

Raybelle almost dropped the receiver. "Really? When can you be here?"

It had been so long since she'd fallen in love that her own body felt alien to her, as if the person she was used to being was just someone she watched on TV.

It had never been okay for her to feel the way she felt now, and so she'd pushed it down, so far inside that she supposed her capacity for love had diminished forever. Instead, it had hardened like a diamond, and now wherever she tried to look within herself, it drew her eye.

Raybelle had dreamed of the presidency, and reached the senate, the premier body in the United States, before crashing to earth (or as she preferred to think of it now, returning to her roots). Nothing in her life's trajectory had prepared her for the desire to throw herself at the feet of anybody, still less a woman. The expression "might as well be hanged for a sheep as a lamb" came to mind. She'd gone out of her political career in style, guns blazing; no final press conference featuring hookers or money laundering or sleaze. No, leave that to the men who ran the country. If, in her fifties, Raybelle McKeehan were finally to make a fool of herself for love, then let it be for someone as outrageous, who had made her as angry, who had disrupted her life as much as Tomas Jefferson. Where was the grand passion otherwise?

***

A few days later, Tomas paid her second visit to the Tri-Cities, Tennessee. A place she'd never expected to see at all.

A senator, even out of office, still had so much clout. What was Raybelle planning to do with hers? Someone like Raybelle could never really retire. Men who left public life "forever," on the high heels of some sex scandal, generally found themselves back sooner or later, hawking a magazine interview or a book about all they'd learned from the experience.

In the small terminal Tomas's new shoes clacked on the newish tile floor. She wasn't sure why she'd felt the need to buy new shoes to impress a Tennessean. But she was conscious of them, how loud they sounded in the quiet airport. She was used to airports being lined with carpet, to absorb all the noise of a lot more people than she saw here. Airports like Chicago's. Or Washington's.

At the single set of glass doors she saw Raybelle waiting, in short sleeves and blue jeans. It looked as though she'd gotten a bit of sun on her skin, on her hair.

"Hey." Tomas swung her carry-on from her back to her hand. She held it there, dangling.

"Come on." The former senator dragged her in the direction of the luggage carousel. "We only have a minute to get to the luggage before they take it in back."

"What, and blow it up?" Tomas said, then slapped her own hand over her mouth, mindful that the joke might be overheard in such an acoustic environment.

Raybelle tsked. By the time they got over to the carousel it had already started to move, and oversized people were hoisting oversized cases off the conveyor belt. Before Tomas could reach for hers, Raybelle had snatched it up.

"How did you know which was mine?"

Raybelle tapped an elegant long finger on the name badge. Remembering those fingers made Tomas's heart skip.

They proceeded out the automatic exit doors, across a lane

with little traffic and up the ramp to the parking lot. They still had not touched, and Tomas couldn't stand it anymore. So she stopped and threw her arms around Raybelle and squeezed the breath out of her.

"Thanks," Raybelle said when Tomas released her.

"What are you thanking me for?"

"For coming. Remember, I've never done this before." At Tomas's look of consternation, Raybelle explained, "Asked anybody out. I'm not a young woman, Doctor."

Tomas stopped Raybelle with a hand on her arm, took control of the luggage. "I wasn't asking about your past. Enough people have done that."

Raybelle opened the trunk. Then she opened the passenger side door, which touched Tomas somehow. After she'd buckled herself in Raybelle reached over, once, and squeezed her hand, but that was it for the rest of the trip. Tomas was boiling over inside with anticipation and uncertainty, but Raybelle scarcely took her eyes from the road, which was as winding and rural as Tomas remembered.

They approached the McKeehan estate, or so Tomas had called it in her mind. It was a nice place, certainly too big for one person, but not by any stretch a plantation, and set right near the road.

Raybelle let her in the door of the house, still not looking at her. "Make yourself at home."

Tomas followed, put her suitcase down. Then Raybelle took her hand and led her outside, showed her the sky and land.

"I want you to feel as at home here as you do in your own home," she said.

That wouldn't be difficult. Tomas didn't really feel at home anywhere. Aloud, she said, "I like Chicago. I've considered making a change, but I can't."

"I understand."

Tomas stopped walking. She looked at Raybelle. "You do?"

Raybelle slung a comradely arm around her shoulders. "You're talking to someone whose entire life has been about a job, and the place I was born. I never envisioned anything that would make me reconsider that."

"But?"

"But nothing." She waved her arm in an arc, following the Canada geese migrating south overhead. "This little spot, these trees, this field. It's my land, my home. Can't imagine leaving it any more than I can imagine losing my legs."

"No person should ever ask anyone to give up that much."

"Agreed." Raybelle tapped her on the nose with one playful finger.

Tomas wondered if Raybelle had ever shared this much contact with someone in an ordinary day, when it really meant something.

Raybelle added, "And the fact that we agree on this is one of the reasons I feel so close to you."

"Here." Tomas beckoned her inside, fiddled her suitcase open. "I got something for you."

She handed Raybelle the WE CAN DO IT! T-shirt. She hoped it wouldn't seem like a cruel joke. That Raybelle's whole career didn't seem like one.

"Thanks," Raybelle said. "Thanks, that's real, real nice of you, Tomas." She was quiet, holding the shirt up to herself, then folding it neatly, as if to wear later. "There's someone I want you to meet," she said.

"In the barn?" That seemed to be the only place they were headed.

Raybelle looked like she might have been in high school. Tomas supposed these were her high school stomping grounds. Maybe that explained the youthfulness in her face. Tomas wanted to reach out and touch it.

Raybelle opened a door, just inside the barn, and something small and furry came bounding down a narrow set of steps. "My dog."

The dog in question must have been trained, for it sat its white body down at Tomas's feet, but trembled all over with the urge to jump. She wasn't crazy about dogs she didn't know, but felt she should reward the anticipation on Raybelle's face. "Is it a boy or girl dog?"

"What a medical question!" Raybelle laughed. "I was hoping I could just tell you her name."

"Which is?"

"Angel." She looked as expectant as her dog did. "Go ahead and pet her, if you like. She won't hurt you."

Raybelle McKeehan was asking her to take this on faith. She did reach out, this time, and stroke the fur on top of Angel's head. The dog's body shook with excitement. Tomas was weirdly touched by what seemed to be the McKeehan family's eagerness to please.

"I never thought I'd have another dog here." Raybelle joined in the petting. Angel settled down on her paws to enjoy the affection.

"Well, you wouldn't have had time to take care of a dog in Washington. Not even a little one like Angel." At the sound of her name, she yelped ecstatically. "A dog needs attention every day."

"There've been plenty of presidents with pets," Raybelle said in a wry tone. "But they always have other people to take care of them."

"Probably their wives!"

Raybelle looked serious again. "I never wanted one of those."

"Never?"

"Maybe a lover. Never a wife." Raybelle's eyes were clear, but they seemed to be focusing farther than she could see out the barn door, with those mountains on the horizon.

Tomas squatted down to better scratch behind Angel's ears; on her haunches, they were each in a similar posture. "Do you miss it?"

"What, Washington?"

"All of it. The Capitol. The dream of running for president."

Angel had given up all restraint and was whirling round after her tail. Raybelle gestured at the dog. "Remind you of anyone? You know, I've got influence that only a few people in this country ever have, Tomas. To fight the good fight. Speak out against what I don't believe in. Against what's truly un-American." Then she unfolded the T-shirt again. "'We can do it,' huh? What can we do?"

"Maybe you can work on the Defense of Marriage Act. Signed by a Democrat, and totally unconstitutional. Instructing states not to recognize other states' contracts—forbidding them to."

"I meant you and me," Raybelle said. "We slept together."

"Technically, we didn't."

"Well, is that it?"

"No," Tomas said. "That's not 'it.' We're good together. I don't just mean as a couple; we work well together."

"But we're a couple too. Well, I want to be." Raybelle spoke in her politician's voice, to convince. "I'm not saying conventional; I may be on the road a lot. Speaking out, using that soft power."

"I promise you," Tomas said, "no cozy domesticity with me. The stories my patients tell me now, I'm lucky to sleep at night at all."

"I'd like to at least be there. Some of the time." Raybelle pulled Tomas over to the most convenient seat, a bale of hay. "See if we *can* sleep together."

Tomas kissed her and kept on kissing her. For the first time in her life there was not a prescribed next stage, a rung on the ladder.

"You're staying here, right?" Raybelle said. "Not at the Ramada."

Tomas shuddered. "I've had it with hotels for a while," she said. "Still haven't gotten over what happened in London."

"You know that embassy," Raybelle said. "I don't suppose you had a chance to see the statue out front."

"Of Reagan?"

"No, the other one. Eisenhower."

"Oh, both Republicans. Figures."

"Are you ever going to let that go?" Despite her words, Raybelle looked happier than Tomas had ever seen her. "Before he became president, Eisenhower said something about every tomorrow having two handles. We can either take hold of tomorrow with the handle of anxiety or the handle of faith."

"I'm not very faith-based."

"I know." Raybelle kissed her again. "But it sure beats anxiety. So let's just take the future by that handle. Shall we?"

Bella Books, Inc.

Women. Books. Even Better Together.

P.O. Box 10543
Tallahassee, FL 32302

Phone: 800-729-4992
www.bellabooks.com